The Living Year

This edition published 2025
by Living Book Press
Copyright © Living Book Press, 2025

ISBN: 978-1-76153-752-3 (hardcover)
         978-1-76153-763-9 (softcover)

First published in 1950.

A catalogue record for this book is available from the National Library of Australia

The Living Year

by

RICHARD HEADSTROM

Contents

January

It snowed all day. The snowflakes began to fall shortly after daybreak. They were light and airy, and the slightest breeze blew them merrily along in whirling clouds.

The storm appeared to be much like those we have in early spring, which last but a short time and then pass away. But as the morning advanced, the flakes continued to come down, and before long, patches of brown earth could be seen only around the base of a tree or in a sheltered corner of the house and barn. It had become colder, too, and the wind had begun to blow with more intensity. Perhaps a real snowstorm was in the offing.

By mid-afternoon, the stone wall that bordered the road had become all but lost from view. The wind now howled about the house and blew the flakes into drifts that grew higher and higher. Grotesque shapes took form on the landscape as trees and shrubs became wreathed in snow. All life outdoors seemed to be suspended, waiting for the storm to run its course. A lone chickadee appeared, however, in a nearby apple tree. He seemed gay and happy, in spite of being buffeted by the wind and snow, and went about his business of finding insects with cheerful industry.

It was still snowing when darkness fell. But during the night, the storm passed, for when I awoke, the sun was just beginning to rise above the eastern horizon. Through a window all but frosted over, I looked out at the whitened landscape and was dismayed at the amount of snow that had fallen. Only the tall evergreens in the distance might provide fare for those who were fitted to eat at their table; for a while, at least, fruit-laden shrubs and the withered stalks of weed plants would be no festive board. Even the feeding stations, which I had put up around my house, were so completely covered as to be wholly inaccessible; and when some time later I managed to get to them, wandering prints testified to disappointed visitors.

Prints are easy to read if you are acquainted with them, and those which I found in the snow told tales as clearly as if I had been an eyewitness to the behavior of my feathered and furred visitors. The almost undecipherable prints of a sparrow revealed the futile attempts of the little bird to gain entrance to a sheltered feeding station, which, by some malicious quirk of fate, had been entirely filled with snow. The lone print of a woodpecker at another station was a telltale sign that the bird had made a brief appearance but, finding nothing to eat, had presumably flown off to more productive feeding grounds.

On the ground, I found the prints of a crow and a robin. I knew the crow would find food somewhere, but the robin seemed faced with the bleak prospect of starving to death. Several starlings had also left their calling cards, but at the moment they were nowhere to be seen, although I was sure they would return. The tracks of a gray squirrel, who was in the habit of visiting daily a tray I had set out for his own private use, marked an erratic course about the grounds. I could read his tracks as clearly as if I had watched him running out of the woods and hurrying eagerly to the tray containing his breakfast. I could see him, in my mind's eye, grubbing about vainly in the snow that covered it, and, with disappointment in his heart, search the grounds before he reluctantly returned to the woods, where he doubtless hoped to find a nut or two. He did return later in the day, when his visit was not unrewarded, for I had, meanwhile, cleared the feeding stations of snow and replenished them for any hungry callers.

Some people abhor squirrels and consider them a nuisance; personally, I cannot help liking these frisky, bright-eyed little creatures and would willingly suffer the loss of a few apples or a few ears of corn rather than forgo the pleasure of their visits. I have always found them responsive to my overtures of friendship and have long since discovered that their companionship provides a few moments' pleasure and comfort in this disquieting world. If you have ever had one of these little beggars climb your coat and take a nut or two from your hand, you know what I mean. The gray squirrel has been indicted for robbing birds' nests, but the number of birds he might destroy in the course of a year are certainly few compared to the number that lose their lives because of other enemies or other causes, such as storms. He has also been charged with stealing the food we set out for the birds in feeding stations and trays, but why shouldn't he, if we fail to take the proper precautions to safeguard it? I have seen food scattered on the ground and placed on window sills and other similar places, and then have listened to complaints that the squirrels ate most of it.

The gray squirrel is not a fair-weather friend, and if you treat him right, he will always remain near at hand. Even during the winter, he is abroad except during a severe storm, when he retires to his home until it passes. He does not hibernate and does not have to lay up large quantities of food to see him through the winter, being confident he can find what he needs by diligent search. But he has the habit of digging holes and hiding a nut here and there for future use. The next time you see a squirrel so engaged, stop and watch him for a few moments. After he has dropped a nut into the hole and refilled it with loose soil, observe how he presses the soil firmly in place with his front feet. He is careful, also, not to leave any trace of his excavating, for before he goes off to hide another, he covers the spot with grass and leaves.

These hidden nuts do not wholly sustain him during the winter, and he must scurry about to find other food, such as the nuts which still remain on the trees. Of course, he is not the only claimant for the nuts and must compete with the red squirrels and redheaded woodpeckers. The woodpeckers seem to think the nuts are exclusively theirs and enforce their claim with their sharp bills. The red squirrels, too, resent their larger relative and, strangely enough, will not hesitate to attack him.

I don't know whether the gray squirrel is an out-and-out coward or just pacific by nature; at any rate, he will not engage the red squirrel in combat and usually retires upon the latter's appearance. In the face of the competition offered by the red squirrels and woodpeckers, it would seem unlikely that he would get many nuts, but he has solved the problem by rising early and gathering his share before the others arrive.

During the days following the snowstorm, I took several walks through the nearby fields and woods, and in the snow I found the tracks of many two-footed and four-footed creatures. I discovered the prints of a deer mouse among some wild rose bushes, and in a clump of sumacs, the tracks of a cottontail. I also found the tracks of the ruffed grouse in a wild grape thicket. With some curiosity, I followed them across an open field to the edge of the woods, where they disappeared in a profusion of bushes and undergrowth. I had no way of knowing whether the bird was in the immediate vicinity or had vanished, for it was impossible to follow the tracks any farther or, for that matter, to locate them in the tangled undergrowth.

Apparently, I was closer to the bird than I suspected, for, as I poked about, there was a whirr and buzz almost at my feet, and with hysterical notes of alarm, the grouse rose from the ground and flew off into the woods. The noise set a blue jay to screaming in the distance, and I was reminded of Thoreau's description when he wrote of "that unrelenting steel-cold scream of a jay, unmelted, that never flows into song, a sort of wintery trumpet screaming cold, hard, tense, frozen music, like the winter sky itself..." A moment later, I saw the bird, a brilliant spectacle against the snow, but only for a moment, as he quickly flew to a nearby tree and was lost among the snow-covered branches.

I shifted my position a few feet and saw him perched on a limb. I need not have moved, for a jay has an insatiable curiosity and would soon have reappeared to learn, if he could, what I was doing there. Call the jay a thieving rascal or whatever name you will, he nevertheless has many engaging qualities, and we would miss him were he to vanish forever from our woods and thickets.

Although nature appears at its lowest ebb in January, there is still much of interest to be found in the outdoors. To be sure, it is the time of the year when I prefer to sit snug and complacent beside my warm fireside; yet if I do not occasionally get outdoors and roam through the fields and woods, I have missed something vital and stimulating. Even though there is a sharp bite to the air and the snow makes walking difficult, all discomfort is quickly forgotten when I spy among the naked branches of a tree a little mote of gray and white moving about with lively abandon. I see the chickadee at all seasons, but it is in the winter that I really notice and appreciate him. For when all nature seems to have retired before the icy blasts of the north wind, the chickadee is a-wing, gay and happy, enlivening the winter scene with his amusing acrobatics and merry chatter of "chick-a-dee-dee-dee-

dee." He actually seems to enjoy a snowstorm, and in the most bitter weather, I find him frolicking from tree to tree, laughing and joking in his own inimitable way. He is the bird of whom Emerson wrote:

> This scrap of valor just for play
> Fronts the north wind in waistcoat gray,
> As if to shame my weak behavior.

I often find a white-breasted nuthatch or two in company with the chickadees, for they hunt together all winter for beetles, caterpillars, and the pupae of insects among the cracks and crevices of trees. Watch these birds cavort about a tree and you may get the impression they like to view the world upside down since the chickadee often hangs head down from a twig while the nuthatch usually alights head down on the trunk. The latter has feet adapted for clinging to the bark and is able to run so rapidly about on the tree that he is often called the "tree mouse." He is a most industrious little bird, always on the move, climbing easily up or down the trunk, straight up or straight down, or circling it, according to his mood.

I have always thought that the chickadees and nuthatches get along well together, and I believe they do if they confine their activities to their own hunting grounds. But I am not sure they remain on friendly terms if one of them should invade the other's territory. I have noticed, for example, that whenever a chickadee is feeding on one of my trays and a nuthatch appears, the newcomer pecks and harasses the chickadee until the latter flies away and leaves the nuthatch in sole possession.

Many visitors call at my feeding stations during the course of the winter. One year, several evening grosbeaks visited a tray I had erected outside my study window. I mention their unexpected visit because it was the only time I had ever seen these birds in my grounds. I had just finished lunch and had entered my study when I happened to glance out the window. At that very moment, two evening grosbeaks alighted on the tray and proceeded to feed. The appearance of these birds from the Canadian North was startling, and before I could recover from my surprise, they were joined by several others. I approached the window warily and saw on the ground a flock of possibly fifty or more, though an accurate count was impossible, for they suddenly took flight and disappeared into the sky. I have always wondered why they did not tarry longer, or return, or why I have never seen these birds in my grounds since, as they are rather quiet and sedentary, especially where food is plentiful, and make friends easily, and when well treated become unusually tame. Every winter, I have looked forward to another visit, but though I have occasionally seen them in the woods, feeding on the seeds of conifers and various deciduous trees, I have never had the opportunity, so far as I know, of playing host to them again.

As I write, I recall another winter's day. It was bitterly cold, with the thermometer hovering about the zero mark. A thick blanket of snow covered the landscape, and the wind whirled the snow in maddening gusts. But in spite of driving flakes and low temperatures, a flock of tree sparrows found good cheer in a nearby field, where brown stalks of weeds and grasses stood in phalanxes against the sky. They flew, with cheerful industry, from one brown patch to another, clinging to the dead stalks as they carefully explored them, picking out the seeds.

Every now and then, one or more, made thrifty by the wintry dearth, would hop around upon the snow, searching for seeds that had been scattered by the wind. It was not alone a serious quest for food; it was also a frolic in which the sparrows' gay notes fell upon the air like the tinkling of sleigh bells.

Weedy and bush-grown fields are also hunting grounds for goldfinches and juncos. Only yesterday, a flock of goldfinches descended upon the field back of my house. These birds are at their best in late summer or early September, when they may be seen in flocks, feeding upon their favorite thistle seeds. But even in January, when their bright summer colors have faded to a more somber hue, they are a delight to watch as they meticulously search for seeds on the dried and withered stalks which, in the bright sunshine, trace delicate and intricate shadows on the snow.

With the exception of one or two species, such as the snow bunting and Lapland longspur, which habitually seek open fields far from all cover and which in January can be found along the coast, feeding on the seeds of the beach grass, most of our winter birds prefer sheltered places: thickets and bush-grown roadsides, orchards, cedar and alder swamps, and stands of pine and other coniferous trees. In an alder swamp, I have occasionally come upon a flock of redpolls, fearless and usually friendly little birds, but sometimes during the winter season, extremely wild. Crossbills and pine grosbeaks frequent stands of coniferous trees when these trees bear fruit; golden-crowned kinglets and brown creepers apparently prefer woods of oak and maple. In hemlock groves, I often find the juncos, merrily chattering away, although these birds, as I have already remarked, may also be found in fields. These birds are truly winter birds for they seem to enjoy the cold and snow and as long as they can find enough to eat, are frequently seen throughout the winter months.

As January advances and heavy snows begin, hairy woodpeckers leave the forest and appear in villages and orchards in search of food. The downies, of course, are always near at hand, and the silence of the winter woods is often broken by the tapping of their bills as they search for insects on the trunks and branches of trees.

It is a mystery how the woodpecker can unerringly drill into the very spot occupied by an insect beneath the bark or wood. Some believe that the vibrations produced by a grub as it cuts away the wood with its strong jaws are conveyed through the beak and skull of the bird to the brain, but this does not explain how it can locate small grubs that make no audible sound or grubs and ants that lie dormant and motionless in winter. Perhaps the bird can fix the exact location of the burrow by tapping with its beak in somewhat the same manner that a carpenter, by striking the wall of a room with a hammer, can determine the position of a timber hidden under laths and plaster.

The woodpecker is a familiar bird, and yet few of us realize how eminently successful he has been in the struggle for survival. Long ago, he discovered that to have his mate lay her eggs in a hollow tree or in a cavity which he excavated would protect her eggs better against the elements and enemies than if they were laid directly on the ground, or in a comparatively frail basket made of twigs, grasses, or other material.

But even earlier in his development, he had become so modified in form and structure that he could assure himself of a constant supply of food in the form of the insects that are to be found at all times of the year in burrows and beneath the bark of trees. His short, stout legs and toes, furnished with strong, sharp claws for clinging to the bark, are well adapted for climbing. Even his tail of stiff feathers, terminating in sharp spines or quills, can be pressed against the bark as a prop or brace to hold him in an upright position while at work. But such equipment would be useless did he not have the means of penetrating the wood and dislodging the insects hidden there. His hard chisel-shaped beak, however, forms an exceptionally effective wood-cutting instrument and his hard skull is constructed to absorb the shock of constant hammering. For spearing and conveying the insects to his mouth, he has a highly specialized tongue that is long and cylindrical, with a tip hard as horn and with many strong barbs, and operated by a marvelous mechanism that can extend it far beyond the beak. Thus while most birds, of necessity, must be content with such insects as they can find on the surface of plants, in open crevices, or flying in the air, or with such seeds and berries as are readily available, the woodpecker is able to find food at any time.

Although much animal life is in a state of dormancy or rest, the January scene is not wholly one of inactivity. This is the month when raccoons mate and bear cubs are born in caves or

in hollow trees. Mink forage along the frozen banks of brooks
and streams, and foxes prowl the silent woods in search of cottontails, mice, and other food.

Few animals have as many enemies as the cottontail. Hawks,
owls, crows, skunks, foxes, red squirrels, weasels, mink, and
snakes — all animals, indeed, that can catch him — consider
him legitimate prey; and then there is your hunter, man and boy,
who, with the odds overwhelmingly in his favor, hunts him in
the name of what he likes to call sport.

Every year millions of these little animals lose their lives, and
if Nature in her omniscience had not made him a prolific breeder,
he would long since have become extinct. Yet in spite of his many
enemies, the cottontail lives and flourishes.

Anyone not familiar with this little inhabitant of the brier patch
and hedgerow might think him wholly defenseless against his
enemies. This is not so, of course, and I doubt very much if any
animal that Nature has created is without some means of defense.

Many a cottontail has saved his life by "freezing" or remaining
quite motionless, except for the trembling of his whiskers and the
almost imperceptible movement of breathing. I have seen a cottontail "freeze" and while no amount of staring would disconcert him,
I admit that when I approached too closely he quickly raced away.

The cottontail is by nature a timid animal and at the slightest
sound of danger will usually seek safety beneath some cover. He
can travel with considerable speed over the ground, his long legs
propelling him forward in a series of jumps which sometimes
cover a distance of eight feet or more, but he has none of the
specializations for speed seen in the jack rabbits and depends for
safety more on the protection afforded by the undergrowth than
by flight. He often makes use of a deserted burrow of a woodchuck
or skunk, especially during the colder months, as a retreat in
which to spend the daylight hours or as a place of refuge in time
of danger, though sometimes such a retreat fails as a sanctuary
if he is pursued by a mink or weasel, for these animals can enter
almost any burrow, however small.

It is questionable if many of these animals succeed in following a cottontail to his burrow, for, as a rule, the cottontail, when pursued, uses the runways leading to the burrow. These runways crisscross and twist and turn so much that he can usually elude any pursuer or at least escape long enough to find a place of safety. Yet, the goshawk will follow these paths on foot in a most unhawklike manner, to drive him out into the open and into the waiting talons of his mate, for goshawks usually hunt in pairs during the winter.

Several years ago, I spent a pleasant afternoon with a group of young naturalists, following the wanderings of one of these rabbits. It was an elementary lesson in tracking, but one which I think they enjoyed immensely, as we traced the somewhat erratic course made by the animal the night before on his search for wild rose hips and other hardy berries. As rose hips and berries, however, are not too plentiful in the winter, the cottontail also feeds on the twigs and bark of small trees and bushes. He is partial to sumac bark, as I pointed out to my young friends, for as we followed the tracks we came to a clump of sumacs where the little animal had recently been at work.

That same afternoon, we found pellets of bone and fur under various trees, evidence that owls had been hunting in the vicinity. Owls are beneficial birds and in the field of usefulness are the complement of hawks, the hawks working by day and the owls by night. They feed on mice and other ground animals which they capture with their feet, the prey, unless it is too large, being swallowed entire and the hair and bones disgorged afterwards in the form of pellets.

We also found other things of interest. We encountered some flies, for instance, and I explained to my astonished audience that they were not true flies but species of stone flies that complete their nymphal lives in ice-rimmed streams in winter and appear in the frosty air as adults which mate on the banks. True flies, such as bluebottles and greenbottles, however, may be seen in January. They emerge on warm days from their winter retreats in the corners of attics and crevices of outbuildings, and usually starve as a result of appearing out of season.

Insects are rarely seen during January, but a few species, such as the springtails, are in evidence. These are small, grotesque-looking creatures with a device that permits them to jump or spring when disturbed. They may frequently be seen as dark patches on the quiet waters of still unfrozen ponds.

Insects seem to be rare in winter compared to the countless numbers that we find during the summer months; yet they abound in a less active state if we know where to look for them. They may be found everywhere, passing the winter in all the stages that comprise their life cycles. The light buff oval egg masses of the gypsy moth, for instance, may be found on the trunks of trees, on fences, in the crevices of rocks, on piles of wood, and in similar places. This is the insect that a well-meaning amateur entomologist imported from Europe about 1868 with disastrous results. Many millions of dollars have been spent in trying to get rid of the gypsy moth, but all that has been accomplished so far is to confine it to New England and a small area in New York and New Jersey.

Another familiar and occasionally troublesome insect that passes the winter in the egg stage is the tent caterpillar, whose protectively varnished egg bands are conspicuous on the twigs of the wild cherry. Some years ago, children were urged to destroy the eggs and we were admonished to burn the nests and destroy the caterpillars in the spring. We were even advised to cut down the wild cherry trees if necessary. If we had cut them down as advised, what would have happened? We would simply have forced the females to lay their eggs on apple trees and other related plants with the result that we would have changed the tent caterpillar from an eater of wild cherry leaves to an eater of apple leaves, since experiments have shown that when a leaf-eating species is deprived for several generations of its normal food and reared on the leaves of some other plant, it will adopt the new food as "normal."

Perhaps it is not even advisable to burn the nests or destroy the caterpillars, for it has been found that the egg masses contain parasites that keep in check the tent caterpillars and probably other caterpillars as well. Should we destroy these parasites, it is possible we might upset a whole chain of delicate balances.

Equally conspicuous on the twigs of deciduous and evergreen trees are the curious egg sacs of the bagworm. They are made of silk, in which are fastened leaves or bits of stick. If we examine these bags, we will find many of them empty, others full of soft yellow eggs. These bags are made by the full-grown larvae which pupate within them. When the male moths are ready to emerge, the pupae work their way to the lower end of the bag and halfway out of the opening at the extremity. Then their skins burst and they emerge. The adult females, however, partly emerge from the pupal skins and push their way to the lower end of the bags where they await the approach of the males, since they are entirely destitute of wings and legs. After mating, the females work their way back into the pupal skins where they deposit their eggs, mixed with the hairlike scales from the ends of their bodies. Then they work their shrunken bodies out of the bags, drop to the ground, and perish. The eggs, meanwhile, remain in the pupal skins until they hatch the following spring.

Fallen logs and rotting stumps serve as a winter retreat for many insects, and in the soft wood we may find the nymphs of the wood cockroach, the only outdoor roach that winters in the north. Frayed cattail heads may seem a poor place in which to winter, but the larvae of the cattail moth find them quite serviceable. The half-grown larvae of the viceroy butterfly spend the winter in silken cases, suspended from the twigs of willow and poplar, and the larvae of the pistol-case bearer hibernate in pistol-shaped cases attached to apple twigs. The odd-shaped cases are usually overlooked unless you know where to look for them. If you are in the habit of getting outdoors during the winter, you will be more apt to find the large and conspicuous silken cocoon of the cecropia moth, the largest of the giant silkworm moths. Children call this cocoon the "cradle-cocoon," because it is shaped like a hammock and is suspended lengthwise beneath a branch or twig. Cleverly made, it consists of two walls of silk, the outer one being thick and paperlike and the inner one thin and firm; between these walls is a matting of loose silk which provides excellent insulation and makes a snug retreat for the wintering pupa.

Like the insects, spiders spend the winter in all stages of life. Adults and young spiders of various ages hide in a variety of shelters, and many small spiderlings stay through the cold months sheltered within the egg sacs in which they have already hatched. Only yesterday, while examining the dried-up heads of some thistles, I found the pear-shaped egg sac of the orange garden spider fastened to one of the stalks by many ropes of silk so that the storms of winter might not tear it loose. I opened it and found a large number of spiderlings, which immediately crawled all over my fingers. These spiderlings are cannibalistic, the stronger feeding upon their weaker brothers and sisters so that from a sac which in early winter contains a large number of spiderlings, there emerge in the spring a much smaller number of partly grown spiders. Sometimes the egg sac of this spider is infested by ichneumon parasites, which in turn are preyed upon by secondary parasites.

Quite sure that I would also find the egg sac of the banded garden spider if I searched diligently, I spent several minutes looking about before I discovered one between the dried leaves of a goldenrod. This egg sac is quite different in form, being cup-shaped with a flat top. In making it, the spider makes the flat side first, then attaches the mass of eggs to it, and finally covers the eggs with the cup-shaped portion.

Later that same afternoon, in turning over a field stone, I found on the underside several brown papery disc-shaped egg sacs of a drassid spider. I also found beneath the stone a carabid beetle, a millipede that immediately disappeared into the soil, and several sow bugs.

Thus January is not the month of desolation which it might appear to be to the unobservant and uninitiated. Even your ardent fisherman need not be without his sport. True, many freshwater fish rest quietly upon the bottoms or hide among leaves and rocks and take little or no food. But some move about beneath the ice and feed more or less regularly. Some of them even bite freely for baitfish (the pickerel, for instance) and may be taken through the ice.

January is not without beauty, too. Along roadsides, the purplish-red stems of the red osier dogwood give warmth to the wintry landscape, and in rocky crevices of woodland hillsides, the common polypody, with its rich foliage, softens into beauty the rugged outlines of the barren winter landscape. In the woods, the green fronds of the Christmas fern add their touch of winter cheer as the ground pine and ground cedar, in heavy ermine cloaks, brave the wintry elements to color the shadowy woodland floor. While the beech's upright bole casts purple shadows on the snow and its polished brown stems describe an exquisite tracery against the sky, other trees silhouetted against a cloudless sky assume a form and character lost to us when robed in leafy splendor. We see them now in a different perspective, not as a means of shade from the hot summer's sun but as living things each with its own individuality, with its own composition, like so many pictures in an art gallery — many, varied, and ever-changing.

They have their own name plates, too, if one can read them. There is, for instance, the red maple with its red buds and twigs, the tupelo with its dark blue fruit clusters, and the poison sumac, its globular ivory berries hanging from the naked branches in long, slender, drooping pendants mutely reminding one, "Do Not Touch." Even old tree stumps, decrepit and unsightly, gradually crumbling into eternity, attempt in a lavish display of fairy candelabra to pass gracefully from the scene by becoming decked with the branching coral-like cladonia, whose red tips are in rich contrast with their frosted green branches. And if you want to peek into fairyland, examine these lichens with a magnifying glass.

NATURAL EVENTS IN JANUARY

- Foxes hunt for rabbits, field mice, and other food.

- The silence of the winter woods is broken by the tapping of woodpeckers searching for insects on the trunks and branches of trees.

- The light buff oval egg masses of the gypsy moth may be found on the trunks of trees, on fences, in the crevices of rocks, on piles of wood, and in similar places.

- The purplish-red stems of the red osier dogwood add a touch of warmth to the wintry landscape.

- Crossbills, pine grosbeaks, and redpolls feed on the cones of evergreens.

- Various stoneflies complete their nymphal lives in ice-rimmed streams, appearing in the wintry air as adults and mating on the banks.

- Pickerel bite freely for baitfish and may be caught through the ice.

- Cottontails browse on buds and tender twigs. The bark of the sumac is particularly favored.

- Flocks of juncos animate hemlock groves.

- The protectively varnished egg bands of the tent caterpillar are conspicuous on the twigs of wild cherries.

- The globular ivory berries of the poison sumac hang from the naked branches in long, slender, drooping clusters.

- Tree sparrows and goldfinches may be seen in fields and bushy growth, feeding on weed seeds.

- Springtails mass in dark patches on the quiet waters of still unfrozen ponds.

- Except on extremely cold days, red and gray squirrels enliven the woodland scene.

- The green fronds of the Christmas fern brighten the snow-covered woods with their winter cheer.

- Heavy snows begin, and as the snow cover deepens, winter birds flock in numbers to feeding stations.

- Mink forage along the frozen banks of brooks and streams.

- Bear cubs, remarkable for their diminutive size, are born.

- Pellets of bone and fur, under trees, indicate that owls have been hunting in the vicinity.

- Raccoons mate.

- The curious egg sacs of the bagworm hang starkly from the twigs of trees.

- Larvae of the cattail moth winter in frayed cattail heads.

- The dark blue fruit of the tupelo, in clusters of two or three, are conspicuous on the naked branches.

- Ground pine and ground cedar, in heavy ermine cloaks, brave the wintry elements to give color to the shadowy woodland floor.

- In the soft wood of rotting stumps may be found nymphs of the wood cockroach, the only outdoor roach that can winter in the north.

- In a lavish display of fairy candelabra, old tree stumps are decked with the branching coral-like cladonia, whose red tips are in rich contrast with their frosted green branches.

- Hairy woodpeckers leave the forest and appear in villages and orchards in search of food.

- Evening grosbeaks may make a surprise visit.

- Larvae of the pistol-case bearer hibernate in pistol-shaped cases attached to apple twigs.

- The white or brown papery disc-shaped egg sacs of the drassid spider may be found attached to the undersides of field stones in dry fields and along roadsides.

- Lapland longspurs may sometimes be seen in company with snow buntings, feeding on the seeds of the beach grass.

- The beech's upright gray bole casts purple shadows on the snow and its polished brown stems describe an exquisite tracery against the sky.

- Pupae of the cecropia moth may be found within large silken cocoons attached lengthwise to twigs of various trees.

- Half-grown larvae of the viceroy butterfly spend the winter in silken cases, suspended from the twigs of willow and poplar.

- On warm days, bluebottle and greenbottle flies emerge from their retreats in the corners of attics and the crevices of out-buildings — and usually starve as a result of appearing out of season.

- In rocky crevices of woodland hillsides, the common polypody, with its rich foliage, softens into beauty the rugged outlines of the barren landscape.

- Chickadees and nuthatches hunt for insects in the cracks and crevices of trees.

- The red buds and twigs of the red maple are seen against a background of snow.

- Spiderlings of the orange garden spider spend the winter within pear-shaped egg sacs, suspended from the withered stalks of thistles and other herbs.

- Carabid beetles, millipedes, and sow bugs may be found under stones and logs.

February

The ground is covered with a white shroud and trees and shrubs are hung with icy pendants that glisten brilliantly in the sunshine. February is here; and, as winter advances, my thoughts turn to the birds and mammals still abroad in field and forest, battling chill winds, swirling snows, and freezing temperatures, and gambling their lives against a diminishing food supply.

As I observe these brave and hardy creatures, I am amazed at their physical vigor. The chickadees think nothing of being out in a driving snowstorm. The kinglets feed unconcernedly, though the north wind howls and pine branches groan beneath heavy burdens. The shrews hunt even during sub-zero weather, when biting winds sting our faces and crusted snow crackles underfoot.

I am so accustomed to seeing the chickadees that I take their presence for granted. But whenever I see the kinglets, I never cease to wonder how these dainty birds, seemingly so delicate and fragile, manage to survive. Even more surprising is how the shrews get through the winter. I should expect such diminutive animals to seek refuge when the first frosts whiten the ground in the autumn and remain hidden until the rays of the spring sun begin to warm the earth. Instead, they are as active as in summer, hunting at all hours and in all sorts of weather. I frequently find their elfin-like tracks in the snow, but I do not often see these mouse-like animals because of their size, quick movements, and habit of working under cover. Occasionally, I do come upon one of them poking his delicate snout into a crevice in the bark of a tree trunk in search of insects, or ferreting about in the leaf mold or among decayed pieces of wood.

How these little animals hold their own against adverse climatic conditions and a host of natural enemies is beyond understanding. Yet the shrews are widely distributed and are abundant in many places. I suspect one reason for their successful fight for survival is that they seem able to adapt themselves wherever there is shelter and food, apparently as much at home in the dark, moss-carpeted spruce forests of the north as in our own deciduous woods, grassy fields, and marshes.

We often mistake shrews for mice or moles. They resemble both, but they may easily be distinguished from the mice by their pointed noses, small eyes, and finer fur, and from the moles by their smaller size and mouse-like feet. Perhaps if shrews were seen more often we might recognize them, but one seldom gets more than a glimpse of them as they rustle among fallen leaves or dart from one fallen log to another.

Their food consists of insects, snails, small annelids, and other food that they can capture. It doesn't seem possible they can find enough of such fare during the winter to subsist, but apparently there are sufficient dormant insects to supply their needs. Plants are eaten sparingly, but if their preferred diet is not available they can live on a plant menu for many days. Because of a very rapid rate of digestion, they require an enormous amount of food and literally eat all the time. If deprived of food for several hours, they starve to death, as I discovered when I tried to keep them as pets and found that they require almost constant attendance.

Despite their small size — they measure barely four inches in length and weigh only a few grams — they are highly predatory, courageous, and pugnacious little animals and will not hesitate to attack creatures several times their own weight. Except for repellent scent glands, which do not seem too effective, they have no defense against their natural enemies. Owls, hawks, shrikes, herons, and mammals such as foxes and weasels prey upon them with impunity. That many shrews fall victim every winter may be seen by the large number of their bones in owl pellets alone.

Thinking of the shrews, I cannot help comparing these tiny yet hardy animals, who must hunt constantly for food, with the clumsy, lumbering porcupines, who find plenty to eat in the bark and leaves of evergreen trees and need bestir themselves so slightly for their meals. Deer, too, have food ready at hand in twigs and the foliage of evergreens, but heavy snows and drifts often make travel so difficult that many perish from exhaustion and starvation. And other animals find the season one of hardship. As the snow cover deepens and food becomes scarce or unavailable, gray squirrels make use of tunnels to hunt for buried nuts, and weasels, mink, and others, made bold by hunger, roam far and wide in search of prey.

This is one time of the year when the weasel is not likely to kill for the mere pleasure of killing. I know of no animal who has a greater lust for blood. Here, indeed, is your true predator. Bold and inquisitive, with a high degree of cunning, and utterly without fear, he is quick, sure-footed, keen of scent, and relentless in pursuit. It is probably true, as has been said, that he is the most perfectly organized machine for killing ever developed among the mammals. His teeth are designed to seize prey and his jaws are provided with powerful muscles. His ears are attuned to catch the faintest squeak of a mouse and his extraordinary wiry, lithe, and muscular body permits him to follow his prey to the deepest recesses of their retreats. Add to all this a sharp nose and a low forehead in which are set a pair of small, penetrating eyes with a cunning gleam and without the faintest suspicion of mercy, and you have an animal which might be described with one word — rapacious.

And yet, paradoxically, the weasel, of all our wild animals, is, perhaps, of the greatest value to the farmer. At times he inflicts considerable damage on poultry, but on the credit side of the ledger he is one of the most effective checks on the hordes of meadow mice and other rodents which so often destroy forage crops, orchards, vineyards, and garden produce. Providence seems to have assigned him the mission of keeping these pests under control, for whenever a weasel appears mice and other rodents rapidly diminish in number.

I do not doubt his change of coat from brown to white helps him to capture his prey, but I rather suspect his change of dress is of more value as a means of protection for, surprisingly, this fierce marauder is subject, in his turn, to the law of fang and claw and often falls victim to wolves, foxes, and birds of prey, although how such animals succeed in catching him is something of a mystery.

The mink, unlike the weasel, though a member of the same tribe, does not bother to change his coat but remains brown throughout the entire year. I have often found his tracks along a snow-covered bank and have frequently seen the animal dodging in and out of the ice-free water, or swimming beneath the surface in pursuit of prey, for the mink is an expert swimmer and is as much at home in water as on land.

At this time of the year, when still waters are frozen, the mink will haunt open rapids and warm springs in the woods. Frequently he will run beneath the ice of a closed brook, if he can find an opening in it and if the water in falling away has left a narrow strip of unfrozen turf beneath ice and snow, for it is in such places that meadow mice spend the winter, their burrows opening out from the banks in the same manner as those of muskrats. But water is not essential to his happiness, and if streams freeze he will enter the woods and hunt rabbits and such other animals that he can capture.

I wonder what would happen to preying animals, such as the weasel and mink, if the meadow mice and other rodents were suddenly to diminish in numbers; certainly they would find it difficult to exist. But the meadow mouse, for one, is a prolific breeder and one large litter follows another in rapid succession, until it seems as if the countryside would be overrun with them. But their enemies are many, and from air, land, and water a constant menace threatens, ready to snuff out their lives in a savage rush of wings, feet, or fins.

Meadow mice are active throughout the winter, scurrying about in their runways beneath the snow on trips of exploration for the blanched shoots of grasses, seeds, and hardy rootstocks. Many doorways lead to the upper air and at night the mice scamper back and forth across the snow. If we could read their tracery of footprints on the white surface, as they lead from tree to tree and to stump and rock, what tales they might tell, tales of adventure and daring. For what other reason would they leave the comparative safety of their tunnels to venture forth where danger lurks from fox and owl?

I have been curious, too, to know why the deermouse stores up vast quantities of seeds, nuts, and other edibles, and then, instead of staying home like the chipmunk, runs about when cold weather comes. Even on the most bitter nights of winter, when countless stars form a canopy over the tree tops, biting winds hiss through stiff branches, and snow is piled high over tangled brush, the deermouse is abroad, skipping along the snow from tree to tree and shrub to shrub.

Doubtless it is the call of high adventure that lures him forth. To maintain a nightly revel, however, he must draw heavily on his stored-up food supply and, as winter begins to wane, his supplies are often nearly exhausted. So, too, are the seeds and berries which remain on shrub and tree, for others besides himself have dined on them. Is it any wonder, then, that he is thin and shabby when spring comes, no longer the round-bodied, handsome creature of autumn?

Like the mammals, our wintering birds find it necessary to search assiduously for enough food to keep them alive, and for this reason they often eat berries and other fruits which they normally ignore. The scarlet pennants of the barberry, made sour presumably by a provident nature so that summer residents and fall migrants leave them untouched, now become life-saving food. And the bitter, velvety, crimson plumes of the sumac, showing like flaming torches against the sky, are eaten with avidity by such birds as the chickadees and blue jays. But even such food sometimes becomes inaccessible when winter goes on the rampage; only the crossbills seem unaffected by heavy snows, for the evergreen cones on which they feed are usually above even the deepest snow cover. Actually they don't feed on the cones but on the seeds, which they scoop out with their tongues, after prying the scales apart with their curiously crossed bills.

At this moment of writing, a brown creeper is busily exploring the trunk of a towering elm outside my window. This little feathered brownie reminds me of the nuthatch, for he has the same habit of spiraling around the trunk, though he starts at the bottom and works his way upward. He spends most of his time searching for insects, and while this may seem to us an unexciting existence, he appears to be happy and contented and will occasionally burst into a long and ecstatic song in March and April.

I think most of us are unaware of the many plants that remain green throughout the year. The snowberry, bearberry, checkerberry, partridgeberry, mountain laurel, sheep laurel, pipsissewa, and inkberry are only a few that add a touch of summer to the winter scene. There are the pines, spruces, and hemlocks, too, but somehow they escape our notice, and what a pity, for the spruces and hemlocks, their white robes glistening beneath dancing sunbeams, are never more effective than at this season. The pitch pine, too, at all times a sturdy tree, never seems so rugged as when its spreading, scraggly branches groan beneath a burden of snow.

There are many other features of the February landscape that remain unnoticed by most of us. Stroll along a snow-covered woodland path with an observing eye and you will find much to intrigue you. Note the bracket fungi, in greens and reds and browns, encircling old stumps, or stiff and white, standing out from crumbling or fallen moss-grown boles. Note the naked trees, silhouetted against the winter sky, and the grotesque shadows they cast on the whitened ground. Entirely disrobed, they reveal in complete nakedness their separate individualities. Compare the angle at which their branches grow out from the main trunk, the degree and direction at which these branches curve, the appearance of the bark, the arrangement of the buds, and you will find points of dissimilarity which will enable you to recognize them, much as you distinguish your friends by the color of their hair, the tint of their eyes, the curve of their lips, the tilt of their noses. You will find it, if I am not mistaken, a charming and fascinating study.

You will also discover, as you become acquainted with our silent companions of the woods and roadsides, that they are often disfigured by swellings on the twigs and branches or by other peculiar deformations. Sometimes these outgrowths or excrescences, which are known as galls, are not particularly noticeable, but at other times they flag attention. Irregular bud deformations of the black birch may escape the eye, but the dried remains of the flower-gall so disfigure a white ash that they are rarely passed unnoticed. Occasionally a hackberry is found with so many of the so-called "witches-brooms" that the galls might almost serve to identify the tree, and frequently an oak will be adorned with so many oak apples that it looks like a leafless apple tree with last year's fruit still hanging from the branches.

Frequently the naked twigs of many choke cherries appear from a distance to have been charred by fire, but a closer examination will reveal the branches covered with black, compact, rounded, swollen masses. These masses are caused by a plant parasite, the black knot. To some extent the presence of this parasite might be used to distinguish the choke cherry from the wild black and red cherries, for though the parasite occurs on all three, it is more abundant on the choke cherry.

On the nude branches of many trees you may find the winter retreats of various insects. The trim, leaf-wrapped cocoons of the promethea moth look very much like dead leaves and hang straight down from the branches of such trees as wild cherry and sassafras. Many years ago I found hundreds of these cocoons in a clump of sassafras. I took a number of them home and kept them outdoors in an insect cage. One day, after the warm weather had set in, the moths began to emerge and soon the cage was filled with them. I let most of them escape but kept a few for breeding. Within a day or two the females deposited whitish, brown-stained eggs on some leaves which I had provided, and after the eggs had hatched I reared the caterpillars until they spun their cocoons, thus completing the life cycle. I gave the cocoons to some young entomologists and I am glad to report they kept them safely until the following spring.

If you live in eastern New England you may find the nests of the brown-tail moth on the twigs of such trees as maple, elm, oak, apple, pear, and wild cherry. The nests are small, firm-webbed retreats of silk and leaves, and are usually placed at the ends of the twigs. Like the gypsy moth, the brown-tail came from Europe and made its first appearance near Boston, but unlike the gypsy moth its manner of arrival is unknown. The moths are white with yellowish-brown hairs at the tip of the abdomen. The caterpillars spend the winter within their nests, when a third or half grown, and when fully matured have tufts of white and brown hairs. These hairs, especially the brown ones, carry an irritating poison and if the human skin is exposed to them cause the "brown-tail rash."

Many other insects spend the winter in silken nests. One that comes to mind is the Baltimore checkerspot, a butterfly found in swamps and wet meadows during June and July. Like the tent caterpillars, the larvae have the habit of working together for the benefit of all. As soon as they hatch, they spin a silken tent for their home. They enlarge and repair it as necessary, and though they often wander from it they generally return to feed and molt. After the third molt, the caterpillars stop feeding and become more or less dormant. This fast may begin as early as the middle of August, and the caterpillars cannot be induced to eat until the return of spring. They will not even feed in the southern part of their range, where they would have plenty of time to mature as butterflies and to produce another generation of caterpillars that could pass the winter. Evidently the instinct to bridge the winter as they do has become so firmly fixed after countless generations that it cannot be changed.

Although the caterpillars feed on various members of the figwort family, they seem to prefer the turtle-head. Look for the silken tents on the withered stalks and if you fail to find them, which is not unlikely as the species is not common and very local, look, instead, for pitcher plants, which are to be found in the same sort of environment, and you will discover many other interesting insects hibernating within the leaves.

February, in many ways, is a month of contrasts. Normally a month of cold and snow, there are days when spring is in the air — days when the mercury climbs high and howling winds give way to gentle zephyrs; when a benign sun warms a frozen earth and melting snows cascade along rock-ribbed gullies; when butterflies flit about in a sunny glade. Butterflies are certainly not a part of winter; we think of them as part of the summer scene, flitting about lazily in the sunshine,

> Seeing only what is fair,
> Sipping only what is sweet...

Yet I have often found mourning cloaks in February flying about in the snow-clad woods. These butterflies hibernate as adults in a convenient shelter and often emerge on mild winter days and fly about from tree to tree. They remain abroad only during the warmer parts of the day, and as the temperature begins to drop they disappear one by one, returning to their winter quarters until the sun's rays again call them forth.

So far as I know there is only a single brood of this species in the northern states. The individuals seen in February are the ones that emerged from their chrysalids in July. They are also the same ones seen in autumn flying about in the sunshine before seeking their winter quarters, where they remain, except for brief flights during the winter, until May, when they lay their eggs. Thus they live for ten months as adults, an extraordinarily long time for a butterfly.

The mourning cloaks are not the only insects to be seen at this time. On warm days gnats fly about, sometimes in small swarms and at other times by the thousands; snow flies emerge and walk over the snow; and diving beetles rise to the surface of ponds and streams. The diving beetles spend the winter on the bottoms of ponds or under banks, where they remain in a dormant or semi-dormant state, except when they are attracted to the surface by a rise of temperature. I always delight in watching these insects move through the water, for they swim and dive expertly.

They are well adapted for an aquatic existence, having an oval body, which lessens water resistance, and long, flattened hind legs that serve admirably as propelling organs.

Diving beetles are usually black or brownish marked with yellow. They have slender antennae in contrast to the club-shaped ones of the water-scavenger beetles with which they might be confused. Some of them are an inch and a half long, while others are very minute. But big or little, and in either case quite innocent-looking, they are fierce and voracious and a terror to the other small inhabitants of pond and stream. They frequently hang head-downward from the surface of quiet waters, and if you observe them carefully, you will see that just before they dive, they lift their wing-covers and take in a supply of air in the space beneath them, which they use to breathe while submerged. I have frequently taken these beetles home, as they make interesting aquarium animals if well supplied with food, and, though I have kept them alive for several months, I never succeeded in keeping them as long as Harris, who kept one "three years and a half in perfect health in a glass vessel filled with water, supported by morsels of raw meat."

The appearance of the diving beetles may lead one to suspect they are the first manifestation of renewed activity in our ponds and streams. This is not so, for many animals living in our fresh waters are active throughout the winter season. I distinctly recall a February afternoon when I was poking about in a shallow but swiftly flowing brook and a two-lined salamander suddenly slithered from beneath a flat stone. Since then, I have found many of these salamanders, for they are among the ever-present winter inhabitants of our swift shallows.

Nymphs of various May flies are also abundant in swift rivulets and spring-fed brooks, where they feed on the green algae, which they scrape from the rocks, or on the soft silt, which they sift and swallow. And brook leeches, often with young attached, may frequently be found clinging to the undersides of rocks. These leeches do not suck blood but feed entirely on aquatic insects. They are oval, flat, and olive green in color, with two lines of black dots near the center of the dorsal side. In the colder parts of spring-fed brooks, scuds swim jerkily about, searching for food and in turn being eaten by brook trout. These little animals — distant cousins of the shrimps, crabs, and lobsters — are the acrobats of the water world, for they can climb, jump, swim, or glide with equal ease. They are shaped like fleas, with arched backs and narrow bodies, and have appendages for climbing, swimming, and jumping. Apparently, Nature was in an expansive mood when she created them.

The larva of the dobson fly, commonly known as the hellgrammite, is another active inhabitant of rapid streams. I use the word "active" advisedly, for if the water grows cold, the larva will become sluggish and feed indifferently. As the temperature rises, it springs into renewed activity, probably to the dismay of other aquatic insects, since it is a fierce predator, a devouring enemy of May flies, stone flies, and caddis flies.

Averse to light, it hides by day in a hole or in a crevice beneath rocks and is seldom seen unless a stone is suddenly pulled out. I have found it occasionally but more by accident than intent. It is a queer-looking creature and so unlike the adult fly that the two hardly seem related. But there are countless similar instances in the animal world of the young being unlike their parents, so it is not altogether surprising.

Although the earthworms at this time of the year are deep in the ground, their relatives, the bristle worms, are active by the millions in ponds and streams, where they overturn the ooze of the bottoms as effectively as the earthworms overturn the topsoil of the land. And in small pools, where other animals are very scarce, water isopods crawl sluggishly over the muddy bottoms, feeding on dead leaves and other decaying vegetation. These little crustaceans, which look like miniature armadillos when viewed from above, seem to think that February is as good a month as any in which to mate, so females may be found carrying eggs in brood pouches under their legs. They must believe in frequent matings because from February until summer they have a new brood of young every five or six weeks, and the females are always carrying a brood pouch full of eggs or of developing young ones.

Other animals also feel the urge to breed. Yellow perch begin to migrate to their spawning places in shallows along pond and lake shores; skunks and gray squirrels seek their mates; and the great horned owl may be heard courting with loud hoots.

I know of nothing more disturbing than to be suddenly startled by the loud "who, hoo-hoo-hoo, who-who" of this owl, as his cry speeds through the cold, frosty air, breaking the silence of a winter's night with unexpected shrillness. It has an eerie quality and a suggestion of nameless terror. I wonder if the creatures of the woods experience the same sensation of fear which we sustain when suddenly confronted with danger as this fierce predator announces his presence, for no living thing above ground, except the larger mammals and man, escapes his talons. Even the skunk is not exempt, for this implacable enemy, flitting through the woods silently as a shadow, cares little for the disagreeable consequences of attacking such a pungent animal.

I do not often see the great horned owl, but I frequently hear him on winter nights when the lack of food sometimes drives him to visit an isolated farmyard. Never a really silent bird, he is more vocal in January and February, particularly during his courtship. His mating antics are most curious and something to see. He nods his head, flaps his wings, and bows, using, meanwhile, the choicest words of the owl language in his most persuasive manner. If mating occurs early enough in February, the eggs may be laid before the end of the month. Whatever your opinion of the bird, you cannot accuse it of neglecting its young, for the mother sits closely on her eggs during the cold days and long nights, and it is not uncommon to find her stolidly incubating under a thick blanket of snow.

As February grows old, melting snows gradually reveal patches of spreading strawberry leaves in fields and meadows and mats of lovely gray reindeer lichen in woods and thickets. When I first saw this lichen, it was a summer's day, and I wondered how the reindeer could find its stiff, coral-like growth either palatable or edible. But when months later, I found it again newly uncovered by snow, soft as a sponge, and exceedingly lovely in its freshness, I saw how easily the reindeer, lemmings, and other cold-climate animals could subsist on it and why the Scandinavians once made bread with it.

The strawberry plants, of interest in the spring when their white flowers cover the ground and even more attractive later in summer because of their red, pulpy berries whose delicate flavor is unrivaled by cultivated varieties, attract us now for the dainty lace bugs which spend the winter beneath the leaves. I suggest you find one of these tiny insects and examine it under a lens. You will be surprised, and henceforth you may realize that small things are not always so insignificant as they seem.

Spring is still a month away, yet spring is in the air and signs of it are everywhere. Snow buntings in swirling flocks have begun to move northward along ocean beaches, and the first woodcocks have appeared, though the main flight will not appear until later. The first geese are returning on their spring trip northward, and black ducks are winging their way to their breeding grounds. Starlings are beginning to whistle, and cave bats, awakening from their winter's sleep, are making short flights in their quarters. But spring will not have arrived until I catch my first glimpse of blue among the naked branches of a roadside maple. For only with the arrival of the bluebird will spring have come, though my calendar tells me otherwise.

NATURAL EVENTS IN FEBRUARY

- The trim leaf-wrapped cocoons of the promethea moth are conspicuous on the naked branches of the wild cherry and sassafras.

- Weasels, shrews, and other mammals, not in hibernation, search for food.

- Snow buntings, moving northward, feed along the ocean beaches in swirling flocks.

- The red berries of the barberry are eagerly sought by wintering soft-billed birds.

- Nymphs of various May flies are abundant in swift rivulets and spring-fed brooks.

- Gray squirrels use tunnels under the snow when hunting for buried nuts.

- Yellow perch begin to migrate to their spawning places in the shallows along pond and lake shore.

- During mid-winter thaws, the mourning cloak butterfly may be seen flitting among the trees in sunny glades.

- The great horned owl is heard courting with loud hoots.

- The eggs may be laid before the end of the month.

- Naked trees, silhouetted against the winter sky, cast their tracery on the snow-covered ground.

- On mild days, snow flies may be found walking over the snow.

- Deer nibble twigs and the foliage of evergreens.

- Starlings begin to whistle.

- The larvae of the dobson fly, known as hellgrammites, may be found in holes and crevices beneath the rocks of swift-flowing streams.

- Skunks mate.

- Northward flights of black ducks begin.

- Water isopods begin to breed.

- Females have eggs in pouches under their legs.

- Cave bats make short flights in their winter quarters.

- Two-lined salamanders are active in swift shallows.

- Various insects hibernate in the leaves of pitcher plants.

- Brook leeches may be found clinging to the undersides of rocks in swift riffles.

- Shelf brackets, in greens, reds, and browns, encircle old stumps or, stiff and white, stand out from crumbling or fallen moss-grown boles.

- The larvae of the Baltimore checkerspot butterfly winter in silken tents on the withered stalks of members of the figwort family.

- Scuds swim in spring-fed streams.

- The pitch pine, despite its scraggly appearance, reveals a picturesque ruggedness beneath its burden of snow.

- Dainty lace bugs find refuge from the winter storms under spreading strawberry leaves.

- The first woodcocks appear; these are occasional individuals, the main flight still a month away.

- Bristleworms are active in ponds and streams.

- Spruces and hemlocks, their white robes glistening in the February sunshine, provide a decorative background for winter's stage.

- On sunny days, diving beetles frequently rise to the surface of ponds and streams.

❧ Brown creepers on the trunks of trees industriously search for insects.

❧ Gray squirrels mate.

❧ In patches free from snow, the reindeer lichen carpets the forest floor with a gray coral-like growth.

❧ On warm days, gnats fly forth in small swarms or by thousands.

❧ Half-grown caterpillars of the brown-tail moth pass the winter in small, firm-webbed nests of silk and leaves on the tips of twigs.

❧ The dried remains of the flower-gall persist on the naked branches of the white ash.

❧ The black knot stands out on the naked branches of the chokecherry.

❧ The scarcity of other food drives chickadees, blue jays, and other wintering birds to feed on sumac berries.

❧ The first hardy flocks of geese return on their spring trip northward.

❧ Kinglets feed unconcernedly, though the north wind howls and pine branches groan beneath heavy burdens.

❧ Porcupines feed on the bark and leaves of evergreen trees.

❧ Meadow mice scurry about their runways beneath the snow on trips of exploration.

❧ Crossbills feed on the seeds of the pine, which they pry loose with their curiously crossed bills.

❧ Evergreen plants add a touch of summer to the winter scene.

❧ Oak apples are conspicuous on the leafless branches of oak trees.

# March

When I awoke this morning and looked out of my window, I found the sky heavy with the threat of snow. And some time later, when I left my house, I discovered a chillness in the early air. March has come and I had hopes of an early spring, but it was not a morning designed to convince me that spring was near.

Yet, a few moments later, I did not care if storm clouds gathered, if winds howled among the treetops, and snowflakes whirled over the ground. Let winter sound another note of defiance as it beat a slow and sullen retreat, for when the bluebird comes, spring cannot be far behind, and I had caught a glimpse of blue, vivid against the leaden sky, among the naked branches of an apple tree in the orchard.

March was only three days old and I could already mark two red letter days on my calendar, for yesterday I heard the thin, sweet "pe-ep, pe-ep, pe-ep" of the spring peeper issuing from a woodland pool not far from my house. Early in March some years ago, I tried to trace the source of this sound but without success, as the peeper is an elusive creature and while the air is still chilly, it remains well hidden. No matter how carefully I poked around among the dead leaves and moss at the water's edge or scrutinized every stick and bit of grass, he still remained a mysterious piping voice.

Later in the month, when the twisted horns of the skunk cabbage were high above swampy ground and the golden tassels of the pussy willows swayed with every passing breeze, I renewed my search. It was a bright, warm day. The air was balmy with the breath of the south wind and the smell of the new earth, and countless pools in the meadows mirrored the clear blue sky. As I followed the narrow path through the woods, a tiny blue butterfly lazily winged its way, and now and then I walked into swarms of midges dancing in the air. I saw, too, a cottontail, thin and ragged, scurry about the rustling brush and heard the "kong-quer-ree" of red-wing blackbirds somewhere in the distance.

When I reached the woodland pool, I found that the stiff catkins of the alders, growing along the water's edge, had expanded into soft drooping tresses. I startled a group of rusty blackbirds feeding in the shallow water. They took flight and perched in a nearby tree, whence they watched me with curiosity as I gingerly jumped about on tree roots and tussocks, for the ground was still soft from winter snows. A painted turtle, sunning itself on a log and doubtless frightened by my approach, slipped silently into the water, disturbing the smooth surface in ever-widening ripples that tossed whirligig beetles about like rowboats in an angry sea.

I paused a moment and listened. My solitary peeper had now been joined by countless others, and their voices were all about me. I pushed apart some floating leaves and poked about among the grass and moss but failed to find a single singer. One seemed to be at my very feet, and I bent over and looked carefully among the vegetation growing at the water's edge, but he was not there. And so I spent the afternoon seeking the elusive frogs, who must have laughed with glee at my futile efforts. I finally gave up and went home.

A month of melting snows and chilling winds, March tempts few of us to venture into fields and woods where sodden turf cakes boots with mud and tires muscles. But the nature lover doesn't mind these things. As March arrives with its promise of spring, he is eager to be afield and to note with never-flagging interest the many stirrings of a reawakening nature world.

Wintering purple finches are beginning to sing and the bills of the starlings show touches of yellow. The weasel is changing his winter coat of white to brown, and bluebottle flies dart about in sunny places. Sap has begun to run and buds to swell, and the maples on the wooded hillsides, gray and apparently lifeless since November, are suffused with a rosy hue. The tops of willows are turning a golden yellow and bramble and other shrubs are taking on deep red and purple tints.

Pussy willows are showing their furry coats, the skunk cabbage is appearing above swampy ground, and the hepatica adds its note of cheerfulness to the still-bleak woods, thrilling a strolling wanderer with its unexpected beauty. I recall my delight when I found it for the first time, blossoming beneath a blanket of snow, and even today I experience a responsive thrill when I find its pale delicate blossoms in a hidden nook.

The skunk cabbage, too, evokes a similar feeling as I watch for it to respond to the pulse of life and push its twisted horns, mottled with purple, green, and yellow-green, through the wet earth of gloomy woods. The hive bees are among the first insects to visit it, but being fastidious in their taste in the matter of perfume and color, they leave it when other and more attractive flowers appear. Then the flies and gnats, which have lived under fallen leaves during the winter and are now warmed into active life, swarm about the spathes.

The leaves appear after the flowers. At first, they are to be found in a compactly coiled, pointed spike close beside the ruddy spathe, but later they unfold in vivid green crowns. Frogs and toads sometimes make their home beneath them, and frequently a yellow-throat endures the plant's foul odor and builds her nest in it, seemingly to understand that her four-footed enemies prefer a sweeter-scented atmosphere.

Our ponds and streams, no less than the earth, respond to the warm influence of the spring sun and everywhere, even in the smallest spring pool, there are signs of renewed activity. As the ice breaks up, muskrats leave their homes and feed on the shore, and wood frogs and spotted salamanders slip from the cover of the forest floor and enter the water to mate and lay their eggs.

Water striders and whirligig beetles come to the surface and play about along the water's edge. The whirligig beetles may be seen at almost any time, even in the winter, when they come out during mild weather for midwinter dances. But it is at this time of the year, when rising temperatures lure them from the mud, that they can be seen in the largest numbers, gyrating on the surface and breaking the water into ripples or basking like turtles on logs and stones. Occasionally they fly if they can climb out of the water to "take off," and if captured they squeak by rubbing the tip of the abdomen against the wings and emit a disagreeable milky fluid.

The water striders have always fascinated me, ever since I found them in a bubbling brook that ran through a woodland glen. It is surprising how memories linger through the years, and I still vividly recall the day when I first chanced upon these curious, slender, long-legged insects and was completely lost watching them skate about on the surface of the water. Even today I often pause to watch them play about, darting here and there, or drifting with the current, or jumping up and landing on the water without breaking the surface film. Sometimes they gather in schools in a quiet, sheltered spot, as if to discuss some weighty problem or to exchange the gossip of the day, scattering for shelter if alarmed but quickly congregating again.

It might seem odd that these insects can skim about on the water without breaking the surface film. But they are able to do so for much the same reason that we can float a greased needle. It all has to do with surface tension and related things in which we are not at present interested. A point of interest, however, is the fact that some species of water striders live in mid-ocean and are the only insects that do so. It seems incredible that such fragile-appearing insects can survive the high seas of a storm but they cling, doubtless half-drowned, to some floating object until the storm has passed and they have a chance to dry off.

The striders feed on insects which they capture with their front legs, and in turn, like some other water bugs, they support many young water mites which are now abundant in quiet streams and still pools. The water mites are small but gaily conspicuous as they move rapidly through the water or force themselves among the leaflets of water plants. They look like spiders and sometimes have been erroneously called water spiders, although this term is not a good one, as there are some true spiders that are semi-aquatic in habit and therefore more deserving of the name. The water mites are rather plump yet quite active, swimming freely through the water by means of eight legs attached to the forward part of the body. They are oval or nearly spherical in outline, with a skin usually soft and easily broken, and are brightly, if not brilliantly, colored in various shades of crimson, brown, yellow, blue, green, or purple.

In temporary spring pools, such as are formed by melting snows, fairy shrimps are often seen. They are rather unusual looking animals, measuring about an inch long, with a transparent body in which it is often possible to see the beating heart, and are colored with all the tints of the rainbow. These little creatures always swim on their backs by means of leaflike appendages, which also serve as breathing organs, and as they move through the water the waving plumes are plainly visible.

Females, which can be recognized by the brood pouch on the side of the abdomen, appear to be more numerous than the males, and in some species no males are known, the young developing from eggs which have never been fertilized. The larvae hatch from the eggs in a partly developed state but grow rapidly and mature in six or seven days. In a typical New England spring, the fairy shrimp population may reach its maximum within a week or two after the ice has left, and at that time females, carrying eggs in their brood pouches, and many mating pairs may be seen swimming about.

Fairy shrimps can live only in cold water, and as the water warms or the pools dry up, they gradually fall to the bottom and die, but not before the females have deposited eggs which lie dormant for a considerable period in mud, either wet or dried. These eggs are thick-walled to carry the species through the summer and may be dried and frozen without injury. Some even seem to need drying before they can hatch.

The distribution of fairy shrimps is freakish and fraught with uncertainty. They may be numerous in one pool and entirely absent from one nearby, which to all appearances is exactly like the first one. For several years they may appear as regularly as the seasons and then they may not be seen again for four or five years, although the conditions may be the same, or they may be abundant one season and then not reappear for several years.

During the month of March, I often find the footprints of the raccoon on the soggy woodland floor or along the muddy banks of a stream. I see the animal only occasionally, however, for usually the weather is not yet to his liking and except for short trips abroad, he remains in his winter retreat. The raccoon is not a true hibernator and he will often emerge from his sleep during midwinter thaws to search for animals also active. But such foraging expeditions are short-lived and as the temperature begins to fall, he returns to his den until the sun again lures him forth. His expeditions abroad during the early spring days are actually trial trips and usually also of short duration, and it is not until spring has really taken possession of the woods that he finally emerges to search among the sodden leaves and debris left by melting snows for newly awakened snakes and beetles.

Sometimes appearances can be deceptive. The raccoon appears clumsy and deliberate of movement and yet I have seen him climb a tree with surprising agility. He spends as much time in the trees as he does on the ground, for he sleeps in them during the day, flattening himself out along a thick branch or climbing to the topmost branches and encircling the trunk with his body. It is amusing to watch him adapt himself to the uneven bed, tucking his nose down between his paws, and curling his tail about his body.

The trees also provide him with a refuge when pursued by an enemy, and in the winter a hollow one serves as his home. In thick woods, he often travels considerable distances among the treetops and while traveling frequently comes upon a nest of squirrels, scattering the terrified occupants.

Unlike the raccoon, the skunk is now abroad rather regularly. He is not so heavy a sleeper as other hibernating animals and awakens early, although, like the raccoon, he often leaves his lair for an excursion abroad during the winter. At first, he confines his activities to the woods, where he feeds on whatever insects he may find and such other small animals and birds that he can succeed in capturing, but when the spring thaw sets in and the snow gradually disappears he abandons the woods and thickets for more open land, where he hunts meadow mice on the newly exposed areas of turf or snakes that may have been lured from winter quarters by the sunshine.

As the frogs and salamanders begin to migrate to breeding ponds and streams he adds these to his diet, as well as mollusks, crayfish, and other aquatic animals. Before long I expect to find evidence of a nocturnal visit to my yard and perhaps I will hear of an expedition to a neighboring chicken coop. The harm he does, however, is more than balanced by his destruction of injurious rodents and noxious insects.

Farmers are rapidly learning that the skunk is a valuable ally in reducing the population of farm pests, and in many states he is protected by law. He is charged with being a killer of domestic fowl and it is true that he will enter a poultry house, but he does so only upon occasion. Furthermore, this preying on poultry is a perverse and abnormal tendency and is practiced only by individuals; it is doubtful if more than two percent ever taste chicken. Even with a higher percentage, his marauding proclivities could easily be curbed with the proper housing of poultry and protection of the beehives, which he is also inclined to rob.

The skunk is doubtless the most misunderstood of our native animals. We instinctively shy away from him as if he were a loathsome, leprous thing, yet there is probably no animal more harmless and inoffensive than this little denizen of our fields and forests.

Occasionally he offends our sensibilities, but only if threatened. At all other times, he is exceedingly neat and particular in his personal habits. He minds his own business, and he is attractive. He likes the companionship of man, and as he has a gentle disposition, can easily be domesticated, proving an affectionate and entertaining pet, as tame and playful as a kitten and far more intelligent and amusing.

The skunk prefers to rest by day and hunt by night, but I have seen him in the fields and woods during the daylight hours. One day last summer, I was walking along a narrow path dense with tall grasses when suddenly they quivered excitedly. I stopped and peered down, and when I saw what was at my feet, decided that rather than debate the right of way, I would wait until my little friend had put a safe distance between us. He was in no hurry to do so and made no effort to move until some moments had passed, when he quite deliberately ambled off. His actions were typical, for the skunk is normally fearless of any living thing, and if left alone will continue on his way with genteel and dignified indifference. Molest him, and you do so at your peril.

The powerful effluvium which he discharges is stored in two glands under the tail and may be ejected a distance of ten feet. It is yellow in color, and somewhat phosphorescent, and resembles musk in its extraordinary volatility. It is also intensely acid, burns the skin like fire, and in extreme cases has been known to produce blindness. The discharge at any time is scarcely three drops, and yet this small quantity will pollute the air for half a mile or more in every direction. The mephitic odor holds terror for most animals and provides the skunk with immunity against attack, although at times he falls victim to the horned owl, fox, and bobcat.

The woodchuck is another animal of which I have yet to hear anything complimentary. Everyone seems to think he is an unmitigated nuisance. He frequently does considerable damage to crops, especially vegetables in field and garden, and often proves annoying to the farmer by digging holes and earth mounds in the fields and feeding on and trampling down grasses and grains, but after all, he does these things without malice and simply because he has to live.

I would dislike to see the woodchuck become extinct, for he is such a familiar feature of grassy field and hedgerow. To my mind, he is also a rather likable animal even though he is fat, lazy, and stupid. But I doubt if he will ever vanish because his natural enemies, with the exception of the fox, have largely disappeared from his haunts, and as for the farmer and gardener, he can successfully contend with them.

The woodchuck seeks his burrow in early fall and remains there until the warm March sun lures him forth. As yet, I have not seen him, but I expect any day to catch sight of him waddling across the field back of my house. Or perhaps I shall come upon him in his characteristic pose, sitting upright and motionless, surveying the countryside with undisguised curiosity.

The raccoon, skunk, and woodchuck are not the only hibernating mammals enticed from their winter retreats by the seductions of returning spring. Female black bears, followed by their cubs, emerge from their dens and search for food, feeding, for the most part, on buds and twigs. And, about the middle of the month, the chipmunk awakens from his long winter sleep. Excited at the prospect of many pleasant days of adventuring and activity and full of joy to be released from his underground confinement, he mounts a log or tree root and starts a loud, chirpy "chuck-chuck-chuck." Other chipmunks, deep in their burrows, hear the clarion call and with a rush scamper out and add their loud and vigorous notes in a spring salute.

I know of no inhabitant of our fields and woods so appealing as the chipmunk, with his bright dress, airy grace, and bird-like vivacity, or so delightful to watch as he scampers merrily about; and, what is more, I know of no wild animal who is such cheery company, once you make his acquaintance. The chipmunk delights in the open woods and rocky pastures, where stone walls, half-rotted logs, and thick underbrush offer safe retreat on the approach of an enemy. In such places I find him during the daylight hours, for he loves sunshine. I often stop to watch this elfin creature frolic on a stone wall, pausing now and then to scan his surroundings with alert, inquisitive eyes. He is an extremely wary and timid animal, and if alarmed will immediately dash away among the rocks or otherwise disappear from view, with his tail quivering excitedly. He has, however, much curiosity, and if disturbed by the appearance of anything unusual will seek some safe vantage point from which to peer at it with every sign of interest, sometimes chattering away like a red squirrel.

In chipmunk land, spring is the time for love-making and before the month is over the males go in search of mates. Other animals, too, feel the same urge, and from isolated woods may be heard the barking of foxes or the noisy caterwauling of wildcats as they seek their mates. Meadow mice are more silent.

In March, the gray squirrels begin to build their nests and before April showers caress the earth the young may be born.

Porcupines may also give birth to precocious young, though frequently they are not born until May; and beneath stones and logs that have long lain on damp ground, wood lice have their first brood of young ones.

Few birds mate at this early date, though sometimes bluebirds, robins, and crows will try to get an early start, often with tragic results, for the weather is not yet conducive to nest building and family raising. But the English sparrows and the barred owls are indifferent to the temper of the elements; and, as the owls engage in their grotesque love-making, weird sounds disturb the silence of the woods at night.

Various forms of animal life are now to be found under stones and logs, and if you should turn them over you will find millipedes and centipedes, insects, snails, and spiders gradually being warmed into active life. You may also discover a small brown snake or two, and perhaps a red-backed salamander. Both of these animals are quite common, the salamander being abundant in woods, where it lurks under moss, bark, logs, and stones. It is a very secretive and timid little animal, and when revealed in its hiding place rarely attempts an immediate escape but remains quietly curled in the position in which it was found. Prod or even touch it, however, and it will usually run off, though run may not seem quite the word as its legs are relatively weak and must be aided by looping movements of the trunk and tail so that the animal seems to progress over the ground by a series of rapidly executed leaps.

One Saturday afternoon several years ago, I took a group of young naturalists on an early spring collecting trip and we found dozens of these little plum-red salamanders in a woodland glen. The young collectors were elated at finding what they persistently referred to as "lizards," and many of the little creatures were placed in bottles and taken home as pets. They do very well in a vivarium, but the vivarium should be covered as the salamanders are excellent climbers and can easily mount the vertical sides and escape. Later their dried bodies will be found in a corner.

Salamanders are often confused with lizards, but it is easy to distinguish between them because salamanders have a smooth skin whereas lizards have a scaly one like the snakes. Except for one species, the common five-lined skink, which has been recorded from Massachusetts and Connecticut, lizards are not found in New England. I don't know why, but doubtless other species will eventually make their way into this part of the country.

The little brown snake is very common, even in urban regions, where it may be found in vacant lots under all kinds of trash, such as pieces of old linoleum or roofing. It is an extremely inoffensive creature but very secretive and seldom seen because of its habits, small size, and drab color, although I have discovered it basking in the sun in early spring, when the grasses and other vegetation have not yet begun to grow. When I first began collecting the various creatures I found in the fields and woods, this little snake was my introduction to the science of herpetology. I remember with what triumph I carried a specimen home and how I pored over a snake book to learn what to feed it.

I know of no month that offers such a succession of delightful and unexpected surprises as March. On an early morning, I might awaken to the gay carol of a song sparrow as he voices his arrival in clear, ringing notes, and later in the day discover the starry blossoms of the spring beauty expanding in a sunny hollow or in the still naked woods the spring azure butterfly flying about like a "violet afloat." Butterflies are such ethereal creatures that they seem out of place in our blizzard-swept winters, and yet, as we have seen, the mourning cloaks are often abroad during midwinter thaws. It is surprising to find that one of the first butterflies to appear in the spring is the small, dainty spring azure; it would seem more fitting that some larger and seemingly hardier butterfly would be the first to venture forth after the snows have melted.

The spring azure is a creature of many fashions, for over a territory ranging from Labrador to Alaska and south to the Gulf of Mexico, we find one form in one locality, a different one in another. It is a source of endless labor to those of us who would study its protean forms, for even seasonally it differs to a marked degree. For instance, we have in the vicinity of Boston an early spring form which is small with large black markings on the under surface of the wings, a later variety which is larger with smaller black spots, and finally in summer a third form, still larger and with considerably fainter spots.

The spring azure is not the only butterfly to be seen during the month. On warm days, mourning cloaks appear in sunny glades and similar places and occasionally the tortoise butterfly. I have also seen a violet tip on the branch of a maple, sipping the sweet sap from a wound made, possibly, by a red squirrel. The little rodent is fond of the maple sap and taps the trees by gnawing through the bark on the upper side of a branch. The cut forms a cavity in which the sap collects and serves as a "drinking fountain" which the animal may visit several times a day.

The red squirrel, always a noisy animal, seems unusually so at this time of the year, or perhaps it is because he and his cousins, now out of their vermin-infested retreats, are busy building clean, cool nests against the day when their families will be increased by young ones.

If the winter has been a mild one, the downy woodpecker will begin as early as March to advertise for a mate by drumming loudly on a resonant tree or pole. I have often seen two males pay court to a female, and if she happens to be somewhat of a coquette, she may seem to encourage first one suitor and then another as they vie for her affections. This may continue for a week or more, the males, I suspect, meanwhile being kept in a state of suspense. When the female finally makes her choice, she and her newly-found partner immediately begin hunting for a suitable home site. This may take some time, but when a desirable site is finally located, usually a dead stub or a branch that is decayed at the heart, they both drill until a gourd-shaped hole has been dug. Here the eggs are laid and the young reared until fledged.

For the first few days of March, our avian friends are those that have wintered with us, but as the days pass, new arrivals appear on the scene. Some of them stay for a few days or a few weeks and then go on to more northern breeding grounds, while others remain until the chill of approaching autumn warns them to return to warmer regions. A day or two after the bluebird appears, I am sure to see the robin on the lawn or to hear his sharp clucking call from a nearby tree. For some reason, the first robin of spring always seems to be alone, and yet a day or two later, he may be seen in company with several others as if they had been close at hand but timid about showing themselves. But this explanation seems unlikely, for the robin displays a most charming confidence in the friendliness of man and walks unconcernedly about our lawns in search of worms. Frequently, his trusting nature leads him to build his nest and rear his family on the woodwork or in the vines of a porch within a few feet of a window or door.

It may be days before the robin bursts into song, but then some early morning, his simple song of faith and hope falls upon our ears. But even before the robin begins to sing, the song sparrow sounds his gay carol from every quarter. Little does this feathered creature care what the weather is. Once he starts to sing, he will sing on the brightest morning or bleakest day; even though winds may blow and snow and ice still decorate the landscape, he will pour out his liveliest carol in a spirit of optimism and in defiance of the raging elements, as if to speed departing winter on its way.

While the chill and blustering winds of March still sweep over frozen fields or through snow-clad woods, the familiar note of a newly arrived phoebe may be heard about the barn, in the orchard, or along a rushing stream. Over still ice-bound swamps, their scarlet epaulets flashing in the bright sunshine, red-wings break the silence with their cheery "kong-quer-ree." And bronzed grackles, whirling into a leafless tree, their iridescent plumage twinkling greens and purples in dancing sunbeams, advertise their return by discordant chatterings.

Later in the month, a marsh hawk appears out of the blue sky and flies in his buoyant but unhurried manner over a meadow; a cowbird, notorious for his belief in free love, arrives like a silent shade and struts over the ground; and on a windy morning, a fox sparrow is blown in like an eddying gust of dead leaves, announcing his presence by noisy scratching in a thicket as he searches for still dormant insects, but pausing now and then to burst into a song that falls upon the air like the soft tinkling of tiny silver bells. And as the month draws to a close, a vesper sparrow runs along a country road where the whitlow grass blooms, flirting his white-tipped tail, while from a neighboring treetop comes the loud call of a meadowlark.

NATURAL EVENTS IN MARCH

- Young porcupines may be born.

- Under the warm rays of the spring sun, the stiff catkins of the alders expand into soft, drooping tresses.

- Marsh hawks return from the South.

- Meadow mice begin to breed.

- The delicate, starry blossoms of the spring beauty begin to bloom in sunny hollows.

- On bright days, tortoise butterflies may occasionally be seen on the wing in open glades of woods.

- Cottontails, thin and ragged, scurry about the rustling brush and sere meadow.

- The whitlow grass opens its small white flowers in barren fields and along roadsides.

- Rusty blackbirds, in small groups, may be seen feeding in swamps and about woodland pools.

- Skunks are now seen regularly.

- Brown snakes may be found basking in the sun before the grasses and other vegetation have begun to grow.

- Weird sounds that disturb the silence of the woods at night announce that barred owls are performing their courtship rites.

- Cowbirds put in an appearance.

- Chipmunks emerge from hibernation and soon after the males begin to seek their mates.

- The hepatica, often covered with a mantle of snow, opens its pale, delicate blossoms to herald the approach of spring.

- English sparrows begin their nesting.

- Wood frogs and spotted salamanders slip from the cover of the forest floor and enter the water to lay their eggs.

- Female black bears, followed by their cubs, emerge from their dens and search for food, feeding on buds and twigs.

- Water striders and whirligig beetles appear on the surface of ponds and streams.

- Male red-wing blackbirds, arriving in noisy flocks, end the winter silence of swamps and marshes.

- The buds of pussy willows show their furry coats.

- Returning song sparrows salute departing winter with their lively carols.

- The first brood of young wood lice appear.

- Wintering purple finches begin to sing.

- Some of the wintering young males begin to show a little red in their plumage.

- As the ice breaks up, adults and larvae of the fairy shrimp may be found swimming in ponds and spring pools.

- The violet-tip butterfly emerges from hibernation and seeks the sweets which drip from wounded maples.

- Red-backed salamanders lurk under stones and logs.

- The twisted horns of the skunk cabbage appear in swampy ground.

- Bluebottle flies, enticed forth from their retreats by the warmth of the spring sun, fly about in sunny places.

- Bills of the starlings show touches of yellow. Following mild winters, downy woodpeckers begin to advertise for mates by drumming loudly on a resonant tree or pole.

- In the still naked woods, the spring azure butterfly, like a "violet afloat," searches for an early flower.

- Water mites are abundant in quiet streams and still pools.

- Millipedes, centipedes, snails, and spiders are gradually warmed into active life.

- Meadowlarks call loudly from treetops.

- Woodchucks venture out of their burrows.

- The nocturnal barking of foxes, issuing from isolated woods, hints of the mating season.

- A flash of blue among the naked branches of a roadside maple or a tree in the orchard announces the arrival of the first bluebird.

- Sap begins to run.

- Red squirrels slit the bark of maples to suck and nibble on the sweet icicles of sap.

- Robins arrive from the South.

- The wildcats' mating call resounds through the still silent woods.

- Raccoons make trial trips out of hibernation.

- The familiar note of the phoebe may be heard in an orchard or along a rushing stream.

- Weasels change their winter coats of white to brown.

- Bronzed grackles, whirling into a leafless treetop, advertise their return with discordant chatterings.

- Muskrats, freed from their winter imprisonment by the breakup of the ice, leave their homes to feed on the shore.

- Swarms of midges dance in the air.

- A thin, sweet "pe-ep, pe-ep, pe-ep," coming from a pond, pool, or marshy swamp, is the call of the spring peeper, awakened from his winter's sleep.

- ❧ Gray squirrels begin building their nests. (The young are often born during this month.)

- ❧ A noisy scratching in a thicket reveals a transient fox sparrow industriously searching for seeds and insects.

- ❧ Tree buds begin to swell.

- ❧ The golden tassels of the pussy willows sway with every passing breeze.

- ❧ Maples become suffused with a rosy hue.

- ❧ Brambles and other shrubs take on deep red and purple tints.

April

In April the south wind, fragrant with the smell of spring, gently caresses the landscape and the spring sun, mounting higher in the sky, dissolves lingering snow wreaths. Countless shoots, with early leaves snuggled close, push their way through rain-moistened soil and tinge the earth with vernal green. Ant-like stars of the night, tiny blossoms appear in gloomy woods and rocky hillsides, in sun-kissed fields and shaded roadsides, perfuming the air with subtle fragrance.

I am afield as often as I am able to escape from routine chores, poking among the dead leaves that still clothe the forest floor, or exploring dark retreats and craggy nooks. Among the dead leaves I seek the wild ginger and its small bell-like flower, hiding modestly under woolly leaves, as if in apology for having blossomed; and in rocky places, where great boulders are covered with lovely little gardens, I hunt the corydalis, whose kinship with the Dutch-man's breeched and squirrel corn is evident by its pale foliage and attenuated saclike blossoms.

The skunk cabbage remains a relic of March, but its mottled spathes have given way to leafy green crowns, soon to blend with the leaves of the hellebore, now beginning to unfold. Huddled on little islands, the marsh marigolds are opening their golden petals to provide a festive board for bees and brilliant flower-flies. I am particularly careful not to bypass places where the turf is sodden and uninviting, for in such places I find the dainty little lilies of the yellow adder's tongue. These pale yellow flowers nestle between mottled leaves and play host to hive and mining bees, and those frauds, the bee flies, whose larvae feed on the eggs and young of other insects.

Occasionally, I find the purple trillium growing with these gilded lilies. Bees and butterflies do not visit the carrion-scented purple flowers; not because they are fastidious in their taste but because they cannot obtain nectar from them. Since these insects are not available for cross-pollination, the plant must depend on the carrion flies, which are doubtless attracted to the flowers by their resemblance, in color and odor, to decaying flesh. They lay their eggs in these flowers, and in return for a monopoly of pollen food, which probably tastes as it smells, transport the pollen grains.

Growing in the shelter of evergreens, the lovely arbutus opens its chalices to scent the air of the spring woods with a delicious, spicy fragrance that blends with the odor of pine and the smell of snow-soaked soil just warming into life. It is almost a sacrilege to pick the dainty blossoms, which seem to have been placed in our early spring woods as messengers of hope and gladness, and whenever I pass an itinerant vendor hawking the forlorn, withered blossoms tied together in nondescript bunches, my soul rebels against such vandalism.

Along woodland borders and on shaded hillsides, the tremulous starlike blossoms of the anemone quiver in the slightest breeze; and in rocky places, on hillside slopes and bordered roadsides, the early saxifrage, rooted in the clefts of rocks, sends up tufts of tiny flowers, crowding the feathery, fern-like leaves of the Dutchman's breeches. And in hidden copse and shaded thicket, the solitary buds of the bloodroot slowly disengage themselves from the embrace of silvery-green leaf-cloaks and expand into white-petaled, golden-centered flowers of evanescent beauty.

In fields and rocky pastures dotted with juniper, the wild strawberry, cinquefoil, and ground ivy carpet the ground with trailing vines and open their blossoms to the sky. Here, too, the pussy-toes, or early everlasting, unfold their little clustered heads, tufts of silver-white silk on stems rising from charming rosettes that could have been found throughout the winter. And everywhere, the pestiferous chickweed opens its small white flowers.

As a rule, our early spring wildflowers are small, shy, and delicate little plants, and we find them more by accident or by painstaking search. Of course, there are exceptions, such as the yellow rocket, which sends upward from a single root crown a dozen or more sturdy stems a foot high, each bearing a showy, panicled spike of small brilliant yellow flowers that brighten meadows and the banks of neglected runlets in early April. This showy plant is a relative of the lowly shepherd's purse, already flowering along roadsides and in waste places, for both have flowers in which petals and sepals are arranged in the form of a cross and hence are members of the *Cruciferae* or mustard family. The word crucifer means cross bearer, but the crucifers are no martyrs. They are, on the contrary, a group of vigorous plants adapted to succeed in the struggle for existence.

The shepherd's purse is no exception and if you examine it,

you will find that it makes one stem serve for many flowers, none of which develops at the tip of the stem, for to do so would be to stop its upward growth. You will also observe that the flowers, though small, are not entirely inconspicuous. They are clustered together to attract those insects which aid in pollination and which otherwise might pass them by if the small flowers were arranged separately on the stem. This is one reason why the plant has been able to march around the world and compete successfully with other plants. Notice, too, as summer passes into autumn, that the plant continues to blossom until frost covers the ground. By thus extending its flowering season far beyond that of any native flower, it avoids the fierce competition for insect trade it would encounter were it to flower during a shorter period. In your daily journeyings, note the places where you find it growing and you will discover it is not a proud plant but will take root wherever it may, being satisfied with unoccupied wasteland and locations where other plants refuse to grow. Is it any wonder, then, that the plant has been eminently successful in its struggle for survival?

The buds of trees, which began to swell in March, begin to open as April arrives and before the month is half gone, red maples fringe the woods and brighten swamps with the scarlet of myriad blossoms; elms appear as if wreathed in a coppery mist; willows gild the landscape with their golden catkins vivid against the blue April sky; and poplars and aspens shake out countless tassels that dance upon the south wind.

From my window, I can look out across the fields and see the shadbush in bloom, its silvery-white chandeliers brilliantly white against the background of leafless trees. And should I take the path that leads across those fields into the woods beyond and follow its twists and turns for half a mile or so, I would find the aromatic spicebush in blossom, its golden knots threaded on naked branches gilding the swampy April woodland, and the small yellow flowers of the leatherwood, twinkling in the sunlight as it filters through the leafless trees.

As the spring sunshine warms the air, many insects emerge

from their winter retreats, and the eggs of others hatch into nymphs, grubs, and caterpillars. Within the dark recesses of their burrows, tree borers resume their nefarious activities, and in the ground, the larvae of click and May beetles begin to feed on various roots. Ladybird beetles come out of retirement and wander about in search of food; carabid beetles hide by day beneath stones and logs and roam at night in search of prey; ants repair their colonies; and Polistes wasps begin to build their nests.

The eggs of the tent caterpillar hatch, and soon the small silken nests may be seen on the branches of the wild cherry. The wingless females of the spring canker worm climb up the trunks of trees where the winged males search for them; a few other brave and hardy moths and butterflies emerge from their hibernating places and fly lazily about, visiting the early spring flowers; bees and wasps and various flies hum about the blossoming maples and willows; and the industrious ichneumons chase them all.

We eagerly await the arrival of the bluebird and excitedly search for an early spring flower, but we casually accept the appearance of the first bumblebee. Yet the bumblebee, in her rich velvety costume of black and gold, and her wings yet untorn from long foraging flights, strikes a welcome note as she emerges from her resting place and hums her way over field and meadow.

The bumblebees we see in April are queens and the only survivors of last year's colonies. Their mission in life is to establish new colonies, but instead of getting to work immediately, they fly about for a week or so, sipping the nectar of early flowers and filling the bags on their hind legs with pollen grains. Such activity is not without purpose, for after a fast of eight or nine months, they must store up energy in preparation for their domestic duties and obtain the food necessary to feed the growing grubs of the new colony.

For a place in which to locate the nest, the queen usually selects the abandoned nest of a field mouse or chipmunk. Frequently it means a diligent search until she finds one to her liking, but as soon as she has made her selection, she mixes the pollen and nectar which she has gathered into a loaf about the size of a bean. She places this mass — the so-called "beebread" — on the floor of the nest and lays a few tiny eggs in it. Then, covering the eggs with wax, which she secretes from between her abdominal segments, she fashions a thimble like honey pot and fills it with honey to serve as food while she broods over the eggs.

The grubs feed on the "beebread" under the waxen coverlet, and as they feed, they burrow deeper and deeper into it. After a week or so of stuffing themselves, they become full-grown and then each spins a thin, papery but tough cocoon in which to pupate. Meanwhile, the queen broods on the cocoons and sips from the honey pot.

About ten days or two weeks later, the grubs are transformed into worker bumblebees whose immediate duties are to gather more nectar and pollen and to help rear the next brood of workers. They also have the responsibility of maintaining the entire colony, for the queen henceforth does nothing but lay eggs. In addition to rearing successive broods, they strengthen the silken pupa cradles with wax and convert them into cells for storing honey.

The first generation of workers is followed by others, and the colony gradually increases in size until the climax is reached in late summer, when young queens and males are produced. The males are sluggish creatures, and their one purpose in life is to mate with the young queens. After they have performed their marital duties, they die, and as summer wanes, the workers also begin to die off. The mother queen, having fulfilled her destiny, also dies, leaving only the young queens to spend the winter in some cozy retreat, each one by herself, until the following April, when they emerge to establish new colonies.

Most of the moths and butterflies that appear in early spring are small, dull-colored forms — the advance guard of the brilliant hosts of midsummer. An exception is the common white or cabbage butterfly, which flies over fields, meadows, and gardens in April, sipping the nectar of early flowers through its long coiled tongue.

This butterfly — one of the major pests of garden crops — is of particular interest because it is one of the few imported insects of which we have been able to keep a complete record. The insect, which has been a pest for centuries in Europe, came to our country by way of Quebec during the Civil War and has since spread over practically all of the United States and Canada. Before it came, we had our native species but, like the Indians, it retreated before the invader and is now confined to the wilder parts of the country.

In our ponds and streams, various forms of water insects are also beginning to appear. A few have been active all winter, and others, like the whirligig beetles and water striders, have already made their appearance. In a field back of my house, a spring pool forms every year, and just about this time, I find the caddis worms crawling along the bottom with their cylindrical houses of leaves and straw. They live, for the most part, on vegetable matter and move about with only their heads and legs exposed, ever on the alert to withdraw into their dwellings when faced with danger. Although similar in habits, all caddis worms do not construct the same type of home. Some species use bits of leaves or bits of stick; others use sand; and still others small stones, the material being fastened together with silk, which is not, as a rule, spun into a thread but is poured forth in a gluelike sheet upon the objects to be cemented. Most of them build dwellings in the form of a cylinder, but some construct a house shaped like a horn, while others prefer a more ornate habitation reminiscent of a small seashell.

When the caddis worms become full-grown, they anchor their homes with silken cords to some underwater support, seal both ends, and enter the pupal stage — the remarkable period of transformation when the wormlike larvae change into adult flies. Most pupae, when ready to emerge as adults, slowly make their way out of their dwellings and then rest on a twig or other vegetation until their wings are dry and strong, but those which live in swiftly flowing streams fly away immediately, since the rushing stream would otherwise impair their wings for purposes of flight.

Besides the insects, other forms of water life become active in April. Sponge gemmules, the winter buds of the freshwater sponge, are germinating and colonies have begun to form; freshwater mussels are spawning; and painted and spotted turtles, having emerged from the bottom mud of the ponds in which they have hibernated, are swimming about or basking on a protruding stone or partially submerged log, ever alert to plunge into the water upon the approach of danger, real or fancied.

I often come upon them sunning themselves on a rock or derelict timber and am always amused at the clumsy way in which they tumble into the water at the sound of my approach. As soon as they touch the water, their broadly webbed feet take an immediate hold, and they quickly make for the bottom where they hide among the water plants. They remain hidden until they sense that danger has passed and then swim to the surface. But only their eyes and snout break the water, and in this manner, they swim about, inspecting the outlook until satisfied that all is safe, when they climb back one by one to their roost to resume their interrupted sunbath.

As worms, insects, snails, and other small aquatic animals become abundant in the ponds and streams, the fishes, on short rations through the winter, feast and soon grow fat and brisk. The yellow perch has already begun to spawn, and the agile, bloodthirsty pickerel and pugnacious stickleback are getting ready to discharge the duty of egg-laying so the young may be hatched and get a fair start for growth during the summer.

The stickleback, a small fish with a row of sharp upstanding spines on its back, lives among the weeds of small streams and has quite a reputation for industry in nest-building — the male, that is, for he alone does all the work. One year I observed him build his nest in an aquarium, and it was quite a revelation.

He first bit off small algae filaments and attached them to the submerged stem of a water plant, keeping them in place with a sort of cement or glue, which he spun out in fine threads through an opening near his anal fin. When he had these firmly in place, he obtained some more and attached them in like manner. I don't recall how many trips he made for building materials, but as he worked, I noticed that the structure gradually assumed the shape of a small hollow sphere, and when finally completed was about the size of a glass marble. It was a pretty structure, quite durable, with reinforced walls, and wholly utilitarian, with a little circular door on one side. Even though I was a witness, it seemed incredible that the little creature could accomplish such a feat with the simple means at his disposal, yet he did it with no apparent difficulty.

His home completed, his next task was to persuade the female to enter it. This seemed more of a problem than that of building, but after several attempts, he succeeded in driving her through the little door. Then, while he guarded the nest by swimming around and around it, she laid her eggs. When all her eggs had been deposited, the female swam out, and the male immediately entered and discharged his sperm cells over them. He then took up a position outside the nest and stayed there until the eggs had hatched and the little sticklebacks had emerged and floated off.

As our native fishes recover from the stupor of winter and once again swim briskly through the waters of ponds and streams, many migratory fishes — herrings, alewives, shad, and eels — crowd to our watercourses from the sea. For years the complete life history of the eel remained a mystery, and only recently (1925) have we learned the missing chapters.

The eels which ascend our rivers in the spring are young specimens and measure only about two or three inches in length. They work their way up the rivers, feeding by day and traveling by night. Only the females persevere to the headwaters; the males stay in the lower parts. They live six to eight years in these places, feeding on both animal and vegetable matter on the muddy bottom, although at times they come out of the water and hide under stones in swampy ground a few feet from the shore, and then undergo a remarkable change. They stop eating, turn white and shimmering, and begin to migrate downstream. On reaching the open sea, they journey to the West Indies where, in the deep waters, they spawn, each female laying from one million to ten million eggs. The stages between the egg and the young eel were once the missing chapters in the life history of this familiar inhabitant of our inland streams and lakes, but comparatively recent researches have filled the gap. Soon after the first and only breeding season in their lives, the male and female eels die, leaving the newly hatched larvae to provide for another generation. These larvae are thin, flattened creatures and so transparent that ordinary print may be seen through their bodies. They retain this form for about a year and drift near the surface. Then they are caught in the current of the Gulf Stream and carried toward the American coast. Meanwhile, they grow rapidly and by the time they near the coastal waters are ready to transform into the young eels that ascend our rivers.

By the time April arrives, the spotted salamander and the common newt have begun to mate and to lay their eggs in ponds and pools, and by the end of the first week most of the wood frogs have come out of hibernation and their clucking chorus may be heard issuing from a woodland pool. But the leopard frogs are just beginning to assemble in the ponds, and the toads to emerge from their winter burrows beneath flat stones and logs. By the middle of the month, the low, guttural croaking of the frogs, in sharp contrast to the shrill notes of the peeper, may be heard day and night but the sweet, tremulous calls of the toads may be heard only here and there, for the full toad chorus does not begin until the end of the month.

The first time I heard the wood frogs, I mistook their clucking for the quacking of ducks, and even today I momentarily think of ducks when their call notes break the silence of the woods. These frogs mate soon after they enter the water, and the eggs, which are laid in masses about four or five inches in diameter, may be attached to twigs and grasses or left free. The masses contain from one thousand to three thousand eggs, and after they have been in the water a week or so, they flatten and spread out on the surface of the water when they are not so easily recognized, for the jelly about the eggs turns green, and the masses look very much like floating pond scum. The color is due to countless microscopic green plants which provide oxygen for the developing tadpoles. The advantage is not one-sided, for the plants utilize the carbon dioxide expelled by the tadpoles for food manufacture.

The year I tried to find the elusive peeper, I resumed my search about the middle of April. The third attempt proved successful, for I had hardly arrived at the pool when I saw a little brown body swim vigorously through the water and climb upon a floating twig. He did not remain on the twig very long but plunged into the water and swam to the protecting cover of some floating leaves. He began singing at once, and I saw his swollen throat gleaming like a great white bubble.

Watching the peeper sing, I realized why he is so elusive. He is so small — only about an inch long — and in color so much like his surroundings that it is surprising he is ever seen. I often look for him among the leaves on the forest floor, for I enjoy watching him chase insects, leaping after them with careless abandon and then hiding beneath a leaf or among the moss until some other insect engages his attention.

The peeper makes a delightful pet. He requires almost no care, takes up very little room, and will amply repay you for your efforts. A small bowl, such as a goldfish bowl, planted with moss and a few small ferns, is all that is necessary to keep him happy. Of course, you have to feed him — in the summer on small insects such as gnats, mosquitoes, and ants, and in the winter on mealworms (which you can obtain at any pet store) and earthworms cut up in small pieces—but this is no chore. In return for this little trouble, he will amuse you with his antics, but don't expect too much, for he will probably sleep much of the day.

He may be kept throughout the year, and often on winter evenings, he will climb up the sides of the bowl or cling to a fern and sing a few cheerful notes. The peeper is able to adhere to smooth surfaces, such as glass, for his toes and fingers end in small round disks which secrete a sticky substance. Watch him as he climbs up the sides of the bowl, and you will see how he does it. You will find, too, that he will not seek to escape. His small moss garden is his home, and if provided with a companion or two and enough food, he will be satisfied and content in his little world. Better cover the top of the bowl, however, with a piece of cloth, or he may inadvertently get out and not be able to find his way home.

In April, the naked young of the deer mouse are born in a warm nest of leaves and shredded bark; the kittens of wildcats and young mink are brought forth in hollow logs and burrows; the flying squirrel introduces her young ones to the world in a tree cavity; the red fox gives birth to pups in a secluded den; and baby raccoons are born in lofty chambers in hollow trees.

Now that domestic cares have been thrust upon him, the raccoon can no longer idle his time away and at last emerges from his winter quarters. Food is not yet plentiful, and he is often compelled to go hungry, but in the mad scramble for food, he has a decided advantage over the woodchuck and other vegetable eaters, for he will eat almost anything. He has a special liking for fish and will sit on the bank of a stream and catch any fish within easy reach. He is also fond of crayfish, and clams are a delicacy, although you may wonder how he can open them. With one crunch, he breaks the hinge that holds the two valves together, and his paws complete the work of getting out the meat. He is also a skilled frog catcher and pursues these amphibians both in the water and in the marshes. At times, he will stoop to rob a chicken roost, and being a night wanderer, he often surprises sleeping birds, both on the ground and among the branches of trees. He has a special predilection for corn, and in the summer often invades the garden to strip down the husks. In sheer wastefulness and wanton extravagance, he often destroys several times as much as he eats. Later on, like many other mammals, he feeds on myriads of crickets and grasshoppers and is not averse to rifling beehives and to digging young bumblebees and wasps out of the ground, for his long thick fur enables him to do so in comparative safety. And to round out his diet, he eats fruit, especially berries and wild grapes, nuts, and grains.

Despite his omnivorous tastes, I have never known a raccoon to eat mushrooms and have wondered why more animals do not eat these lowly plant forms. If we can eat them without injury, certainly many of the herbivorous mammals should be able to do so. There are, of course, a few animals that include them in their diet. The common slug, whenever it chances upon a mushroom, usually stops and gormandizes until there is practically nothing left of the plant. Insects are especially fond of a mushroom diet, and I dare say that the larvae of certain kinds are among the happiest creatures on earth, for the mother is particularly careful when depositing her eggs to seek out only the tastiest mushrooms to serve as a food-bed for her offspring. The tortoise, too, will often stop in its wanderings to nibble at a mushroom, and deer and cattle have been known to feed on them. But the prime mushroom eater is the red squirrel. This little animal is especially fond of them and even stores them in the forked branches of trees for future use. Incidentally, though April is not a mushroom month, several species may be found even now, such as the glistening coprinus and the sponge mushroom or edible morel, the latter one of the most sought after.

The glistening coprinus may be found at the base of trees or on covered stumps, particularly after a shower, and the sponge mushroom in orchards and open woodland areas. I am not fond of mushrooms, but I enjoy looking for them, and occasionally when I am afield, I make a special effort to find these early forms. I am not always successful, but while looking for them, I often find the wolf spiders which can easily be seen at this time of the year, before the grass or other vegetation has become too thick and high, running over the ground or along a woodland path. You may have seen them running along fence rails, and if you are of a curious nature and like to overturn stones and logs and poke among dead leaves for what you may find there, you certainly must have found them.

As a rule, they may be seen running about only in the late afternoon or early evening, for they dislike intense light and during the day hide beneath some shelter. Frequently, one of them may be found dragging a tiny, globular, parchment-like affair covered with silken threads. This is the egg case; and when the eggs hatch, the spiderlings climb upon the body of the mother and are carried around papoose-fashion for some time.

These spiders capture their prey by stalking it or chasing it over the ground after the manner of wolves, hence the name of wolf spiders. Many of them have acquired the habit of digging burrows in the ground, to which they retire when not out hunting. A few merely dig a shallow depression beneath a log or stone and line it with silk, but others dig a vertical tube in the ground, going down as much as a foot or more. Some of these build around the opening a circular wall of earth and pebbles which they bring up from below, or a turret of grass and dirt which they fasten together with silk or bits of twigs.

The turret is more than an ornament, for the spiders who build these structures use them as a watchtower. When not out hunting, they spend much of the day perched at the top of the turret with their heads projecting just far enough so they can view the immediate neighborhood. From such a vantage point, they can detect their prey more readily and can also observe the approach of an enemy, from whom they can escape by merely dropping into the burrow.

On my April walks, I invariably find garter snakes basking in the sunshine, for by now most of them have emerged from their hibernating quarters. These snakes are the most abundant and most generally distributed of our snakes. They are also the hardiest. I have come upon them sunning themselves in early March, even though patches of snow still remained in the woods. In March, however, they come out only on warm days and remain close to their hibernating quarters, to which they return when the sun goes down. Not until the weather is settled and the need for shelter has passed do they mate and scatter.

One of the familiar notes of spring is the scream of the red-shouldered hawk as it circles high in the pale blue sky. The bird is a resident throughout the year, but except during the breeding season, when it becomes quite vociferous, it is rather silent and secretive, and I see it only occasionally.

The flight of this hawk is a never-failing source of delight, and I invariably stop to watch it sail through the air on outstretched wings, ascending and descending, balancing on the cool currents high above the ground, sometimes stationary on motionless wings, sometimes climbing an invisible staircase until it is a mere speck in the sky, then suddenly lifting its wings and swooping toward the ground with meteoric speed.

The purple martin is another bird I delight to watch in flight. Several years ago, I saw a flock of these birds flying over a meadow. They were not flying fast, but they cut through the air like arrows. With rapid strokes of their narrow, pointed wings, they would climb into the sky and then suddenly turn and drop toward the earth in one long, sloping sail, suddenly picking up speed and skimming over the top of the grass, tilting to one side and then the other. Sometimes when flying into the wind, they would remain stationary for a few moments on rapidly beating wings.

Martins catch their food on the wing but, like many other capable flyers, also delight in flying for the sheer joy of it. They are fond of bathing and often do so on the wing. Audubon was the first to observe their habit, when flying over a large lake or river of "giving a sudden motion to the hind part of the body, as it comes in contact with the water, thus dipping themselves in it, and then rising and shaking their body, like a water spaniel, to throw off the water."

It is a pity that such delightful and beneficial birds — they destroy vast quantities of harmful insects — should have been driven from our dooryards by such interlopers as the English sparrow and starling. We can, however, do much to get the martins to return by excluding these birds and by erecting martin houses, even though we have no assurance that they will take possession of them. For some reason, they may pass up a house spring after spring, and there appears to be nothing we can do about it. However, since they prefer a locality with running water, a bird bath will often influence them to settle if other water is not available.

In March, only the hardier of our migratory birds arrive from the south, but in April, there is such a great influx of visitors that you have to be on the lookout constantly to greet them as they return. Early in the month, ducks begin to pass northward, and many of those that wintered with us join the migrants, their place on the coast and the marshes being taken by coots, rails, and members of the heron family.

About the second week of April, I usually see the Savannah sparrow searching among the grasses for his insect food, and about a week later, I hear the trill of the chipping sparrow in the early morning. Every day I try to save a few moments to follow the road that passes my house for half a mile or so, to peer into the bordering thickets until I catch a glimpse of the yellow palm warbler. It may be early in the month or sometimes later, but eventually, I find the little wagtail, and I always stop to watch him as he flits from bush to ground or from branch to branch, wagging his tail up and down with the same unhurried motion as the phoebe. Sometimes along this same road, I hear the scratching of the brown thrasher as he rustles the dead leaves, but I do not often see the bird, for he is rather shy and furtive, and on my approach, he retires into the thicket. I see him more often when he calls to his mate in loud, clear tones from some sapling.

The catbirds and tree swallows have already arrived, and yesterday I was watching the swallows curvet in the air. I also saw a killdeer searching for grubs in a newly plowed field, and from a thicket, I heard the peculiar whistle of the white-throated sparrow. It was one of those rare April days that we have only too infrequently. The soft south wind flowed gently over the landscape and barely stirred the leaves on the ground; billowy cumulous clouds drifted so slowly across the blue sky that they appeared as if some giant hand had pinned them there; the perfume of blossoms filled the air; and the warm sunshine kissed the earth tenderly. It was a day designed to make one happy with the magic of the great outdoors.

In a woodland clearing, I came across a towhee, scratching about in the leaves like the fox sparrow, and in a wooded swamp, watered by a brook that had its source in a hidden spring, I caught sight of a myrtle warbler, its yellow rump flashing in the sunshine as it chased flying insects. As I left the woods and followed the path homeward, I saw a male house wren carrying a stick for nest building. I don't know how many sticks the bird had collected or would continue to collect or, for that matter, whether he was even building a nest, but he could have saved himself the trouble of doing so, for the female would use neither the sticks nor the nest. But you could not have convinced him that all his labor was wasted; he was performing an age-old ritual. The practice of building "dummy nests" appears to be a part of the courtship ceremony, for the male arrives earlier than the female and, while waiting for her, spends his time filling every nesting box and cranny in the nesting area with sticks and even building well-shaped nests. The nest to be used eventually is built by the female, who will have no part of any nest that her mate may have built. She may use a nesting box or cavity which he has selected, and in that case, she usually throws out all the sticks he has laboriously collected, or she may select an entirely different site.

Although the robins and bluebirds have turned their thoughts to domesticity and the chickadees, which have been around the house all winter, have scattered to the seclusion of the nearby woods to nest, it is really a little early for nest building. But several birds, among them the meadowlark, have begun to court their mates, and almost any day I expect to see the catbirds perform their courtship antics in the seclusion of the lilac bushes that line the driveway of my house.

Meanwhile, other birds have arrived in great numbers, displaying themselves joyously to each other, singing loudly in rivalry or for pure delight; and as the month draws to a close, the trees unfold their young tender leaves, viburnums and dogwoods show signs of blossoming, violets begin to appear, and horsetails shoot out of the ground. Everywhere ferns are breaking through the soil in watch-spring fashion, the interrupted and cinnamon ferns wrapped in brownish wool, and others less warmly clad.

NATURAL EVENTS IN APRIL

- Horsetails shoot out of the ground.

- The towhee, newly arrived, scratches noisily for dormant insects in the leaf-strewn ground of thickets.

- Kittens of wildcats mew in warm nests in hollow logs.

- Bee flies appear on the wing, visiting blossoms of willows, arbutus, and other early flowers.

- Toads may be heard singing in swamps.

- Larvae of click beetles and May beetles begin feeding on plant roots.

- Poplars and aspens shake out countless tassels that dance upon the south wind.

- Young mink are born in hollow logs and burrows.

- Adult ground beetles become active.

- The wild ginger hides its bell-like flowers beneath young woolly leaves.

- The chipping sparrow adds his song to that of the robin as the sun appears above the eastern horizon.

- Ants repair colonies and resume activities for the season.

- The purple trillium unfurls its unattractive, carrion-scented flowers.

- Freshwater mussels spawn.

- Ladybird beetles emerge from hibernation and wander about in search of food.

- The poppylike golden-centered flowers of bloodroot brighten copses and shaded roadsides with fleeting loveliness.

- The Savannah sparrow searches among grasses for its insect food.

- Catbirds perform their courtship antics in the seclusion of a thicket.

- Flying squirrels give birth to young in tree cavities.

- Willows gild the landscape with their golden catkins vivid against the blue April sky.

- Meadowlarks court their mates.

- The small yellow flowers of the leatherwood, appearing on still naked branches, twinkle as sunbeams search them out in damp woods.

- Young deer mice are born in bush nests, often constructed in a bird's old nest.

- The peculiar whistle of the white-throated sparrow issues from a thicket or brush heap as the bird pauses to eat while on its way to northern feeding grounds.

- The shepherd's purse flowers along roadsides, in fields, and waste places.

- Myrtle warblers, on their northern flight, pause in sheltered, bushy bogs and feed on early insects dancing in the sunshine.

- In fields and rocky pastures, wild strawberry, common cinquefoil, and ground ivy carpet the ground with trailing vines.

- Killdeers search for grubs and worms in newly plowed fields.

- The sponge mushroom or edible morel, one of the most sought-after mushrooms, appears in old orchards and open woodland areas.

- Queen bumblebees, in their rich velvety costumes of black and gold, appear on sunny days.

- The two-spined stickleback nests and spawns in the soft, sandy mud of inlets.

- Leopard frogs assemble in ponds, their low guttural croaking contrasting with the shrill notes of the peeper.

- White cabbage butterflies fly over fields, meadows, and gardens, sipping the nectar of early spring flowers.

- Meadows and river banks twinkle with the golden eyes of marsh marigolds.

- The yellow rocket decorates roadsides and meadows with showy spikes.

- Violets bloom.

- Viburnums and dogwoods show signs of blossoming.

- Trees begin to unfold their tender leaves.

- A flash of yellow in bush or tree reveals the yellow palm warbler, flitting from branch to branch in search of insects.

- Polistes wasps begin to build their nests.

- Young foxes are born in secluded dens.

- The brown thrasher, mounting a sapling, announces his arrival in a song loud and clear.

- Sponge gemmules germinate and colonies begin to form.

- April showers bring forth clusters of the glistening coprinus (mushroom) from covered stumps.

- Painted and spotted turtles emerge from their winter hibernation in the mud of ponds and streams.

- Adult moths of the spring canker worm emerge from pupal cases in the ground.

- The early saxifrage, rooted in clefts of rocks, whiten rocky hillsides with tufts of tiny flowers.

- Garter snakes emerge from their winter quarters, mate, and scatter.

- Pickerel spawn in grassy shallows.

- Ducks fly north.

- The trailing arbutus, often hidden beneath fallen dead leaves, opens its chalices to perfume the air with spicy fragrance.

- Elm trees are wreathed in a coppery mist.

- Wood frogs mate in ponds.

- Caddis worms may be seen moving about with their cases on the bottom of ponds and pools and in submerged vegetation.

- The spicebush gilds swampy woodlands with golden knots threaded on leafless branches.

- Baby raccoons are born in lofty chambers in hollow trees.

- Robins and bluebirds start nest building.

- Tent caterpillars hatch from their eggs.

- The flowers of the red maple, appearing long before the leaves, paint the landscape a rich red.

- Male house wrens build "dummy nests."

- Chickadees retire to the woods to mate and raise a family.

- Ferns break through the soil.

- In swampy woodlands, the solitary, pale yellow flowers of the adder's tongue nod between mottled leaves.

- The scream of the red-shouldered hawk, circling high in the pale blue sky, strikes a familiar spring note.

- The corydalis blooms and reveals its kinship with the Dutchman's breeches and squirrel corn by its pale foliage and attenuated saclike blossoms.

- The hellebore begins to unfold its leaves.

- The tremulous starlike blossoms of the anemone quiver in the slightest breeze.

- The pussy-toes unfold their little clustered heads on stems rising from charming rosettes.

- The shadbush blossoms, its silvery chandeliers brilliantly white against the background of leafless trees.

- Tree borers resume their nefarious activities.

- The parasitic ichneumon flies chase bees, wasps, and other insects.

- Spotted salamanders and common newts mate and lay their eggs in ponds and pools.

- As worms, insects, snails, and other small aquatic animals begin to get abundant in the ponds and streams, the fishes, on short rations through the winter, feast and soon grow fat and brisk.

- Herrings, alewives, shad, and eels crowd to the watercourses.

- Wolf spiders can easily be seen before the grass or other vegetation has become too thick and high, running over the ground or along a woodland path.

- The pestiferous chickweed opens its small white flowers everywhere.

- Bees, wasps, and various flies hum about the blossoming maples.

May

April showers have fallen, and where a few short weeks ago the earth was white and the brook was fettered by the ice, the ground is now a carpet of tender grasses and mosses, and the brook is gurgling noisily over its stony bed. The tender young leaves of trees and shrubs are pushing their way out of their protective armor and unfolding in all their pristine beauty to dress the landscape in a cloak of shimmering green. Countless blossoms perfume the air, and gaily dressed songsters fill the woods, thickets, and roadsides with the tinkle of their singing.

Everywhere the violet is in flower

> Half hidden from the eye;
> Fair as a star, when only one
> Is shining in the sky,

and in the shaded thicket, where the redstart whirls and dashes like a flaming will-o'-the-wisp, the feathery flowers of the early meadow rue, its delicate foliage suggestive of the maidenhair fern, hang in clusters like fleecy clouds, and the plumes of the wild spikenard wave in the soft May breezes.

On the distant hillside, the lupin mirrors the sky, and along the woodland border, where cottontails play, the spreading branches of the flowering dogwood appear as if laden with drifts of snow. In a brushy swamp where the yellow warbler cavorts like an animated sunbeam among the leafy branches of willows, alders, and red maples, the curious and beautiful cancer root opens its lavender flowers on yellow, leafless stalks. Rocky uplands sparkle with blossoming chokeberries, and in rocky woods, where chipmunks romp, the scarlet and yellow cornucopias of the wild columbine dance in the breeze with elfin charm.

Along the woodland path, bordered with the dainty flowers of the Canada mayflower, the frosty-white little star flower, poised above the whorl of pointed leaves, nods a welcome. Beneath a canopy of oaks and hickories embroidered with drooping catkins, I follow its winding course through the green spring woods, where the pink-striped stars of the painted trillium shine like jewels, the bellwort droops, and the fiddleheads of the cinnamon and interrupted ferns unroll above the ground like countless wraiths. Brilliantly colored warblers flit among the treetops, and the wood thrush tunes his lyre amid the misty greenery of a shady nook, where the small white blossoms of the foam flower appear like flecks of foam and the crinkleroot is now full grown.

Where the brook crosses the path, the hobblebush, with its clusters of white flowers, throws its straggling branches across the rushing stream, and beyond the brook, in the shade of the hemlocks, the showy orchis blooms. I pass through a sunny glen, aglow with the fragrant, rosy masses of the pinkster flower, and follow the path upward to where the glacier broke and crumbled a rocky cliff into boulders and jagged rocks and where receding cliffs with moss-grown shelves harbor the feathery tufts of the bladder fern. Above a leafy brown carpet, the striped pinkish pouches of the moccasin flower swing balloon-like in the murmuring wind, and in the nearby thicket, the ovenbird struts along the woodland floor.

I continue on my way, past striped maples with long, graceful drooping racemes of yellow blossoms and the white waxy flowers of the May apple, all but hidden by the glossy umbrella-like leaves, to where a quaint little preacher rises in his parti-colored pulpit, erected beneath leafy cathedral arches, and delivers to the elves and spirits of the woodlands, in a language understood only by them, a sermon perhaps as solemn and as profoundly wise as any we mortals might hear in our places of worship. In the words of the poet:

> Jack-in-the-pulpit...
> Preaches today,
> Under the green trees
> Just over the way.
> Come hear what his reverence
> Rises to say
> In his low painted pulpit
> This calm Sabbath day.

Among the tangled shrubbery, a yellowthroat nervously voices his alarm with scolding chirps and chattering notes, and where the path leaves the woods and becomes lost in a country lane, I hear the plaintive "pee-wee" of the wood pewee, hidden on a leafy branch, and find blossoming thorns and blueberries and the delicate flowers of the wild geranium shining like stars along the wooded roadside.

I stop to examine the bright blossoms of the fringed polygala, frail in their butterfly beauty, growing at the base of a stone wall where garter snakes lurk, and note the incessant activity of bees, wasps, and flies about the drooping racemes of the choke cherry. Above an open field, where buttercups and clovers bloom and dancing sunbeams play upon the delicate blossoms of the blue-eyed grass, the scarlet tanager flashes red against the blue sky, and in the distance, among countless tinted apple blossoms resplendent in the sunshine, a Baltimore oriole weaves his way, singing his song of joy.

As I turn into the walk that leads to my home, I hear the catbirds mewing in the lilac bushes and observe that the lawn is studded with the yellow heads of the dandelion. I make a mental note to do something about it, but in spite of my good intentions, the dandelion continues to flourish, for no plant is better adapted to survive. Examine it and you will discover why.

Note how deeply the stocky root penetrates into the ground far below where heat and drought can affect it or where nibbling rabbits, moles, and grubs can break through and feast. Watch the winds buffet and bend the stem and, though a hollow tube, how invincibly strong it must be since no harm befalls it! Why are not grazing cattle tempted by its rosettes of leaves when other succulent plants are devoured indiscriminately? Is it because they secrete bitter, acrid juices?

Examine the golden yellow flower head and what will be revealed? Not one flower but often three hundred minute, perfect florets, all co-operating to ensure cross-pollination from small bees, wasps, flies, and other insects that come seeking the nectar secreted in each little tube and the abundant pollen, which is greatly appreciated in early spring when food is scarce. After flowering, it transforms its golden head into a globular, white, airy mass of tiny parachutes, each one a seed and each one ready to sail away on the slightest breeze, to be carried untold distances before finding a resting place.

One morning in early May several years ago, I was awakened by a curious tapping. I listened to it for a few moments and then, unable to account for it, rose to investigate. I traced it to the kitchen, but when I got there, it had stopped.

Without warning, the tapping started again. I glanced up at one of the windows and saw a robin pecking at the pane with his bill. I watched him until he flew into a cedar tree which he had appropriated as a nesting site. Apparently, on one of his many trips fetching building material for his mate, for she does the actual building, he had spied something through the window which had taken his fancy; or it is possible he had seen his image in the glass and had attacked it, a thing robins are known to do.

How birds can build a nest, following the same design and using the same materials as their ancestors, without being shown, remains an inexplicable mystery. We call it instinctive behavior, yet I wonder if a certain amount of intelligence doesn't modify their instinctive actions. Birds select nesting sites with the greatest care. They usually build their nests in inaccessible places, where they will be most completely hidden from their enemies and get the maximum protection from the elements. The selection of a site is said to be instinctive, yet, when birds have a selection of several sites, it would seem that something more than instinct determines their final choice. The robins doubtless had examined several sites before finally selecting the cedar tree, and I am inclined to question the view that their selection was wholly instinctive; I prefer to believe it a matter of judgment and if they could have spoken, they would have justified their choice with a rational explanation.

A few birds, as we have seen, mated and began building their nests in April, but nest building on a large scale does not begin until May. Meadow larks and house wrens have already begun to woo their mates and only a few moments ago, I watched a pair of catbirds perform their strange courtship capers in a clump of lilacs. Other birds, too, feel the instinct to mate, and everywhere the air is filled with song expressing the rapture of courtship. Before the month is out, most of them will have settled down to nest building and the rearing of their young.

The nests which our birds build vary almost as much as the birds themselves. They range from a hollow scooped out in the ground by the killdeer, and the shallow, frail platform of the cuckoo, which is so loosely constructed that the eggs appear to be in danger of falling through the interstices, to the robin's compact, thick-walled structure of mud reinforced with grass and straw, and the exquisitely woven affair of the oriole, or the trim, dainty nest of the hummingbird, so wonderfully camouflaged that it is found only by accident, or, as I did one time, by the behavior of the female. It was fifteen feet from the ground and apparently not quite finished, for though it had taken shape, she was still busily at work on it. Every now and then, she flew away, returning a few minutes later with a piece of down. She tucked the down into the inside wall with her bill, which she used like a needle, and, when she had it firmly in place, adjusted the lichens on the outside.

Birds use all sorts of material in the construction of their nests — bark, bits of dead wood, down, paper, and even hairpins, wire clippings, and cellophane — and they build nests in almost every conceivable place. A house wren once built her nest in the fold of a blanket hanging on a clothesline. Even though nest building is instinctive, the birds are not necessarily bound by a predetermined pattern of behavior. They often depart from the normal and use different materials and quite frequently adapt themselves to varying or changing environmental conditions, like a redwing, for instance, which built a much deeper nest in a place subjected to strong winds. Most of our birds nest singly, but a few species, such as the herons, nest in colonies.

Several summers ago, I learned of a nesting colony of great blue herons and on the following day set out to visit it. It was in a swampy woodland about half a mile from the road, and since no path led to it, I had to cut my way with an axe through hurricane timber and tangled undergrowth. After a while, the ground became so soggy that I frequently sank into the ooze over my ankles, and had it not been for the tree roots, tussocks, and fallen logs, I should have had to abandon the attempt.

Occasionally, I had to stop to listen for the croaking of the herons to get my bearings. I finally found the colony and counted twelve nests. They were placed in the topmost branches of dead birch trees and all contained well-grown young. A number of adults were perched on the branches, their statuesque poses silhouetted against the blue sky, and every now and then, one of them would open its broad wings and silently glide into the air and become lost over the treetops. It was a memorable sight and worth all the labor, bruises, and torn clothing.

As April passes into May, the winter bands of the white-tailed deer break up and in secluded thickets the does nurse spotted fawns. Early in the month, muskrats are born. And on a bright, sunny day, young woodchucks, now about a month old, are taken to the entrance of their burrow by their mother and with wondering brown eyes gaze for the first time on the outside world.

This "coming-out party" is doubtless quite an event for the chucklings. The fragrance of the fields and meadows whisper of clover and sweet grass, and the merry tune of the bobolink and the whistle of the meadow lark, rising above the hum of countless insects, reveal the presence of other creatures in this new and strange world. They know nothing of the farmer's dog and their arch-enemy, the fox, but mother, of course, is acquainted with both and before permitting her offspring to leave the burrow, scans the surroundings carefully. If satisfied there is nothing to fear, she leads them to the grass and begins to nibble the juicy clover leaves.

The chucklings instinctively imitate her and when they can eat no more are shepherded back to their burrow. They do not enter at once but remain outside and play about in the grass or sun themselves. The mother, however, keeps them close to the entrance so she can hustle them down into the burrow upon the approach of an enemy.

Thereafter, they venture forth each day from their burrow and are taught how to fend for themselves. They learn how to distinguish the plants which are good for them, either as food or medicine, from those that they should leave alone, and to recognize among the many sounds that come to their ears those that spell danger. Doubtless, too, in the days that pass they have more than one adventure with dogs and as they hurry into the dark recesses of their burrow, their little hearts beat with excitement and the exertion of the chase.

When I went outdoors this morning, I found hundreds of the familiar earthworm "castings" on my lawn. To most of us, the earthworms seem of no possible use except as bait for catching fish, yet they are among our best friends, for unseen, they work day and night, plowing, harrowing, and fertilizing the soil for our benefit. They dig into the ground from twelve to eighteen inches and bring the subsoil to the surface. They also grind it in their gizzards and turn it into a finer texture than we are able to do; and they even fertilize it by secreting lime that neutralizes the acids.

The earthworms, however, are not merely tillers of the soil but are also agriculturists, for they plant fallen seeds by covering them with soil and care for the growing plants by cultivating the soil around the roots. Furthermore, they enrich the soil by burying the bones of dead animals, along with shells, leaves, twigs, and other organic matter which upon decaying furnish the necessary minerals to the plants. They even provide drainage by boring holes to carry off the surplus water.

The earthworms, you see, are not so useless after all. The changing character of the landscape and much of the beauty of our fields and forests can be attributed to the labors of these diminutive workmen; even the ruins and many ancient works of art have been preserved by them. And the success which you have with your garden may be determined in no small measure by the number of these creatures in your plot. Remember this the next time you impale one of them on a hook.

Earthworms are strictly nocturnal and are not found outside

their burrows during the day unless "drowned out" by a heavy rain. During the hours of sunshine, they remain stretched out in their burrows with their heads near the surface. You have doubtless seen a robin tugging away at a protesting worm and perhaps you have even tried to pull one out yourself, only to find that it is not an easy thing to do.

For some reason, the earthworms cannot seem to find their way back to their burrows if they leave them, so they anchor themselves to the walls as they stretch themselves over the surface of the ground in search of food. Strangely enough, they have no eyes and yet are sensitive to light. They have no ears and are completely deaf, yet they respond to sound vibrations. They also have a well-developed sense of taste, for they exhibit preferences for certain kinds of food, and an acute sense of touch, for they apparently like to feel their bodies in contact with solid objects. But I am not sure I can agree with Dr. Jordan when he says that the earthworm is perfectly at home on a hook and that in such a position it rests "peacefully."

May is the mating season for the earthworm, and if you were to go out on a moist night with a flashlight, you would unquestionably find many mating pairs on your lawn or in your garden. The eggs are laid in yellowish-brown capsules shaped like a football and about the size of an apple seed.

A heavy rain will bring not only the earthworms to the surface of the ground but quite frequently it will also bring forth the so-called fairy rings. The rings are formed by various mushrooms that have the habit of growing in circles, but the best known are the rings formed by the mushroom called the fairy ring mushroom, or Scotch bonnet, or, if you wish, by the scientific name of Marasmius *oreades*.

These fairy rings have attracted the attention of man from the earliest times, and in the absence of a scientific explanation, he has drawn freely on his imagination. One belief was that fairies "tripped the light fantastic" on misty moonlit nights, whirling in circles as they danced, thus wearing down the grass. Another belief was that gnomes and hobgoblins buried their treasure within the rings, and still another that they were caused by dragons who scorched the greensward about them by breathing living fire. Later, in an attempt to seek a natural cause, it was thought they were formed by thunderbolts striking the open, or by passing whirlwinds, or by ants and moles and even by haystacks. Today we know that a fairy ring is merely a grass disease.

Mushrooms are not too common in May, but a few species may be found in addition to the one just mentioned. The shapely little brownie cap frequently springs up on our lawns and in pastures, and I have often found the hedgehog mushroom on living oaks, locusts, and beech trees. The uncertain hypholoma is sometimes common as early as May, its white, fragile caps quite conspicuous among the grasses of a lawn, pasture, or roadside; and only yesterday, I found the reddish caps of the waxy laccaria in a woodland grove, although it may also be found in swamps and wet places.

Yesterday was one of those unforgettable days in May when the nature world is in a gay and happy mood. I had awakened as the sun streamed in through my window, and after a hasty breakfast, I went out to my garden, where the tree swallows and bluebirds flew gracefully through the air and in and out of their houses. A song sparrow sang from a neighboring tree, and an oriole appeared, swinging his way in and out among the apple blossoms and lilacs and azaleas and other gaily colored garden shrubs, rivaling their brilliant colors, as he searched for food and material with which to build his swinging home in the elm tree. And as I watched, a hummingbird flew out of the sky and streaked his way across the garden toward the sweet-scented blossoms of a cherry tree.

You would hardly think that such a spritelike bird could travel several thousand miles to his winter home in tropical America, or across the Gulf of Mexico, an incredible journey of five hundred miles, without stopping for food or rest. Or that he would have the temerity to attack an owl. Such were my thoughts as I wandered down the lane where the yellow blossoms of the star grass and wood sorrel peered upward among the grasses, and blossoming thorns revealed their kinship to the apples with their white, round-petaled flowers and pink-tipped stamens.

In a ditch, I found some horsehair snakes, which are not snakes at all but worms, and as I stopped to watch a chipmunk, I heard the song of a water thrush. The bird was off the road somewhere to my left, and it was not easy to thread my way through the tangled undergrowth. I had to be careful, too, that I did not frighten him by stepping inadvertently on a twig or letting a tree branch suddenly swish back. Once I thought I might have alarmed him when a brier provokingly caught in my clothing and I made some slight sound in freeing myself. But there was no retracing my steps, so I continued until in a few moments I came upon an open glade through which a murmuring brook flowed lazily on its way.

Here indeed was a paradise such as only the poet could describe. Warm breezes but faintly stirred the tender young leaves, and overhead fleecy clouds moved across an azure sky, briefly interrupting the sunbeams as they danced upon the water that dimpled over moss-grown rocks and fallen logs. On one of the logs, the thrush teetered up and down and wagged his tail in a thrushlike manner, apparently unaware of my presence.

Insects were there, too, in great numbers. Bees and flower flies, gorgeous little creatures which seem to favor blossoms as gaily colored as their own lustrous bodies, were breakfasting on marsh marigolds. Dragonflies darted swiftly here and there, alighting now and then on a leafy blade. Damselflies were abundant and fluttered about with the uncertainty of butterflies; occasionally one would alight among the forget-me-nots that blossomed along the brookside.

Water striders skated over the limpid water, doing their best to avoid the ripples sent out by whirligig beetles, and beneath the surface, a backswimmer dived to the bottom, where it clung to a plant stem. One or two water boatmen appeared for a moment, and several water beetles crawled among the filamentous algae, from which a scud suddenly emerged and disappeared as quickly. What appeared to be a brown, water-logged stick proved to be a water scorpion. Numerous snails were attached to the submerged vegetation; pill clams and planarians that glided slowly over submerged stems were there too. From behind some algae-colored rocks, gently washed by the brook, a black-nosed dace glided into the sunshine. I found more of these minnows in a cascade some distance upstream, for after the thrush had suddenly taken flight, I followed the brook through the woods.

The character of the brook had changed completely. Here was no slow-moving stream that meandered lazily and somewhat erratically through a sunny glade but a swiftly flowing current of water that fell and jostled as it hurried over the rocks, breaking into droplets that bounced into the air and scattered the sunbeams into spectral colors. Here was no place for water striders, or whirligig beetles, or water scorpions, or dragonflies, or other insects that prefer more quiet waters. Here instead were such insects as the larvae of the black flies, that attach themselves to the rocks by suckers on the hind end of their bodies and, thus securely anchored, swing themselves out into the water, spreading their fan-shaped food-brushes to sweep the diatoms and floating algae into their mouths. There were the nymphs of Mayflies that, facing upstream with tail and rear legs firmly braced, hold hairy front legs close beneath bewhiskered mouthparts to catch whatever food the water carries to them. Stonefly nymphs clambered over the stones, holding on by their strong claws, and midge larvae in vast numbers found pasturage in tufts of algae. In crevices lay net-building caddis flies, their nets facing upstream to catch their dinner as the water rushed by; on the undersurfaces of some rocks, water pennies, smooth-backed and copper-colored and looking like small pennies, held on tenaciously; and when I curiously turned over one of the stones, I discovered a two-lined salamander lurking there.

The Mayfly nymphs leaped and dashed about in the water,

more active than usual. They live, according to species, from a few weeks to three years. When full-grown, they crawl out of the water as beautiful fragile insects and live only three or four days, though some may live only a few hours.

In some species mating occurs almost immediately, in others within a day or two. Most of them mate only while in flight, usually in the cooler hours of sunlight or later in the evening, just after sunset. Thousands may participate in the mating flight, swinging up and down through the air in a joyous rhythmic dance. They move up and down together, swinging downward in a swift descent toward the surface of some stream or pond and then bounding upward as lightly as if they were thistledown wafted by a gentle breeze. Most of them die an heirless death, for there are many males but few females. The females lay their eggs almost immediately, some laying them in the form of egg clusters, which rapidly disintegrate upon reaching the water, the eggs sinking to the bottom of the stream or pond; others drop their eggs gradually, a few at a time. These females either alight on the surface of the water at intervals to wash off the eggs or creep down into the water, enclosed within a film of air, to lay their eggs on the undersides of stones and then float up to the surface and fly away.

The Mayflies are not the only insects that mate in May, for on some predetermined day, probably toward the end of the month, the winged males and females of all termite colonies in a given locality rise in dark funnel-shaped swarms on their nuptial flight. Birds and predaceous insects take a large toll, but those that remain drop to the ground and pair. The paired males and females, known as kings and queens, at once seek separate nesting sites and begin the work of excavating the galleries of a nest in the ground or in wood. They do not mate immediately, however, nor are the eggs fertilized for some time, but they remain together indefinitely and later mate repeatedly.

That most annoying of pests, the squash bug, has made its appearance in my garden and in spite of my efforts to get rid of it, will probably remain there until the first frosts. Aside from being a well-known pest, its chief claim to fame is that it was used in research in the germinal relations of sex. Of far more interest is the froghopper or spittle insect, whose white frothy masses are beginning to decorate various grasses and herbs in the field in back of my house, where countless bluets trace a milky path of tiny floral stars. The insect is called froghopper because at one time the froth was called "frog-spittle," as it was believed tree frogs voided it from their mouths. The name is not inappropriate, however, for the insect is a small, broad, squat creature and looks not unlike a miniature frog.

The adult froghoppers do not live within the frothy masses but wander about on herbage, shrubs, and trees; only the young live within them. Usually only one may be found within the curious dwelling, but in some cases, as many as four or five may inhabit the same mass. The spittle is a viscid liquid which the insects expel and then beat up into a froth by the whisking about of their bodies. At one time it was an open question what purpose the frothy mass served, but it is now believed that it offers protection against parasites and other enemies.

The resemblance of the froghoppers to frogs calls to mind certain moths — the hummingbird moths — that not only resemble the hummingbirds so closely in appearance that they have often been mistaken for them, but also imitate them in behavior, having the unmothlike habit of flying freely in the bright sunshine and hovering about various flowers. Speaking of moths, now is the time when codling moths begin their depredations. These are the insects that harm our apples to the sum of some twelve million dollars annually.

The moths begin to appear about the same time as the apple blossoms and lay their eggs on the leaves. On hatching, the grubs feed sparingly on the leaves and then make their way to the young apples, entering at the blossom end and tunneling to the core. Here they live for about a month, feeding on the pulp and destroying the beauty and appetizing quality of the fruit.

When full-grown they burrow out through the side of the fruit and crawl to the ground where they pupate; that is, if they have not been disturbed by someone picking the fruit and biting into it, as perhaps you may have done.

Yesterday I walked into some small black caterpillars with yellow and white stripes, hanging by silken strands from the branches of a tree. When you see these caterpillars, stop and watch them for a moment, and you will find that they lower themselves partway to the ground and then climb back again, like a sailor going up a rope. Perhaps you can discover what happens to the thread as they make their way upward.

These caterpillars are the larvae of the spring canker moth and belong to a group of insects called the *Geometridae*. Geometrid caterpillars are familiar to most of us because of their peculiar locomotion. They move along by a series of looping movements and we call them measuring-worms, or loopers. To learn why they loop along as they do, examine one and you will find they have legs only at each end of the body and thus have no other way of getting from place to place except to hump themselves along.

Sometimes, when resting, the measuring-worms cling to the branches by their hind legs and hold their bodies out straight, stiff, and motionless. They look so much like the twigs that they are often mistaken for them. You may wonder how they can remain in such a position without becoming exhausted. There is no mystery about it nor are the caterpillars endowed with special powers. They merely spin a thread of silk from their mouths and attach the free end to the twig. The thread serves as a sort of guy rope and if you think there is no tension on it just cut it and you will find that the caterpillars will fall back with a sudden jerk.

When the lilacs perfume the air with their sweet fragrance the tiger swallowtail emerges from its chrysalis. This is the large, showy, familiar yellow and black butterfly that flies lazily about our gardens. The butterfly is of interest in that two forms may develop from the same lot of eggs. In the northern region of approximately the fortieth degree latitude there is only one form, the yellow and black striped butterfly, but south of this latitude there may be two forms of the female, the familiar one of the North and another which is almost wholly black or dull brownish with the hind wings touched with lines of blue and bordered with crescents of yellow and orange.

At one time the two were described as separate species and for many years were so considered, until breeding experiments proved they are the same.

The black swallowtail is another butterfly that appears during this month. The swallowtails have been given their unusual name because their hind wings are prolonged into curious tail-like projections. I might add that we have swallowtails without tails, which have facetiously been called "tuxedos," and butterflies with tails that are not swallowtails.

Anyway, the black swallowtail is a most graceful butterfly, with velvety black wings having three rows of yellow spots across them. It is an efficient pollen carrier and visits flowers frequently, sipping the nectar which they provide as refreshment for carrying their pollen.

The caterpillars are often found on such garden crops as celery, parsnip, parsley, and carrot, but they are not a serious pest. The female has the uncanny ability of selecting only these plants or other members of the *Umbelliferae* or carrot family, for the caterpillars will feed on no others. This ability is not restricted, however, to the female of this particular butterfly, for the females of other species have the same gift. The female monarch butterfly, for instance, lays her eggs only on the milkweed.

A third butterfly appearing in May is the pearl crescent. I saw one of these butterflies this afternoon when I stopped to watch a bobolink, mad with joy, fly in pursuit of his fleeting inamorata in a meadow aglow with early parsnips, whose yellow umbels suggest their kinship to the wild carrot of summer. The pearl crescent is a small species with a wing expanse of only about an inch and a quarter, with wings of a reddish brown called fulvous and more or less marked with black wavy lines and dots. This butterfly has different forms in spring and summer, which vary so greatly that once they were considered separate species. In the spring form, the hind wings are heavily and diffusely marked beneath with strongly contrasting colors, but in the summer form, which is somewhat larger, they are plain and but faintly marked. A number of years ago Edwards showed by some interesting experiments that the smaller, darker spring form is due to cold or low temperatures. He placed a number of chrysalids, that normally would have produced the summer form, upon ice and found the specimens so treated produced the spring form.

During May an ichneumon fly called the lunate long-sting busily drills in trees infested with the pigeon horntail. The long-sting is a wasp-like insect with a slender body from which extend three "hairs" measuring sometimes as much as three inches. These "hairs" are not hairs at all, or stings either, for that matter, but the ovipositor or egg-laying apparatus.

The long-sting is a parasite of the pigeon horntail. The female horntail also has three "hairs" extending from her body but they are considerably shorter. Like the ichneumon fly she uses them to drill a hole in a tree in which she deposits an egg. This egg hatches into a small grub which makes a small burrow as it feeds on the tissues of the tree. If lucky, the grub will feed and grow and finally emerge from its burrow as an adult horntail, but more than likely it will be eaten by a grub of the long-sting before it becomes an adult. This in itself is not unusual, for among all forms of animal life we find species feeding on other species. The uncanny thing is the manner in which the grub of the long-sting finds its way into the burrow of the horntail.

The ichneumon fly, when ready to lay her eggs, flies about looking for a tree infested with grubs of the horntail. How she finds such a tree I don't know. When she has found one she selects a spot which she judges is near the horntail burrow and starts to drill. On penetrating the burrow she deposits an egg, and as soon as the egg has hatched the grub begins to crawl along the burrow in search of the horntail grub. It starts feeding on it immediately and eventually destroys it altogether, but not before the ichneumon grub itself has become full-grown. When that time comes it pupates in the burrow and emerges sometime later by gnawing its way out through the bark and taking flight as an adult ichneumon fly.

In May, redfins and small-mouthed black bass spawn in brooks and creeks; in local ponds where the bullfrogs call in their bass voices, the tree frogs joyously paddle about among the lily pads and sing in their high resonant voices — their vocal sacs so extended that it would seem as if they would balloon right up into the air. The sunfish is building his nest where blue flags tinge the shore with royal color and the royal fern flushes the neighbouring meadow with tender red. I have a warm spot in my heart for the sunfish, for he brings back memories of another day — of the summertime, of a small boy, and a homemade fishing pole. And how that small boy, flushed with excitement, found pure joy in matching his skill with the gamy little fish.

The sunfish is a most beautiful creature when viewed in the bright sunlight, for his sides are a rich iridescent blue and green, flecked with orange and dimly barred with olive. The male is more handsomely marked than the female, and during the breeding season his colors are even more pronounced. He puts his colors to practical use, exhibiting them before his lady love with all the vanity of a peacock. If we are so lucky as to find him in the act of courtship we would see him strutting before her with his gill covers puffed out, the scarlet spot standing out bravely, and his black ventral fins spread wide to show their patent leather finish.

Should he succeed in winning her he invites her to the nest which he has prepared. This nest is a saucer-like basin, perhaps a foot across and several inches deep which he has excavated near the shore, usually in a mass of dense vegetation, but not so dense as to exclude altogether the heat and light of the sun. Strange as it may seem, the sunfish actually excavates the nest, fanning the gravel away with his tail and pulling the heavier stones with his mouth.

On reaching the nest, the male and his bride swim around in circles with their ventral sides close together. While thus swimming the female deposits her eggs, which fall to the bottom and become attached to the small pebbles forming the nest bed, the male at the same time discharging his sperms into the water. Their marriage is short-lived, for soon after depositing her eggs the young bride departs, leaving her husband to guard and attend them, a task which he performs faithfully. After the eggs have hatched he also swims away, leaving his progeny to take care of themselves.

NATURAL EVENTS IN MAY

- The small white blossoms of the foam flower, massed in soft clusters, spot the woods as with flecks of foam.

- Like a flaming will-o'-the-wisp, the redstart whirls and dashes in skilful pursuit of insects among the misty greenery of sunny nooks.

- The white waxy flowers of the May apple blossom among the glossy umbrella-like leaves which all but hide them from view.

- Oaks and hickories are embroidered with drooping catkins.

- The northern yellowthroat plays among the tangled shrubbery of the brookside.

- Codling moths lay their eggs on tender apple leaves.

- The royal fern flushes wet meadows with tender red.

- The soft, feathery flowers of the early meadow rue, its delicate foliage suggestive of the maidenhair fern, appear like fleecy clouds in shaded woodlands.

- The hobblebush brightens deep woods with its flat clusters of white flowers.

- Poised above the whorl of delicate, pointed leaves, the frosty-white little star flower nods a welcome to a strolling wanderer.

- Squash bugs may be found on food plants.

- The curious, beautiful cancer root strikes an odd note in moist woods and thickets as it opens its lavender flowers on yellow leafless stalks.

- Chokeberries blossom in moist woods and rocky uplands.

- The ovenbird may be seen walking on the forest floor like a diminutive chicken.

- The pink and white flowers of the showy orchis, the first of the family to appear, open in the shade of hemlocks.

- The wood pewee calls plaintively from some well-shaded branch.

- Chucklings leave their burrows for the first time.

- Fairy rings appear in fields.

- Brownie caps spring up on lawns and in pastures.

- The uncertain hypholoma is often conspicuous among the grasses of pasture and roadside.

- The reddish caps of the waxy laccaria may be found in woodland groves.

- Receding cliffs with moss-grown shelves harbor the feathery tufts of the bladder fern.

- The yellow blossoms of the striped maple hang in long, graceful drooping racemes.

- Redfins spawn in brooks and creeks.

- The fiddleheads of ferns unroll above the ground like countless wraiths.

- Young muskrats are born.

- The plumes of the wild spikenard grace shady thickets.

- The Baltimore oriole weaves his way among countless tinted apple blossoms, singing his song of joy.

- The spring form of the pearl crescent butterfly appears.

- Jack-in-the-pulpit blooms in deep and shady woods.

- Wild cherries lighten waysides with their white clusters.

- Bobolinks frolic in spring meadows.

- The ichneumon fly, the lunate long-sting, drills in trees infested by the pigeon horntail.

- Above a leafy red-brown carpet, the striped, pinkish pouches of the moccasin flower swing balloon-like from tall stems.

- The tiny white flowers of the Canada Mayflower carpet the woodland floor.

- Tree tops sparkle with flitting forms of gaily dressed warblers.

- The bull frogs call in their deep bass voices and the tree frogs joyously paddle about among the lily pads and sing in their high resonant voices, their vocal sacs so extended that it would seem as if they would balloon right up into the air.

- The larvae of the black flies, forming a moss-like coating on the rocks, abound in waterfalls and rapid streams.

- The pink, striped stars of the painted trillium shine like jewels in the green spring woods.

- The blossoms of the flowering dogwood whiten woodland borders like an untimely snowstorm.

- Dandelions stud lawns and fields with their yellow flower heads.

- The straw-colored flowers of the bellwort droop beneath spreading leaves.

- The wood thrush tunes his lyre amid the misty greenery of a shady nook.

- The water thrush may be seen walking along the bed of a brook or teetering on a fallen log.

- Male catbirds court females in the seclusion of thickets.

- Spittle insects, or froghoppers, make frothy masses on the stems of plants.

- Appearing in meadows and moist fields, the yellow umbels of the early meadow rue suggest their kinship to the wild carrot of summer.

- Wood frogs leave the water and retire to the woods.

- Frail in their butterfly beauty, the bright blossoms of the fringed polygala appear along the roadside.

- Ruby-throated hummingbirds arrive from the South and may be seen buzzing around blossoming cherry trees.

- Tiger swallowtail butterflies visit lilac blossoms.

- The delicate flowers of the wild geranium are conspicuous in woodlands and along wooded roadsides.

- Sunfish begin nest building.

- The scarlet tanager flashes red against the blue sky.

- Countless mayflies, recently transformed, join in joyous dances.

- Sunny glens are aglow with the fragrant rosy masses of the pinkster flower.

- Countless bluets trace a milky path of tiny floral stars in fields and meadows.

- Bees and gorgeous flower flies breakfast on marsh marigolds. In fields and meadows, buttercups and clover bloom in profusion.

- Termites undertake their nuptial flight.

- Blue flags tinge swamps with royal color.

- Small-mouthed bass move into shallow water and spawn.

- Blueberries blossom.

- On moist nights, mating earthworms can be found on lawns and in gardens.

- The hedgehog mushroom appears on oak, locust, and beech trees.

- Horsehair snakes appear in brooks, pools, and ditches.

- Winter bands of the white-tailed deer break up, and in secluded thickets, the does nurse spotted fawns.

❧ Everywhere the violet is in flower.

❧ The yellow warbler cavorts like an animated sunbeam among the leafy branches of willows, alders, and red maples.

❧ The scarlet and yellow cornucopias of the wild columbine dance in the breeze with elfin charm.

❧ Dragonflies and damselflies appear near ponds and streams.

❧ The caterpillars of the spring canker moth may be seen hanging by silken strands from the branches of trees.

❧ Female black swallowtails search for the plants of the *Umbelliferae* or carrot family on which to lay their eggs.

❧ Dancing sunbeams play upon the delicate blossoms of the blue-eyed grass.

❧ The crinkleroot is now full-grown.

❧ Blossoming thorns reveal their kinship to the apples with their white, round-petaled flowers and pink-tipped stamens.

❧ The yellow blossoms of the star grass and wood sorrel peer upward among the grasses. Forget-me-nots blossom along the brookside.

June

June arrives in all its leafy splendor. Everywhere, birds joyously engage in family life, awaiting the arrival of their young ones. The air is filled with their melodious songs, vibrant with the ecstasy of domestic happiness.

Our mammals, too, are concerned with family cares. Spotted fawns of the white-tailed deer receive lessons in woodcraft as they follow the does to their feeding places. Young porcupines come down from the hollows in trees and wander about the meadows, seeking the edges of ponds at night to gorge themselves on succulent water plants. The young of weasels, mink, and wildcats move about with their mothers and learn the art of hunting. On some warm night, when insects are plentiful, young skunks are led forth by their mothers to be taught the methods of getting a living.

I have often seen the mother skunk leading the procession, with her young following in serpentine fashion like Indians on the warpath. Each evening thereafter, the little band sets forth on its nightly hunt for beetles and other insects. Helpless and unprotected young rabbits are eaten whenever found, and nests of wood mice and shrews are dug out from beneath old stumps and logs. Snails, which may be found among sodden leaves and decaying wood in damp hollows, fill in when better things are not forthcoming, and nesting birds are not overlooked.

In June, insect life becomes increasingly abundant. Countless caterpillars, grubs, and flying adults appear everywhere, many of them serving as food for birds and insectivorous mammals, and many others invading our gardens and orchards, fields, and woodlands. Sometimes, I find so many rose chafers on my rose bushes that it seems an impossible task to get rid of them before they damage the blossoms. These chafers are among the worst insect pests of our gardens because they appear suddenly in great swarms and overrun their food plants almost before we are aware of their presence. They attack not only the rose but also grape, apple, and cherry, at first feeding on the blossoms and then on the newly set fruit and foliage.

They remain for about six weeks and then disappear as suddenly as they arrive. The males become exhausted, fall to the ground, and die, but the females burrow into light, sandy soil and deposit their eggs. After they have laid their eggs, they return to the surface, linger for a few days, and then also perish, leaving the eggs to hatch and the grubs to feed on the roots of grasses until the following spring, when the grubs change into adult beetles and the cycle is repeated.

Fortunately, all insects are not harmful, and many are real benefactors. The ladybird beetles, for instance, are among our best friends, for they feed, in both larval and adult stages, on aphids and scale insects. I have often found the larvae in aphid colonies, particularly if the aphids are not attended by ants, and you have probably discovered them too. From experiments or observations, it has been found that an average aphid-eating ladybird larva will eat from twenty to fifty aphids a day, while an adult will eat twice as many.

The adults are also fond of aphid eggs and will devour as many as one hundred eggs a day if they can find them. As a single mother may have from one hundred to two hundred children, the number of aphids they can collectively destroy, assuming they all live to fulfill their destiny of destroying aphids, will run into astronomical figures. Most of them live out their normal life span, for they are ill-scented and are therefore let alone by their natural enemies, the birds.

I remember learning, when a boy, a rhyme which I can, somewhat surprisingly, still recite from memory. It goes like this:

> Ladybird, ladybird! Fly away home,
> Your house is on fire,
> Your children do roam,
> Except little Nan, who sits in a pan
> Weaving gold laces,
> As fast as she can.

The rhyme, quaint as it may be, is meaningless, for the ladybird has no home and never had one. The "children" do roam, however — in search of aphids on which to feed. All, that is, except "little Nan," which is the yellow pupa. She, alas, cannot "roam" because she is securely tied to the plant by the handle of the "pan."

The name ladybird, or lady-beetle, goes back to the Middle

Ages when these insects were dedicated to the Virgin and called the "Beetles of Our Lady." They have given rise to many superstitions and, among children, are probably the most popular insects. The rhyme I quoted was inspired by the custom of the European hop growers of burning the hop vines after the harvest since the vines were usually covered with aphids and ladybird "children."

The robber flies can also be counted among our insect allies. They are large and extremely predatory insects and may often be seen in June over fields and along roadsides, pursuing their victims and swooping down upon them in mid-air, or snatching them off leaves and carrying them to a convenient spot where they may suck the body fluids at their leisure. Some robber flies resemble bumblebees, but it is not known whether this resemblance helps them to get near their prey or serves as a protection against other predacious animals which fear the bee's sting.

Some idea of the ferocity of the robber flies may be gleaned from the fact that they number the powerful dragonflies among their prey. I have always been fascinated by the dragonflies and often pause by a pond or stream to watch them fly back and forth over the water. Only this morning I strolled over to the nearby pond to spend a few idle moments by the water's edge. I found the pickerel weed and arrow arum already in bloom, and where the wet meadow rolled away from the pond, the sensitive fern formed great patches of yellowish-green. Backswimmers, water boatmen, and diving beetles moved lazily through the water; scavenger beetles and water scorpions crawled along the bottom among the water plants. Whirligigs danced on the surface, and water striders hurried to get out of their way. Myriad winged insects — thin, long-legged crane flies, damselflies, dragonflies, and many others — flew about in the bright sunshine, their bodies casting moving shadows on the water.

If you will stop next time you pass a pond or stream and watch the dragonflies for a few moments, you will observe that some of them — the larger and stronger — keep to the higher regions above the water, coursing back and forth, passing and repassing the same point at intervals of a few minutes, while the smaller species are less constantly on the wing, flying usually in short sallies from one resting place to another or hovering about the water before they alight.

The giant dragonflies are exceedingly powerful fliers and, despite their size, have surprising agility, being able to alter their direction with perfect facility. If you want to test your quickness of eye and powers of muscular coordination, try to catch one on the wing with an insect net. You will find it is not easy. These dragonflies roam far from the water and even dash into our houses occasionally. They have a great deal of curiosity and will often remain in one spot, their wings whirring so rapidly as to be only a blur, while they examine some object that has excited their attention. Even today, high school students studying these insects in their biology courses refer to them as darning needles, a name given to them in a bygone age when they were supposed to sew up ears and lips.

But they are entirely harmless and dangerous only to the insects on which they feed. They are especially valuable in combating mosquitoes, for the nymphs feed on the wrigglers in the water and the adults upon the mosquitoes as they hover over ponds and streams while laying their eggs.

The damsel flies, more brilliantly colored than the dragonflies, are slender in form and more delicate. Unlike their larger relatives, they fly leisurely about and often rest on the rushes and grasses that grow along the margin of pond and stream. They are not very strong fliers and often fly tandem. The male, flying in front of his mate, usually accompanies her on her egg-laying expeditions and even submerges with her when she descends to place her eggs on the stems or leaves of submerged water plants. Possibly the males are of real help on such occasions, for the legs of the insects are not particularly fitted for walking, and alone the females would find it difficult to break through the water film. Through their combined efforts, however, the male can break through and then, using his wings, pull the female after him.

Countless toad tadpoles in various stages of development swarmed in the pond, and among the plants that grew along the water's edge, hundreds of newly emerged peepers hunted for gnats, mosquitoes, and ants. As I stood watching them, I wondered if their early escape to land is not a provision of nature, for in the water lurk all kinds of enemies — water beetles, water bugs, leeches, diving spiders, and the larvae of dragonflies, as well as leopard and green frogs and spotted newts. Several newts crawled among the water plants, and occasionally one of them would swim out into open water, but the glare of the sun was too strong and it would immediately seek the shade of a water plant.

I did not see any bullfrogs, but after dusk, I hear their familiar "jug-o-rum, more rum," startlingly weird in the quiet of the night. Several catfish, however, crawled slowly over the bottom with their barbels widely spread. Both the bullfrogs and catfish mate and lay their eggs in June, the former laying ten thousand to twenty thousand eggs in a floating mass that measures nearly two feet across, whereas the latter fastens its opaque yellow eggs to the undersides of stones in masses about two inches wide and an inch thick. The black-nosed dace, a little minnow about three inches long found in small streams where there are rapids and clear pools, also deposits its ova in June. The black-nose is marked with a broad black band that extends along each side of the body from the tip of the nose back to the tail. During the breeding season, the male's fins are tinged with red, and the stripe becomes bordered with bronze.

I spent an hour or so at the pond, and as the morning was still young and I had nothing pressing to do, I decided against returning home and took a path that led from the water's edge into the woods. Along the path, I found the bunchberry, its small greenish flowers surrounded with pure white, showy petallike leaves suggesting a kinship to the larger flowering dogwood; the rattlesnake weed with its flat rosettes of purple-veined leaves and tall clusters of dandelionlike flower heads; and the shy, dainty, deliciously fragrant little blossoms of the pipsissewa or prince's pine.

Everywhere the bracken was spreading its umbrella-like fronds, and in the more open places, the yellow loosestrife had opened its pretty spotted flowers. In an open glade, I found the light feathery clusters of the New Jersey tea, whose leaves were used as a substitute for tea during the Revolution. At one time, I heard the staccato notes of the scarlet tanager. After a few moments of peering about, I discovered him just overhead, partly concealed by the dense foliage. I also heard the hermit thrush, but I did not see this celebrated recluse. As I stood listening to his song, full of charm and bell-like sweetness, I noticed the delicate, graceful Indian cucumber root at my feet, its lily-like flowers hanging from the summits of slender stems. And as I continued on my way, I came across the attractive sheathed amanitopsis lifting its cap above the ground in the middle of the path. At this point, I left the path and explored the woods, and among some fallen pine leaves, I found the oak-loving mushroom and shortly afterwards the wood sorrel blossoming among some moss-grown tree trunks, its pale foliage singularly fresh and delicate.

After a bit of poking around, peering into hidden recesses and examining fallen logs, I returned to the path and followed its twists and turns until I came to the river. The white flower clusters of the arrowwood brightened the river's edge and served as a banquet table to numerous insects. About twenty feet from where I stood, a muskrat broke water and climbed up on the shore. I took a step forward to get a better view of it, and as I did so, a water snake that had been sunning itself on the overhanging branch of a water beech struck viciously at me. It missed, but if it had bitten me it would not have mattered, for the snake is harmless and can inflict only a superficial bite. It looked quite sinister as it glared at me with its beady eyes, but actually, the reptile has no heart for fighting. It will fight if cornered; given a chance to escape, it will quickly take advantage of it. I had proof of this upon the present occasion, for when I retreated into the shrubbery, it dropped into the water and disappeared. The noise it made upon striking the water evidently frightened a kingfisher, for the bird took off from its perch in a nearby tree and flew across the river.

By now the sun had climbed high in the sky, and it was time to return home for lunch. Instead of returning by the path I had come, I decided to follow one along the river's edge to a road that curved homeward. The path led through a swamp, and though I had followed it many times before, I had never found it so wet and soggy or the going more difficult. I was just beginning to regret my decision when I found some pitcher plants among marsh ferns, and just before I reached drier ground and the road, I saw a short-billed marsh wren flit among the reeds and sedges. It is a difficult bird to find since it spends most of its time close to the ground, and when flushed, it flies feebly with fluttering wings for a short distance and then tumbles down into the grass again. It is a great builder of nests, but even so, I could not see any of them, nor could I penetrate very far into the swamp, for the ground was oozy and the going treacherous. The nest is a hollow ball, about the size of one's head, and made of grasses with the entrance on one side. I don't know whether the marsh wrens wait until the reeds have reached a certain height and thickness, or if there is some other reason why they do not begin their egg-laying until about the middle of June, although they arrive early in May.

Cuckoos, warblers, indigo buntings, and red-eyed vireos also wait until June to begin their nest building, although they also arrive early. Goldfinches remain with us throughout the year, and yet they are among the last to assume domestic responsibilities. I saw a flock of these birds, now in their breeding costumes of gold and sable, while on my way homeward, also several buntings perched on a telephone wire, and in a crotch of an apple tree, a red-eyed vireo building her dainty, handsome little basket.

Most of the trees and shrubs have blossomed, but the sumac is just beginning to open its small greenish flowers in terminal spikes that point skyward. And on rocky hillside and woodland border, the maple-leaved viburnum is unfolding small flat-topped clusters of white blossoms at the ends of branches. Along the wayside, the elder is a familiar sight, and though the high tide of bloom comes in July, even now the shrub, "foamed over with blossoms white as spray," is a plant of great delight and equals, if it does not surpass, in beauty and effectiveness, the finest of our garden favorites. Various insects visit the flowers, and when I stopped to watch them climb among the blossoms to seek the nectar, I found the beautiful cloaked knotty-horn whose larvae bore into the pith of the branches. It is a beautiful beetle of dark blue with wing covers of orange-yellow, giving it the appearance of having a yellow cape thrown over its shoulders.

Although many of the April wildflowers are no longer in blossom, most of those that appeared in May are still in flower, while those of June are now in bloom. The showy lady's slipper adds a touch of the tropics to shady peat bogs, where the pale pink flowers of the cranberry nod from erect threadlike stems. The nightshade opens its purple pendant blossoms in a hidden nook or along a wayside wall where lady ferns spread their fronds in first freshness, and the greenbrier twists its prickly stems, with shining ornamental leaves and greenish blossoms, to provide a hiding place for the nest of the yellow-breasted chat. The yellow pealike blossoms of the wild indigo brighten sandy, uninviting places where other plants refuse to grow — except, perhaps, the frostweed, which opens its solitary yellow flower only once in the bright sunshine. Pretty waxen bells of the shinleaf are found along the shaded roadside, and the wild grape swings its graceful festoons along a grassy lane and perfumes the air with the sweet breath of its greenish flowers. The sheep laurel, "handsomer than the mountain laurel," blossoms among clumps of bayberry and wild rose bushes, while stone walls and tree trunks harbor the small white flowers of the poison ivy. Fields and meadows are filled with daisies, the yarrow, black-eyed Susans, the devil's paintbrush, the little yellow heads of the hop clover, and the humble spikes of the selfheal, blooming among waving timothy and orchard grass. And everywhere, blackberry vines wreathe their graceful branches with delicate flowers that all but conceal wicked thorns.

Along the woodland border where the scarlet maple keys of the red maple hang in drooping stems and the berries of the shadbush ripen, to be greedily devoured by the birds, brown butterflies, with such delightful names as the little wood satyr, the pearly eye, and the common wood nymph, float over the nodding grasses, poise quivering above a nectar-laden blossom, or rest on a leafy plant. Along the roadside and over fields and meadows, the common sulphurs become a familiar sight and add a distinctive charm to the summer landscape. And out of the blue sky, the stately monarch appears and searches for the milkweed on which to lay its eggs.

The monarch or milkweed butterfly, as it is also called, is one of the largest and most distinctive of the "frail children of the air," as Scudder happily called the butterflies, and is one of the most conspicuous of our flying insects, with its large orange-red, black-bordered wings. There is another butterfly called the viceroy that closely resembles the monarch, although this similarity did not always exist.

At one time, the viceroy had the prevailing dark color of its genus and was freely preyed upon by the birds. The monarch, on the contrary, remained unmolested because of a rank odor which it exudes; so to secure the same exemption, the viceroy gradually began to imitate the more fortunate monarch in appearance. At least such is the theory, but it is debatable whether protective mimicry is of any value to the mimic. At any rate, these two butterflies are much alike while on the wing; it is only when they are at rest and can be closely examined that they may be distinguished.

One of our most abundant butterflies, equally at home in city park and village yard as in the more open field and woodland, is the dainty little coppery-red butterfly called the American copper. The caterpillars of this species feed on the field sorrel, a common weed in fields and waste places, and quite frequently, the butterfly may be seen flying slowly above the plants, stopping now and then to lay its eggs on the leaves or stems. The color of the insect blends so well with the rusty red of the blossoms and leaves that at such times the presence of the butterfly may be discovered only by an almost imperceptible moving of the wings, or when it suddenly takes to flight. The butterfly also often alights on the daisy and buttercup, and the sharp contrast of colors is a pretty picture indeed.

As I look back to my boyhood days, I can recall how I used to wander through the fields and meadows of a June day with all the abandon of childhood. Today, to recapture that magic freedom, I need only a bright, warm, sunny day, when the blue sky arches over the fields and meadows, when countless insects buzz, and the music of bobolinks bubbles up in a cascade of ecstasy from among the daisies, buttercups, clovers, and waving grasses. You can find much of interest in the fields and meadows of June if you know where and how to look, and in the contemplation of nature's many wonders, you will discover an escape from the unrest which seems to have settled down upon the world.

Examine one of the myriad daisies at random and perhaps you will find small black insects threading their way in and out of the tiny florets. They are the harmful thrips, queer little insects with bladder-like feet and lopsided mouths. Watch a bumblebee when it alights on a clover head and observe how it extends its long tongue down the narrow tubular floret and sucks the nectar. You can imitate the bee, if you wish; all you have to do is to remove one tiny flower from the round head and suck from its slender tube. And while you have the tiny flower in your hand, look at it under a magnifying glass and you will discover it has somewhat the butterfly shape of its kinsman, the sweet pea of the garden.

Examine a yarrow cluster and you will probably find a small greenish-yellow insect with projections from its body and a broad black band across the expanded part of its abdomen. This is the ambush bug, so named because it lies in wait among various flowers and preys upon unsuspecting insect visitors, including large butterflies and even bees. You will also find, if not on the yarrow blossoms, certainly on other blossoms, the familiar stink bug and equally familiar click beetles. The click beetles are the long, slender beetles which, when placed on their backs, spring into the air, turn over and land on their feet, making a distinct clicking sound as they do so. With every step you take, tree hoppers and leaf hoppers will jump in every direction and grasshopper nymphs in various stages of growth will hurry through the grass, anxious to get out of your way.

Upon occasion, I find the eggs of the milk snake in a meadow tussock. This is the snake supposed to suck milk from cows, although no one has ever seen the snake do so. Moreover, it is unlikely that a cow would permit a snake to sink its needlelike teeth into her udders. It is not surprising that many superstitions and fables have sprung up about snakes, for in a bygone age when superstitious people let their imagination run wild, they accepted the most fantastic tales without question. But what is surprising is that many of these superstitions and fables still find favor and that so much misinformation still persists about these unwarrantably persecuted creatures. Actually, most snakes are harmless and of real benefit because they feed on mice and rats and other pests; only a very few are dangerous. The milk snake is a fairly common reptile and is readily seen because of its bright coloring. Though its usual habitat is open woods, fields, and pastures, it is more frequently found about old buildings, barns, and stables, where it hunts for rats and mice. The black snake, on the contrary, remains for the most part in fields and meadows, especially near the woodland border where it can glide into the bushes and undergrowth when discovered. Several days ago, I found fifteen eggs of this snake in the soft, moist soil on the edge of a meadow. They are white and leathery and covered with coarse, chalklike granulations, and measure slightly more than one inch in length.

The hog-nosed snake also lays its eggs in June. This snake is very slow-moving and when encountered rarely seeks to escape by flight; instead, it expands its neck and hisses loudly, making a somewhat terrifying picture. This is done largely for effect, however, since it can seldom be induced to bite.

If the snake fails to scare off an intruder or enemy by such a display, it opens its mouth, rubs it in the ground, contorts its body into irregular undulations which end in a spasmodic wriggling of the tail, turns over on its back, and lies perfectly still. It is a clever bit of acting, the realism being enhanced by the dirt and debris adhering to its mouth. The snake, as a matter of fact, feigns death so cleverly and so patiently that even if picked up it will remain limp and apparently lifeless. There is one flaw, however, in an otherwise perfect performance. If turned over on its belly it will immediately come to life and turn over on its back again to become limp and lifeless as before. Apparently, it thinks it must lie on its back to appear dead.

We usually associate turtles with water, but when the spring sun serves notice that tender leaves and berries may be found on nature's menu, the wood turtle leaves the ponds and streams and wanders through pastures, woodlands, and upland fields. It is like catching the proverbial small boy at the jam jar to come upon the animal feeding on wild strawberries, clawing down the plants in his eagerness to get at the berries, and then lumbering off through the underbrush, his mouth stained with the red juice.

The wood turtle has a beautifully carved or sculptured upper shell by which it can readily be recognized. It is not easily seen, however, in the spring and autumn when its gray-brown color helps to conceal it among the dead grasses and fallen leaves. Because of their hard shells, turtles hardly need such protection; protective coloration is of value, however, to the turtlets, for they are soft, defenseless, and perhaps too brightly ornamented. Infancy is the critical age in the lives of turtles, and they fall easy prey to most of their enemies. But nature, to ensure their survival, has made them masters of concealment and has granted them a remarkable independence as to food. Turtlets that hatch in late summer or early autumn can winter on an empty stomach; those that hatch in the spring can live for weeks without eating.

Turtles have well-developed middle and inner ears but cannot hear in the ordinary sense. Experiments have shown that they do not respond to sound waves through the air. The subject is of more than passing interest, for when courting and mating, turtles grunt and make other sounds. The male wood turtle is known to make a "distinct yet subdued note not unlike that of a tea kettle," audible for thirty or forty feet. The female, too, can emit a low whistle. It has been reported that the male of a mating pair under observation repeatedly whistled at the female, and it is believed that the whistling has sexual significance. The whistling, however, seems, in view of the underwater mating of this species, to be a by-product of a courtship gesture, rather than an overt act to attract the attention of the mate.

In New England, the nesting season appears to be the middle two weeks in June. The female usually lays her eggs in mid-afternoon, and as a rule, she chooses a sandy site near water, although she may lay her eggs in an upland situation. In common with other turtles, she buries her eggs, which number from seven to twelve, and after covering them, leaves them to be hatched by the sun.

Our water species — the painted, spotted, and snapping turtles — also lay their eggs during the month. I once found a female snapping turtle laying her eggs in the middle of a sandy road, though she usually lays them in a sandbank or cornfield. It was early in the morning, and as I watched her, she dug with her hind legs a cavity about six inches deep and not quite a foot wide. When she finished digging, she proceeded to lay her eggs at approximately one-minute intervals, pushing each one to the bottom of the hole with a hind foot. After laying her eggs, she filled in the cavity with the loose sand and then carefully concealed the site by raking the sand over it with her hind feet.

Bats don't particularly appeal to me, but I find them interesting and enjoy watching them fly about in the twilight of a summer's evening. Their flight is swift and erratic as they speed through the air, darting here and there and making sharp turns without visible effort; I never cease to marvel at their agility and uncanny ability to veer off to one side when apparently about to crash into some obstacle.

Bats do not detect obstacles by sight as the birds do but presumably do so by emitting supersonic notes and hearing these sound waves as they are reflected. The membrane, which serves as a wing, is equipped with sensitive nerves which apparently respond to the sound waves, and by localizing the source of the reflected sound, they are able to locate the obstruction.

Artists of a past age fashioned their demons after the bats and thus contributed to the dislike in which these little animals are universally held. Yet, look at the face of the little brown bat with its pug nose, its wide-open pink bag of a mouth, and its mischievous eyes peering out from beneath the woolly eyebrows, and you get the impression of impishness rather than of malice. Actually, it is a most docile and gentle little animal, and when it flies abroad on summer evenings, it seems fond of our company. Perhaps it has an ulterior motive in seeking us out; perhaps the real reason is the mosquitoes and other pests that torment us. The fact remains, however, that when tamed, a bat appears sensitive to the ministrations of the one who cares for it.

As the twilight blends into the darkness of the night and the air becomes fragrant with the smell of sweet grass, animated lanterns begin to flash their beacons against the background of deepening shadows. We are all familiar with the fireflies, but few of us, I think, realize how perfect the light given off by these insects really is. The rays are almost entirely light rays, with practically no thermal or actinic rays. In other words, it is cold light and is said to be between 92 and 100 percent efficient. Just what this means can be shown by the fact that the radiations of an ordinary gas flame contain less than 3 percent of visible rays, those of the electric arc only 10 percent, and those of the sun but 35 percent.

The light of the firefly is not produced like that of a candle nor like that of an electric light. In the burning of a candle, oxygen combines with the carbon and hydrogen of the paraffin to form carbon dioxide and water, with heat and light being given off during the process; whereas, in the electric light, the filament is heated by the electric current until it is so hot that light waves are given off. In the firefly, the process is somewhat different. The insect breathes by means of a network of fine air tubes that open to the exterior, these openings being located on the ventral side of the abdomen. In certain parts of the breathing system, the two chemicals "luciferase" and "luciferin" are produced by certain differentiated cells which form the light organ. The luciferase is what is known as a catalyzer, a substance which promotes or hastens a chemical reaction but otherwise takes no part in it and remains unchanged. Now, when oxygen is taken into the breathing tubes, it combines with luciferin without emitting light, but if the two substances are brought together in the presence of the catalyzer luciferase, which is under the control of the nervous system, they unite so rapidly that light is produced. Apparently, the insect can increase or decrease the brilliancy of the light by regulating the flow of oxygen through the air tubes and can display the light to best advantage by raising its wing covers during flight.

There is much more to the physics and chemistry of the firefly's light, but of more interest to us is of what use is the light to the insect. There are many species of non-luminous fireflies which live much the same as those that give off light and survive just as well. At one time, it was believed that the light served as a warning to nocturnal birds, bats, and other insectivorous animals, a theory supported by the fact that fireflies are refused by birds in general. But it is now believed that the light is used as a signal to their mates since the females of some of the luminous species are wingless. Yet there are wingless females of other insects that do not need light to attract the males; nor are luminous larvae, the so-called glowworms, interested in mating. However, if the light is used to attract mates, the supposition is that they can see each other's light.

I often sit on my porch in the evening and watch the fireflies as a restful pastime after a day of strenuous activity. Each species has a characteristic method of flashing, distinguished by intensity, duration, number, intervals between flashes, and flight levels. Thus occupied in identifying them, the evening passes all too swiftly, and when the flashings cease and I turn on the light, countless insects immediately appear outside the screening and break the silence with their buzzing. Then, suddenly, a thud and a moment later a scratching, as a mahogany brown blunderer crawls up the wire screening. I have known people to be frightened by the loud buzz of the May beetle or June bug and by the insect itself, but it is entirely harmless, although the larvae are sometimes injurious to the roots of various plants.

Moths are well represented among the night-flying insects that gather about our lights. Many moths appear on the wing in April and May; others, such as the tent caterpillars, do not emerge from their cocoons until June when they mate and lay their eggs in the varnished rings that are so conspicuous on the branches of wild cherry in winter.

The so-called silkworm moths — Promethia, Cecropia, Polyphemus, and luna — also wait until June to appear and lay their eggs. They are all large, beautifully colored insects and have conspicuous cocoons. Despite their large size, however, they are rarely seen, as they are all night flyers and to see them, you must be interested in the visitors to porch and street lights. The caterpillars, too, are rarely found since they are protectively colored and blend with the foliage on which they feed. None of them, incidentally, occurs in sufficient numbers to be injurious.

I wish I could say the same for other caterpillars, such as those of the gypsy moth. They are a scourge to our forest and shade trees and are particularly destructive because they include more than five hundred species of plants in their diet. Largely nocturnal, they spend the day congregated in colonies on a limb, trunk, or in some protected place. I have already mentioned that the pest came to us from Europe; in an attempt to control it here, certain Calosoma beetles were brought over to prey upon it. These beetles, of which we have several native species, are large, beautiful insects and are often referred to as caterpillar hunters, a name that should recommend them as it is well given, some of them even climbing trees in search of the caterpillars.

The Calosoma beetles belong to a group known as the Carabidae or ground beetles, which includes several interesting species such as the bombardier beetles. The bombardiers are all similar in appearance — small beetles with a reddish head and thorax and bluish wing covers — and you may find them under logs and stones in damp places. They have a little sac at the hind end of the body, in which is secreted an evil-smelling fluid. This fluid is used as a means of defense, for when they are attacked by an enemy, they spurt it out. The fluid is ejected with a sound like that of a tiny pop gun, and when it comes in contact with the air, it changes to a gas which looks like smoke. When larger insects try to capture the bombardiers and come close to them, they fire their little guns into the face of the enemy. The noise astonishes the pursuer, the smoke blinds it, and when it has recovered from its amazement, the bombardiers are at a safe distance.

NATURAL EVENTS IN JUNE

- The berries of the shadbush ripen and provide a feast for many birds.

- The pitcher plant blooms in bogs and swamps.

- Cuckoos, warblers, indigo buntings, and red-eyed vireos are nest building.

- Toad tadpoles are in various stages of development.

- The silkworm moths emerge from their cocoons. Adults of the tent caterpillars also appear, mate, and lay their eggs in varnished rings on the twigs of wild cherry trees.

- Daisies bloom in profusion in fields and meadows.

- Goldfinches don their breeding costumes of gold and sable.

- The black-nosed dace, rosy in their nuptial dress, nest in the shallow edges of clear streams and ponds.

- Monarch butterflies arrive from the south and search for milk-weed plants on which to lay their eggs.

- Female skunks, followed by their young, emerge from home chambers and set out on nocturnal hunting expeditions. On these nightly excursions, the young are taught how to procure a living. Female wild cats are teaching their kittens the art of hunting at this time, too.

- Sulphur butterflies are common along country roadsides.

- Yarrow blooms in fields and along roadsides. Black-eyed Susans appear in similar places.

- The elongate white eggs of the painted turtle are laid in warm, soft ground. The eggs of the snapping and spotted turtles are also laid during this month.

- Rose chafers appear in large numbers on grapevines and roses.

- Black snakes lay eggs in soft soil.

- Large numbers of wood nymph butterflies appear along woodland borders.

- The beautiful knotty-horn beetles may be found among the blossoms of the elder.

- The wild indigo, with its cloverlike leaves and yellow pealike blossoms, brightens sandy, uninviting places where other plants refuse to grow.

- Along the woodland border, scarlet maple keys of the red maple hang on drooping stems.

- The American copper butterfly alighting on buttercups and daisies makes a pretty picture with its sharp contrast in colors.

- The music of the bobolink bubbles up in a cascade of ecstasy from among the daisies, buttercups, clovers, and waving grasses.

- Thrips thread their way in and out of the tiny florets of the daisy.

- Ambush bugs hide in yarrow blossoms for likely victims.

- Stink bugs are common on various plants.

- Tree hoppers, leaf hoppers, and grasshopper nymphs abound in fields and meadows.

- Hog-nosed snakes mate.

- Wood turtles may frequently be seen feeding on wild strawberries.

- In the twilight of a June evening, bats may be observed chasing flying insects.

- As the twilight blends into darkness, the fireflies begin to flash their beacons against the background of deepening shadows.

- Caterpillars of the gypsy moth feed on the foliage of various trees. Many fall prey to the Calasoma beetles.

- Marsh wrens are busy building their globular nests among the reeds.

- The bracken spreads its umbrella-like fronds along the woodland path.

- Lady ferns are in first freshness.

- The sensitive fern forms great patches of yellowish-green in wet meadows.

- Orchard grass blooms in fields and along roadsides.

- The oak-loving mushroom appears among fallen pine leaves.

- The attractive, sheathed amanitopsis lifts its cap above the ground in woods and copses.

- The yellow hop clover opens its little heads in sandy fields and along the wayside.

- Fields are afire with the devil's paintbrush.

- The pale pink flowers of the cranberries nod from erect, thread-like stems among the slender grasses and moisture-loving plants of peat bogs.

- The wood sorrel blossoms among moss-grown tree trunks.

- The delicate, graceful Indian cucumber opens its lily-like flowers from the summits of slender stems.

- The sheep laurel blossoms among clumps of bayberry or wild rose bushes.

- The wild grape swings its graceful festoons along grassy lanes; the air is heavy with the sweet breath of its greenish flowers.

- The small white flowers of the poison ivy decorate tree trunks and stone walls.

- Pretty spotted flowers of the yellow loosestrife open on hairlike stalks in many circles about the slender stems.

- The blackberry vines wreathe everywhere with their graceful branches and delicate flowers.

- The wet scarlet of wild strawberries glistens among the grasses.

- The nightshade opens its purple pendants in hidden nooks or along wayside walls.

- Along the wayside wall, the greenbrier twists its prickly stems with shining ornamental leaves and greenish blossoms, providing a hiding place for the nest of the yellow-breasted chat.

- The song of the hermit thrush may be heard in the deep woods.

- Catfish spawn.

- Young weasels and mink come out and wander about with their mothers.

- Porcupines may be seen at night feeding on succulent water plants.

- Bullfrogs are laying eggs.

- Larvae of ladybird beetles may be found among colonies of aphids.

- Click beetles visit wild roses to feed on the pollen.

- June bugs fly noisily about.

- Robber flies pursue their victims over fields and along roadsides.

- Viceroy butterflies fly lazily over fields and meadows.

- Milk snakes lay eggs in meadow tussocks.

- The frostweed blossoms, opening its solitary yellow flowers only once in the bright sunshine.

- The humble spikes of the selfheal bloom among the grasses of field and roadside.

- Spotted fawns of the white-tailed deer receive lessons in woodcraft as they follow the does to their feeding places.

- Arrow arum is in bloom.

- Pickerel weed begins to blossom.

- Newly emerged spring peepers hunt for gnats, mosquitoes, and ants.

- Newts are active in ponds and streams.

- The bunchberry blossoms, its flowers suggesting a kinship to the larger flowering dogwood.

- The rattlesnake weed and pipsissewa bloom along woodland trails.

- The light feathery clusters of the New Jersey tea decorate open glades.

- The staccato notes of the scarlet tanager may be heard from woodland thickets.

- The shinleaf hangs out its pretty waxen bells along the shaded roadside.

- The showy lady's slipper adds a touch of the tropics to shady peat bogs.

- White flower clusters of the arrowwood brighten the borders of ponds and streams.

- Marsh ferns are abundant in wet places.

- The sumac opens its small greenish flowers in terminal spikes that point skyward.

- On rocky hillside and woodland border, the maple-leaved viburnum unfolds its small, flat-tipped cluster of white blossoms at the end of branches.

- Bombardier beetles are active beneath stones and logs.

- Timothy is in bloom.

- The elder, "foamed over with blossoms white as spray," is a familiar sight along the wayside.

July

As the sunny, pleasant days of June come to an end and the hot July sun heats the earth, the birds, now that the nesting season is over and they are no longer inspired by the eagerness of courtship, gradually cease their singing. As the month advances, we hear in the early morning or at evening only feeble reminders of the brilliant songs of May and June. And whereas a few short weeks before we found birds wherever we chanced to stroll, they now seem almost to have vanished. Except for those that nest in our gardens, we catch only a glimpse of them along the shaded roadside, in open shimmering fields, or in the woods deep in the shadow of luxuriant foliage.

The mammals, always shy, are also less often seen, and except for the sun-loving woodchucks, squirrels, and chipmunks, we must wander afield on moonlit nights to see the skunk, raccoon, and cottontail rabbit. I frequently encounter the skunk on a summer's night, his white fur a brilliant warning signal, and it is no uncommon experience to come upon a cottontail, sitting on his hind legs, with ears erect for the sound of my approach, and then, as I venture nearer, to have him turn and dash from view, his little white pompon waving defiance.

The summer stage, however, is not without its actors. Though the birds and mammals may have temporarily retired behind the scenes, the insects have taken their place and entertain us with their varied and incessant activities. As we wander about the garden or down a country lane or cut across the field and through the woods, an innumerable company of butterflies dance or rise and dip and curvet in the bright sunshine. July can rightly be called the month of butterflies. The blue spring azure, the American copper, the white cabbage, the yellow sulphur, the dusky meadow browns, and the queenly swallowtails, striped and belted with gay colors, are still with us. They are now joined by the dappled band of fritillaries, variegated by odd dashes and spots of burnished silver, the angle-wings with peacock eyes beneath, banded and spotted purples, and others, with names redolent of romance: the painted lady, the red admiral, the gray comma, the wanderer, the silver-spotted hesperid. How they crowd about the freshly opened flower heads of the thistle and the pendulous clusters of the milkweed! And the moths, no less numerous but of a more somber hue as befits creatures of the night, flock to lighted windows and visit the blossoms of the bladder campion and bouncing bet, familiar along roadsides and waste places. Their larger brothers, the hawk moths, prefer the yellow flowers of the evening primrose, whose nectar they suck with their long coiling tongues.

Go wherever you wish, July, with its hot, dry, sunny days, sees the maximum of insect life, and hardly a plant is without its insect population. In fields and meadows, where the yellow flowers of the St. John's wort sparkle in the sunlight and the fringed orchis sends its showy spikes of blossoms above the waving grass, tarnished plant bugs and four-lined leaf bugs suck juices from punctured stems. And in the woods, tiny white specks of the pine leaf scale perch on pine needles, sometimes in such numbers as to suggest a dusting with flour.

On herbage and the foliage of trees and shrubs, where aphids cluster in colonies, the queer-looking aphis lions, with spindle-shaped bodies and long, pointed, sickle-shaped jaws, stalk the unfortunate creatures. Who would think, looking at these predatory "lions" of the insect world, that they are the young of the dainty golden-eyed lacewing we see flying through the air on green gauzy wings? Follow a flying lacewing sometime if you can and you may see her lay her eggs. It is a sight worth the effort. First you will see her eject a drop of a sticky fluid from the tip of her body and press it firmly down upon the leaf. Then she spins the tiny drop into a thread half an inch or more long which hardens into a stiff silken stalk. She will repeat the performance until she has spun a number of stalks and laid an egg on each.

The egg-laying habits of the lacewing illustrate an interesting provision of nature. The carnivorous aphis lions which hatch from the eggs would just as soon eat each other or the unhatched eggs as hunt for aphids. But as the eggs hatch one at a time and nothing is at hand to eat except an inedible stalk, the newly hatched aphis lions must descend the stalks and search for food. Of course, they could ascend neighboring stalks and feed on their unhatched brothers and sisters, but with foresight, the mother lacewing usually spins her egg stalks in the midst of an aphis colony so that her offspring will not be tempted to feast on her eggs, but, following the course of least resistance, will feed on the more readily available aphids.

Once, I discovered a praying mantis on a neighboring leaf observing a lacewing with greedy eyes. The mantis was too far away to seize her and made no attempt to do so, since it does not pursue its victims but waits patiently for them to come within reach of its long, spiny front legs. If some unfortunate victim alights just beyond reach of its legs, it will, however, capture it by stealth, crawling toward it a step at a time and so slowly it barely seems to move, until it is close enough to extend its deadly, grasping legs. The mantis is the only insect that can look back over its shoulder and see in practically any direction, so it does not really matter where its prey alights if within the grasp of its deadly legs.

Predacious insects employ various means of capturing their prey. Some of them use modified structures, as the mantis; others build snares or traps. An ingenious trap is the ant-lion's. This is really a pitfall and is dug in a rather quaint manner in a sandy location beneath a shed roof or near the foundation of a house, sheltered from the wind and sun. The ant-lion first excavates a circular groove in the sand and then a series of grooves within the first by scraping the sand onto its head with its front legs and throwing it to one side by an upward movement of the head. The conical pit that results varies in size, according to the size of the insect, from less than an inch to more than two inches in diameter. When it has completed its trap, the ant-lion digs in at the bottom and lies in wait for a victim (usually an ant, hence its name) to step over the rim and slide down into its waiting jaws. The jaws, incidentally, are the only part of the insect visible.

Occasionally, a prospective victim manages to halt its descent, whereupon the ant-lion throws up little showers of sand to further its downward journey. Sometimes a larger victim than it can easily handle falls into the pit; in that event, a tug-of-war usually ensues. The ant-lion usually wins in the unequal struggle, for it has a pair of crooked hind legs with which it can anchor itself in the sand and thus hold on until the prey has become exhausted.

The ant-lion can undergo long fasts, another interesting provision of nature, since days and even weeks may elapse before it eats. The length of an ant-lion's life thus is variable and dependent on how often it feeds. Sometimes it may take two or three years to become full-grown. When fully matured, it fashions a loose, globular cocoon of silk and sand, pupates, and emerges a delicate gauzy-winged creature not unlike a dragonfly.

The larvae of the tiger beetles also dig a hole in sandy places. These holes, not traps but burrows in which they live, often extend a foot or more in depth. The larvae, uncouth creatures, with large heads and prominent jaws, lie in a position of watchfulness at the mouth of the burrow and woe to an unsuspecting insect that walks over it or ventures near, for they are able to throw their bodies about in order to seize their prey in their rapacious jaws. They have a hump on their bodies provided with forward-pointing hooks which serve to anchor them in their burrows when wrestling with large prey and to help them drag their victims into their burrows where they may feed at leisure. I have often thrust a piece of straw down a burrow and then pulled it out with the larva clinging savagely to it.

The adults are the slender, beautifully colored beetles we find on bright, sunny days along dusty roads, well-beaten paths, and on the shores of streams. They are fleet of foot and capable flyers and often remain quite still as we approach until we come within reaching distance, when they spring into the air and fly away, alighting a few rods ahead of us. While in flight or just before they alight, they turn so that they face us and can observe our movements.

In places frequented by the tiger beetles, we may find the Carolina locust, which also has the habit of springing into the air as we are about to step on it, flying some distance, and then alighting on the ground. This large, pale yellow insect with dusky spots blends with the sand and soil so well that it takes searching to find it. Try to capture one and you will discover that it is not easy. It is a tantalizing, elusive creature and yet can be caught if you persevere.

Beetles number among their kind some of our most beautiful insects. I am thinking particularly of the tortoise beetles, small, bright, golden green or iridescent insects, with the prothorax and wing covers broadly expanded to form an approximately circular or oval outline suggesting the shell of a tortoise. There are a number of species, but one of the most exquisite is the one commonly found on the bindweed, clinging like a drop of molten gold to the leaves. Look for it where the bindweed winds its way about the shrubbery of a wayside thicket or trails over the ground of fields or meadows, its bell-shaped flowers suggesting their kinship to the morning glories of the garden trellis. Observe it carefully before you pick it up, for the brightness of its colors is said to depend on the emotions of the insect; you may find its shining luster dulled when removed from its happy home to the relative insecurity of your hand.

There is another tortoise beetle found on the milkweed, called the milkweed tortoise. It is a large, brick-red species with its wing covers marked with many black spots. Do not confuse it with the red milkweed beetle which is quite another insect with only four black spots on each wing cover and more slender in form.

Many different species of insects visit the milkweed for the nectar to be obtained from the blossoms, but I know of only five that, in New England, actually live and feed on the plant: the two already described, the monarch butterfly, the harlequin milkweed caterpillar, and a third species of beetle. The latter resembles the Colorado potato beetle in size and form but differs in color, being a deep blue except the wing covers, which are orange with three dark blue spots on each. I haven't been able to find a popular name for the insect, but if you are interested in the scientific one it is *Labidomera clivicollis*.

Although the caterpillars of the monarch may be seen throughout most of the summer, June seems to be the best time to look for them. They feed on the succulent leaves and when full-grown change to beautiful green chrysalids with golden markings. The chrysalis has been variously called "the greenhouse with the golden nails" and the "glass house with the gold nails," but whichever you prefer it is one of the most beautiful objects to be found outdoors.

Clothed with tufts of orange, black, and white, the gay harlequin caterpillars may frequently be seen feeding on the milkweed leaves, in apparent disregard of the birds. Birds don't like hairy caterpillars, anyway, but these may get added protection from the acrid nature of their food.

I have said that July can be called the month of butterflies but sometimes I wonder if it should not be called the month of beetles. The butterflies are the more conspicuous but the beetles are the more numerous in species and the more abundant in individuals. Countless potato beetles, Mexican bean beetles, cucumber beetles, flea beetles, and weevils are to be found in any vegetable garden; flat-headed and round-headed borers in the orchard; elm leaf beetles and willow beetles along the roadside; in the woods bark beetles, timber beetles, borers, and weevils are so numerous as almost to defy listing; and everywhere Japanese beetles seem a step ahead of us in our warfare against them.

Like other major insect pests the Japanese beetle is also an importation. It was first found in America in 1916 in Riverton, New Jersey, but was probably brought over some years before as a stowaway in the soil covering the roots of ornamentals imported from Japan. If prompt and efficient means had been taken when first discovered, the original infestation might have been cleared up. Little was done, however, and the insect spread rapidly into the neighboring states, into Ohio, the Carolinas, and the New England states. The usual methods of combating the insect with chemicals have been of no value, nor have quarantine measures proved more effective. More than two hundred kinds of trees, shrubs, and plants are affected, and the pest will probably continue to spread and cause destruction until enemies brought from Japan are so thoroughly established here that they might control it. That seems to be our only hope, for it is doubtful if we can ever exterminate it.

The adult insect is about the size of the Colorado potato beetle, shining bronze green in color, with tan or brownish wing covers. The larvae live in the ground, feeding on grass roots; the adults live above ground feeding on fruits and leaves. I have found the beetle many times in and around Boston; only last summer a friend spent hours trying to rid his raspberry patch of them, but for every one he killed others appeared to take its place. Both of us filled a quart bottle with them within a matter of minutes without shifting our position. Strangely enough, he had a good crop of berries in spite of the invader.

I have just come in from watching a potter wasp put the finishing touches on her little water jug, a delightful and exquisite little object worthy of the skill of a master craftsman. Neatly fashioned, it is about half an inch in diameter with a delicate lip-like margin, and saddled on a twig of a cedar tree. The water jug serves as her nest; as soon as she provisions it with spiders and deposits an egg she will close the opening. After a few days, the egg will hatch and the grub, after feeding on the spiders, will pupate and emerge as a full-fledged wasp.

I find a water jug only occasionally, although the potter wasp is not a very rare insect. The nests of the mud dauber are far more common, and every summer I have them in my garage. The mud dauber is a slender insect, so slender, in fact, that it is amazing how the heart and the nervous system and alimentary canal can find room within the narrow body. There are two common species. One is colored steel blue, the other, black or brown with yellow spots and legs. The latter has the curious habit of jerking her wings constantly as she walks around in the sunshine. Why, I don't know. Perhaps it is to display her beautiful black wings, which shimmer in the sunlight with a rainbow iridescence. Or perhaps it is nervousness, for she also has the curious habit of turning around constantly as if she momentarily expected to be attacked from the rear.

The mud daubers appear in June, when they may be seen flitting about the flowers or sunning themselves on a fence rail, but it is not until July that they are at the height of their nest-building activities. The yellow species likes to sing while at work. She does not actually sing in the true sense but makes a sound by vibrating her wings. The pitch may be either high or low, according to what she is doing at the moment; when she is in the actual process of constructing her nest she makes a high-pitched rasping sound, but when she gathers the mud she makes a faint hum as if this were a task more to her taste.

I don't know what determines her selection of a nesting site, but I do know that she is rather particular as to what kind of mud she uses. I have seen these wasps spend considerable time near a puddle, running up and down, digging here and there until they find mud to their liking. Then they ram their heads down into it and with their jaws cut out little pellets about the size of sweet pea seeds. Anyone coming upon a group of these wasps for the first time and seeing them standing on their heads and waving their tails in the air might well wonder what sort of rite they are performing.

Every summer wasps of the genus *Polistes* also build their nests in my garage, and one winter I counted more than thirty empty nests. They were not all built the preceding summer but represented wasp labor over a period of years. If you are not a timid soul I would suggest you examine it the next time you find one of these nests. They are the open paper combs that may be found suspended by a single pedicel from beneath window ledges, corners of roofs, within barns and sheds, under rocks, on the warm sides of ledges, and in trees. In some of the cells you will find long, white eggs, in others, chubby little soft-bodied grubs, and in still others pupae in various stages of transformation.

The grubs hang head down and you may wonder how they can remain in their cells without falling out. They are held in place by a sticky disc at the rear end of their bodies and later by their enlarged heads, which completely fill the openings of the cells. They are constantly nursed by the workers and fed first upon the sugary nectar of flowers and the juices of fruits. Later they are fed upon more substantial food, such as the softer parts of caterpillars, flies, bees, and other insects, which have been reduced to a pulp by mastication.

Several days ago I discovered that the yellow jackets had taken possession of a hole in the ground in a secluded part of the garden and had built their nest in it. They were going in and out of the hole, which measured barely an inch in diameter, in a hurrying, jostling throng. Some of them were returning from foraging expeditions and carried food; others were returning from a visit to a weather-beaten fence post, intent upon adding their load of pulp to the nest; while those that were leaving carried pellets of earth which they had scraped from the walls of the hole to make room for further additions to their home. None seemed bent on pleasure; they appeared, on the contrary, to be too busily engaged with their tasks to pay any attention to me though doubtless they were aware of my existence.

Wasps are irritable and nervous creatures at best. Most people are afraid of them and with good reason, for they can inflict painful wounds with their stings. The yellow jackets, in particular, are trim, graceful creatures and do not give the impression of being formidable. Antagonize them, however, and you will learn differently. You may be sure I made no attempt to distract them and as I let them alone they paid no heed to me.

Unlike the ants and honey bees, wasps do not live in permanent communities. When cold weather sets in ants pass into a state of dormancy while honey bees cluster in their hives and remain semi-dormant. But like the bumblebee colony, the entire wasp community dies, except the queens. Accordingly, when spring returns all the bees and ants have to do is to start where they left off, whereas the wasps have to begin all over again. A new nest must be built and a family reared which will endure only a few months.

As June blends into July the tadpoles of the wood frogs complete their transformation, and the froglets leave the water and take to the green moss and delicate ferns that live in the shade of tall trees. The wood frogs are essentially creatures of the woods, where the subdued light and quiet harmonize with their natures. They are not easy to find, for their reddish-brown color blends with the brown pine needles and oak leaves of the forest floor. I have often startled one into action, as I followed a woodland path, and more than once have I discovered one lurking among the pyrola leaves as I stooped to examine the fragrant flowers. Perhaps the best place to find them is along the edge of a woodland pool.

Toads also complete their metamorphosis by July and hop out of the ponds to help us in our warfare against the insects. It has been found that 88 percent of a toad's food consists of insects and other small creatures considered garden pests. It has also been estimated that in three months a toad will eat some ten thousand injurious insects, and of this number 16 percent are cutworms, 9 percent caterpillars, and 19 percent weevils and other injurious beetles. In terms of dollars and cents, a toad was once estimated to be worth $19.44 in a single season, because of the cutworms alone which it devours. (And these figures were based on pre-inflation values.)

I could never understand why many people dislike the toad. Perhaps it is mostly a heritage of a superstitious age that wrapped him in a veil of magic and believed that he brought evil and misfortune. Actually, the toad is a most delightful little animal when you get to know him. As for bringing evil or doing harm or causing warts, as many people still believe, it is all nonsense. I know some people are prejudiced against him because they think he is cold and slimy to the touch. It is true that sometimes he is cold but there are also times when he is quite warm. The reason for this is that the temperature of his body changes with that of his environment. On a very warm day, he might be very warm indeed, and conversely, on a cold day very cold, so cold in fact that he might dig down into the earth and sleep all day.

As for being slimy, he is not slimy at all; on the contrary, quite dry. Of course, if you squeeze him a little too hard or handle him somewhat roughly, he will become slightly damp, but this is his way of telling you that you are hurting him. The fluid he pours out at such times is colorless and odorless and quite harmless. He does, however, secrete another fluid when he is in great agony, which is slightly poisonous. The toad usually reserves this means of defense for such times as when he is seized by an enemy, for the fluid has a disagreeable effect on the mucous membrane of the mouth. I have seen more than one dog drop a toad in a hurry.

Some people consider him loathsome because he lives in a dark, damp place, but the toad seeks such a situation not only for the shelter it provides but also for the moisture. A toad, you see, does not drink water in the ordinary way. All the water he gets he absorbs through his skin. Keep a toad in a dry place and he soon becomes thin and distressed looking; within a few days, he will probably die. But provide him with plenty of moisture and he will remain plump and contented, even though he may not have much food.

A toad may not be as intelligent as other animals, but he is wise in many ways. He sleeps during the greater part of the day when the sun is hot and his enemies are abroad, but when the sun sinks in the western sky he comes out and begins his nightly chase in search of food. The chase is always an exciting one, for he eats only living food; and as he has an enormous appetite, he must hunt almost incessantly to get as much as he needs. To watch a toad eat is well worth a few moments of anyone's time. Observe how still he sits, his head bent slightly forward, his eyes bright and intelligent. A fly alights within two inches of his nose. His mouth opens, his tongue comes out, and the fly is gone. And as he swallows it, he closes his eyes as if to savor the dainty morsel to the utmost.

As the afternoon begins to wane, the tree frog also becomes restless, and it is then I hear his long, reedy tremolo from a tree or vine. This little frog remains as invisible as Perseus in his charmed helmet because he blends with his surroundings and can pass for a green leaf, plant stem, or a small excrescence on the gray trunk of a birch or lichen-covered oak; usually I find him only by accident. He has a rather extensive wardrobe and can change his suit almost at will. He resembles the chameleon in this respect, but unlike the chameleon, his color changes are due more to environmental conditions than emotional disturbances. He usually wears a bright gray suit with dark markings, but in a dark, moist, or cool place he seems to prefer a suit of deep stone-gray or brown; and among green surroundings, his favorite suit is white and green, which he will quickly change for one of yellowish-white if the temperature goes up.

The tree frog is a squat little creature and somewhat clumsy looking, but he is quite the little acrobat and, as he can see objects at a distance of two feet or more, he will unhesitatingly leap through the air after a fly or mosquito, apparently quite unconcerned as to where he is going to land. I have often seen him leap for some slender plant stem, catch it with one foot, and swing in the air with outstretched legs. Then, when it would seem as if he would drop to the ground, he would pull himself up, blink his eyes, and settle himself comfortably. I have yet to see him fall very far, although I admit my heart has often skipped a few beats. He always finds something to arrest his fall, even if it requires a bit of frantic acrobatics. Of course, he is well-equipped for such feats, having sticky disks on his fingers and toes that enable him to cling to vertical surfaces, such as glass.

Though the birds have become more or less silent and we no longer hear the shrill piping of the peeper and the croaking of wood frogs, the days are not entirely without sound. We hear the familiar song of the katydid and the drone of the dog-day cicada among the treetops. Then, as the sun begins to sink, we hear the reedy tremolo of the tree frogs and later, when night has fallen, the singing of the meadow grasshoppers, the loud, sweet notes of the whip-poor-will, and the cry of the screech owl. How the screech owl ever got his name I don't know. Certainly, his cry is not a screech, but a singularly mournful and plaintive wail; I know people who shudder when they hear it. Most people have a horror of owls and regard them as eerie creatures of the night that thread their silent way through the darkness on missions of evil and disaster and whose cries are prophetic of impending death. Actually, owls are beneficial birds and in the field of usefulness, the complement of hawks, the hawks working by day and the owls by night.

It is a pity that hawks are still generally regarded as a nuisance and are often hunted indiscriminately. It is true, of course, that there are certain species which occasionally raid a poultry yard or kill a game bird, but it is senseless to indict the entire group because of a few and to shoot every hawk on sight simply because it is a hawk. Hawks are of immeasurable value, as they destroy rodents and harmful insects, and those that kill game birds more than offset the harm they do by removing game birds suffering from contagious diseases.

Hawks do not seem to be as numerous as they were, although the sparrow hawk is apparently increasing. He is a beautiful bird and doubtless would be a universal favorite did he not prey upon the songbirds. He lets them alone as long as there are mice and grasshoppers to be had, but if such fare is not obtainable, he will drop like a thunderbolt upon a sparrow, warbler, or any small bird. Several days ago I saw one of these birds perched on a fence post, occasionally jerking his tail as he looked about for a victim. Suddenly, he launched himself into the air, hovered for a moment over the ground, and then plunged downward and disappeared in the grass. He reappeared a moment later with a sparrow in his talons and flew back to his perch, where he feasted at leisure.

A few moments before I saw the hawk, I had been watching some kingbirds chase flying insects over a stony pasture, where mullein stalks, with scattered yellow blossoms, stand like senti-nels and the pink spires of the steeplebush point skyward. Ever since I saw a kingbird attack a cat about to pounce on his young in their nest, I have admired these fearless, pugnacious little birds, and whenever I see them, I invariably stop to watch them. There are better flyers, but when a kingbird dashes after a flying insect, you know he is going to get it. His entire behavior, whether on the wing or perched on a tree stump, fence post, or some other support, bespeaks confidence and assurance, if not arrogance, though I dislike to use the word. He often shows despotic tendencies, however, toward other birds and will contest the right of any to infringe on what he considers his own territory. He will brook no interference with his own welfare, and if you call that tyranny, well, then let us call him a tyrant, as many have done. The only birds that seem willing to dispute his sovereignty are the duck hawk and, strangely enough, the tiny ruby-throated hummingbird. Also, the catbird and the militant Baltimore oriole will give battle occasionally.

The orioles, incidentally, have left their swinging nest in the elm tree and with their brood have taken to the woods and thickets to feed on ripening berries. Other birds have, too, and the woods are alive with an increasing number of small birds. Within a few short weeks, they will be heading south and once again we will see the passing migrants. Even now the male bobolinks, who only yesterday, as it seemed, made the meadows ring with their music, are assuming their autumnal garb, and by the end of the month, both the young and old will have assembled in flocks, ready to begin their southward journey in August.

Although there are glimmerings of approaching autumn, summer actually has just begun. The catalpa and basswood blossom belatedly, the sumac is in full bloom, and the fleecy white spikes of the sweet pepperbush perfume the air with a spicy fragrance. Countless wildflowers, more robust and more showy than those of spring, decorate the landscape with all the colors of the rainbow. The butterfly weed fires the pasture with creeping flames of orange-red, and the fireweed enfolds the meadow in a purplish haze. The grass pink and common persicaria decorate the roadside with flowers of pink, and the Indian pipe relieves the gloom of dim-lit woods. Meadow lilies nod in the passing breeze and wood lilies gleam from beds of feathery, gold-tinged ferns. Sweet clovers scent the air, wild mustards are in bloom, and the exquisite flowers of the jewelweed dangle from slender stems along shaded streams. Sundews blossom in swamps and bogs where green berries, with sun-burned cheeks, hang from the branches of cranberry vines. Pickerel weed and long purples line the edges of ponds, where pond lilies spread their golden chalices to the sky. In little pools, the bladderwort lifts its yellow flowers, and in swampy ground, the spotted cowbane and ethereal meadow rue tower above the rushes and sedges. About the beautiful flower spikes of the meadowsweet and the lacy flowers of the wild carrot, innumerable flies, bees, wasps, beetles, and other insects swarm in great numbers, seeking refreshment from the countless blossoms, where ambush bugs and crab spiders lurk for prospective victims.

The crab spiders resemble crabs. Observe the short, broad form of the body, the crablike legs, and the curious fact that they can walk more readily sideways or backward than forward. Some of them live on plants and are colored to blend with the flowers they inhabit, while others live a secluded life under loose tree bark, stones, and in similar locations, such species being for the most part colored brown or gray.

One of the most frequently seen is the common white crab spider, which is of interest because of the way its color changes as it migrates to flowers of another color. In the spring and early summer, it may be found most often in white flowers, such as the white trillium or white fleabane. At this time, it is white in color, so it cannot be seen by the flower-visiting insects on which it feeds. Later in the season, it migrates to yellow flowers such as the goldenrod and tansy, when it becomes yellow or white with yellow decorations. Naturalists have found it in milkweed blossoms when it was white with lilac or purple markings. Some years ago, Dr. A.S. Packard proved experimentally that it changes from white to yellow in ten or twelve days by placing a number of the white spiders on goldenrod.

I was reminded this morning of the following two lines:

> And dew-bright webs festoon the grass
> In roadside fields at morning

when an unusually heavy condensation of dew brought out in bold relief numberless webs of the grass spider. Few of us realize what an immense number of webs are spun by this species except when the dew condenses on them and makes them visible so that the fields and our lawns appear to be covered with an almost continuous carpet of silk.

Should you be curious about these webs and be prompted to examine one, you would find it to be shaped somewhat like a broad funnel, with a tube extending downward at one side. This tube is used by the spider as a hideout in which to lie in wait for its prey, or as a place of refuge in case of danger, and is open at both ends so that the spider can escape from either end if necessary.

Many lines of silk, which cross each other irregularly, compose the web. Collectively they form a firm sheet held in place by many guy-lines attached to grass stems. Above the sheet, there usually is an irregular open network of silken threads to catch flying insects or so impede their flight that they will tumble or fall upon the sheet, where they may be seized by the waiting spider. Touch the web lightly and you will see the spider spring out from its hiding place intent on seizing some unfortunate victim, but jar the web roughly and the spider will take fright and speed out through the back door.

In July, the time to ramble is as the afternoon begins to wane, or, better still, in the cool of the morning, before the sun gets high, the deer flies start biting, and walking along the country road or open upland becomes unpleasant and tiring. I was up this morning for a stroll before breakfast, as the sun began to appear above the eastern horizon. Along the roadside and in the neighboring fields, the chicory was opening its blossoms to "match the sky," and in a thicket, a pair of cuckoos slipped furtively through the tangles. In a shady copse, I found the day flower open and alert, only to close after a visit by a bee, its lovely petals wilting into a wet, shapeless mass. A spring azure butterfly, larger than those I saw in the March woods, winged its way over a stone wall, where a chipmunk appeared and watched me with his inquisitive little eyes. And when I stopped to inhale the lovely fragrance of a wild rose, a leaf cutter bee appeared and began cutting a circular disc from a leaf blade.

Did you know that the bee uses these pieces of leaves to fashion little thimblelike cups or capsules in which to deposit her eggs? The capsules are built in some out-of-the-way place, usually in the pith of a bramble, or perhaps in a tunnel in the ground under a stone, in a cavity of a lead pipe, between shingles of a roof, in a cavity of a sumac branch, or in a piece of hemlock timber. The nest is difficult to find and usually is discovered only by accident.

After the bee had flown away I left the road and cut across a meadow and here I found meadow mushrooms in abundance. Farther on I came across a solitary parasol mushroom, a most graceful and attractive species and one that is delightful to the taste but unfortunately not very common. Mushrooms, incidentally, become increasingly abundant during July. Almost everywhere you go you will find them appearing above the ground — the tall, stately destroying angel, of a shimmering, satiny whiteness, symbolic of innocence, but one of the most poisonous mushrooms known; the equally poisonous fly mushroom with its danger signals of warts and concentric scaly rings; the small chanterelles with the cheerful yellow of their diminutive caps; the beautiful Jack-o'-lanterns in dense clusters; the dainty coral mushrooms that border the woodland path and brighten the somber wood tints with colored branches; and the green and red Russulas that vie with the flowers in the brilliancy of their coloring.

NATURAL EVENTS IN JULY

- In the morning dew the webs of the grass spider form an almost continuous carpet of silk on the grass of fields and meadows.

- Pitfalls of the ant lion may be found in sheltered sandy places.

- The dainty, golden-eyed lacewing is common on herbage and the foliage of trees and shrubs.

- The grass pink illumines the meadow with countless purplish-pink blossoms.

- The erect pink spikes of the persicaria brighten roadsides, fields, and waste places.

- Green berries, some of them already with sunburned cheeks, hang from the branches of cranberry vines.

- White sundews blossom in swamps and bogs.

- The bladderwort lifts its yellow flowers above the water of black pools that border ponds and swamps.

- Among the grasses of moist meadows the white fringed orchis sends showy spikes of bloom skyward.

- The fleecy white spikes of the sweet pepperbush perfume the air with a spicy fragrance.

- The large magenta-lilac flower heads of the pasture thistle provide a banquet table to flying insects.

- The white umbels of the spotted cowbane tower above the grasses of swamp and meadow.

- Borders of ponds and streams are aglow with long purples.

- The yellow flowers of the St. John's wort, gleaming in the sunlight, decorate fields and waste places.

- The tall meadow rue, with its graceful foliage and white pyramidal clusters, provides a sharp contrast with the ranker growth of sunny swamps and low meadows.

- The bindweed winds its way about the shrubbery of wayside thicket or trails over the ground of fields and meadows and opens its pretty bell-like, pink-tinged flowers that suggest their kinship to the morning glory of the garden trellis.

- Mud daubers are at the height of their nest-building activities.

- The open combs of the Polistes wasps may be found hanging from beneath window ledges, corners of roofs, within barns and sheds, under rocks, and in trees.

- Yellow jackets may frequently be seen flying in and out of a hole in the ground, busily engaged in various wasp activities.

- Tadpoles of the wood frog complete their transformation and the froglets leave the water for the green mosses and delicate ferns that live in the shade of tall trees.

- The fragrant white flowers of the pyrola blossom along woodland paths.

- The singularly mournful and plaintive wail of the screech owl may be heard at night.

- The sparrow hawk is sometimes seen on a dead limb or fence post looking about for some luckless grasshopper or mouse.

- Kingbirds chase flying insects over stony pastures.

- The butterfly weed fires dry pastures with creeping flames of orange red.

- Crab spiders hide in flowers, under loose tree bark, stones, and similar places.

- Biting deer flies appear in woods and along country roads.

- Cuckoos may occasionally be seen in roadside thickets.

- Dayflowers open and close in shady copses.

- Mushrooms become abundant; meadow mushrooms appear in grassy places.

- Mullein stalks, with scattered yellow blossoms, stand like sentinels above stony pastures.

- Sweet clovers relieve the drabness of waste places with stalks of countless blossoms, scenting the air with sweet odors.

- Potter wasps construct their miniature water jugs.

- The exquisite mottled orange-yellow flowers of the jewel weed nod from slender stems as soft breezes murmur through the foliage near shaded streams.

- The loud, clear notes of the whippoorwill fall upon the night air.

- Darters play in swift streams.

- Leaf cutter bees are busy cutting out pieces of leaf blades for use in making nests for young.

- The long reedy tremulo of the tree frogs issues from trees and vines.

- Water lilies spread their golden-centered chalices to the sky and sweeten the air with their lovely fragrance.

- Red milkweed beetles are conspicuous on milkweed plants.

- Bobolinks gather in flocks, preparing for their departure south.

- Basswood is in bloom and bees reap a harvest.

- Newly emerged fritillaries, anglewings, and other butterflies fly leisurely over fields and meadows.

- Woods are filled with young birds.

- This is the time of the summer brood of the spring azure butterfly.

- Greenish-white sumac is in full bloom.

- Milkweed blossoms, rich in nectar, entice hosts of insects.

- Baltimore orioles with their young leave their nesting sites to fly to the woods where berries are ripening.

- The beautiful flower spikes of the meadowsweet and the pink spires of the steeplebush point skyward.

- Gay harlequin caterpillars and the caterpillars of the monarch butterfly feed on the succulent leaves of the milkweed.

- Beetles abound everywhere.

- White catalpa is in flower.

- Toads, completing their metamorphosis, begin to hop out of the ponds where they have developed from eggs.

- Blue chicory blooms and the lacy white flowers of the wild carrot offer refreshment to innumerable flies, bees, wasps, and other insects.

- The yellow flowers of the evening primrose open at dusk and are visited by the night-flying hawk moths, which suck the nectar with their long, coiling tongues.

- Other night-flying moths visit the blossoms of the bladder campion and bouncing bet, familiar along roadsides and in waste places.

- The graceful, waxy-white clusters of the Indian pipe appear ghostlike in woods.

- The drone of the dog-day cicada is heard among the tree tops.

- The familiar song of the katydid may also be heard, and at night meadow grasshoppers burst into song.

- Buff yellow-spotted meadow lilies nod from long stems and the vivid orange-scarlet cups of the wood lily gleam from beds of feathery, gold-tinged fern.

- The nodding wands of the fireweed rise in a purplish haze.

- Violetlike spikes of the pickerel weed line the edges of ponds and streams.

- Tarnished plant bugs and four-lined leaf bugs suck the juices from punctured stems.

- Tiny white specks of the pine leaf scale perch on pine needles, sometimes in such numbers as to suggest a dusting with flour.

- Aphis lions stalk aphids in herbage and the foliage of trees and shrubs.

- Praying mantises lurk among the foliage for unsuspecting victims.

- On sunny days tiger beetles and Carolina locusts are common on dusty roads, well-beaten paths, and on the shores of streams.

- Tortoise beetles may be found on various plants.

- Yellow wild mustards are in full bloom.

- The enchanted nightshade opens its insignificant white flowers in the shady woods.

August

It has been a hot, sultry day — one of those typical August days in the midst of a heat wave, when hardly a leaf is moving in the sky and when the sun is almost obscured by the copper shadows of some distant tree, and the cicada droned its monotonous tune. All day long the dog-day cicada droned in some distant tree, and occasionally a long-horned katydid, now as the shadows deepen, called its familiar "Katy." And I can hear the crickets and the grasshoppers tuning their fiddles in preparation for their nocturnal chorus.

I don't know why crickets chirp. At one time it was believed the males chirped to attract the females, but it has been shown that the females are indifferent to their serenades. Presumably there are times when the females might be receptive; as a rule they pay little attention to the chirp of the males. As you listen to their nightly concerts it might seem as if the males strive to play in unison—that they hear one another and that each one governs himself accordingly. But insects are usually soloists, and if they play together it is probably by chance rather than by design. Even if two of them seem to play a duet or four combine to form a quartet, it is likely that their playing together is accidental. Of course, one insect might stimulate another to play, but there is no evidence that they co-ordinate their playing. Under such circumstances you would expect that the continuous chirping of crickets, each one playing for and by himself, would be a nerve-wracking, discordant din. Some people do find it a distraction and are kept awake at night, but I find their nightly concerts soothing and restful and enjoy lying in bed listening to their serenades until drowsiness creeps over me and I fall into a deep slumber.

While listening to the crickets I sometimes think of the many ways in which insects produce sound. I daresay that only man himself has succeeded in producing a greater variety of means, and doubtless there are times when many of us wish he could have directed his energies elsewhere. Bees, flies, and mosquitoes make a sound by vibrating their wings; crickets and the horned passalus by rubbing their wing covers together; grasshoppers and the sand crickets by rubbing their legs against the sides of the abdomen; whirligig beetles by rubbing the tip of the abdomen against their wing covers; the water boatman and backswimmer by rubbing their front legs against their proboscis; a few moths by rubbing the feelers on the lower jaw against their proboscis; the powder post beetles by rubbing their front legs against a projection on the body; the blow flies and May beetles by a vibrating membrane; and the deathwatch beetles by bumping their heads against the sides of their burrows.

Few of these insects can be called musicians; usually the sound which they produce is incidental and the result of some normal activity. We are all familiar with the high-pitched notes of the mosquito and the housefly and the hum of bees as they buzz about gathering nectar and pollen. Most of us are also familiar with Rimsky-Korsakov's delightful and popular "Flight of the Bumblebee" in which the composer has succeeded in capturing the sound of the bee. What most of us do not know is that the bees produce different tones which appear to result from various degrees of activity. Listen sometime to a honeybee worker as it contentedly goes about its business of collecting nectar and pollen and compare it with the note of an enraged bee. Other insects also reveal differences. The mud dauber, when gathering a load of mud at the edge of a pool, makes a faint hum but when she applies this mud to her nest the pitch is raised to a high, rasping sound that may be heard for a considerable distance.

These sounds are incidental and unlike those produced for a specific purpose, such as that made by the sand cricket, which makes a loud noise when attacked to intimidate the enemy, or that made by the deathwatch beetles, which serves as a means of communication. The sounds produced by the cicadas, grasshoppers, crickets, and katydids are also apparently produced for some definite purpose, since these insects have organs for hearing. The female tree crickets, however, have no auditory organ and can therefore not hear the chirps of the male; the chirping of the male is, nevertheless, not without purpose, for when he raises his legs to stridulate a gland is exposed. This gland gives off a liquid which has a pleasing odor and attracts the female for the purpose of mating. These tree crickets, incidentally, are incessant chirpers, and have been known to chirp 2,640 times without stopping. They chirp both day and night but their music, if such it can be called, is more plainly heard at night when other sounds are not so loud.

Several days ago a neighbor asked me to identify a caterpillar of the white-marked tussock moth. In case you do not know your caterpillars, it is a beautiful insect with four white tussocks, three long pencils of black hair, a coral-red head, and two small red swellings which are said to give off an odor disagreeable to its enemies. It is a rather common caterpillar and occasionally is so abundant as to damage various shade trees, such as linden, maple, and elm.

Another caterpillar, common and sometimes quite abundant in August, is the snow-white, black-dotted, black-tufted caterpillar of the hickory tiger moth, which may be found on the leaves of the hickory and butternut. I have never looked into the matter and do not know whether caterpillars are more abundant in August than in any other month, but certainly they seem more noticeable. I remember one time I found a willow so populated with the spiny caterpillars of the mourning cloak butterfly that the leaves were hardly visible. This is also the time of the year when the little velvety black caterpillars of the painted beauty may be found feeding within silken nests on the leaves of the everlasting. Yellow bears also are common in almost every garden.

Insects certainly still dominate the summer scene, for wherever you roam you are sure to find them — bees, flies, wasps, beetles, bugs, dragonflies, and all the lesser-known members of this large group of animals. The beautiful little eight-spotted forester flies daily about my house, and only a few minutes ago I found a rosy maple moth asleep, or intoxicated with nectar, in the wilted blossom of an evening primrose. The spotted pelidnota beetle is a frequent visitor to the grape arbor, and at night stag beetles and the prionids are sometimes attracted to my porch light. You may not be familiar with the buffalo tree hoppers, so-called because of their fancied resemblance to the buffalo, but you must have seen them at times, for they are quite abundant in the fields and meadows. They are grass green in color, triangular in shape, and hop from plant to plant. If you are unacquainted with them, I suggest you learn to recognize them, especially if you have apple or pear trees, since the scars made in the bark by the female when laying her eggs cause considerable injury to the twigs.

Of more general interest are the two-marked tree hoppers. These insects are usually found on the bittersweet, and if, on your rambles, you come across this trailing vine, I suggest you look for them. You may have some difficulty finding them because they look so much like thorns, and it is only when they move that you can be sure you have found them. No matter how much the vine twists and turns, you will observe that they rest with their heads always toward the top so that the sap, which they suck, may flow more easily down their tiny throats.

There are many species of tree hoppers and most of them live on trees, although some live on low shrubs, grasses, and other herbaceous plants. Sometimes they are called insect brownies; if you want to know why, look at them full in the face through a hand lens. Notice that part of the body is prolonged backward over the abdomen and in some species sideways and upward as well. John Henry Comstock once said that "Nature must have been in a joking mood when tree hoppers were developed." Doubtless Nature had a hand in forming them into the many strange and grotesque shapes for which these insects are famous. Nature plans nothing idly, however, and I think she had another intent in mind when she fashioned their bodies, for the majority of the modifications which she evolved have served to bring about protective resemblance, since the insects have been made to look like different plant structures, such as buds and thorns.

The tree hoppers are not the only insects that resemble plant structures or other objects. I have already mentioned the geometrid caterpillars; there is also the walking stick, a curious insect that resembles a twig. Certain weevils, when disturbed, drop to the ground and look like bits of soil or pebbles, and certain moths, when at rest, look like fungus growths.

There is a considerable difference of opinion on how much the insects benefit by such modifications. The popular belief is that they are highly successful in protecting the insects from enemies, but this theory is largely based on the false assumption that the senses of the lower animals are co-extensive in range with ours.

It fails to consider the fact that the birds' ability to detect insects is far superior to our own. The truth of the matter is that in spite of such "protection," the insects do not entirely escape detection. More than twenty different birds prey upon the geometrid caterpillars alone. However, if such protection is not 100 percent successful, it doubtless can be regarded as advantageous, since an adaptation may be successful if only partially perfect.

This morning I found some spiny green and pink galls on my rose bushes. I don't know how many different kinds of galls there are — the number runs into the thousands. They are found on almost every form of plant life and may occur on any part of the plant — root, branch, leaf, blossom, fruit, and even seed. Some are very simple in structure, but others, like the oak apple, are most complicated.

Many galls are highly attractive and striking in form and coloration, such as the oak hedgehog gall, yellow and spiny and sometimes shaded with red; the maple leaf gall, of yellow, red-margined, eye-like spots, which abounds on the leaves of the red maple; and the wool sower, woolly, creamy-white, and admirably set off with blotches of bright pinkish-red, which occurs on the small twigs of the white oak and which is one of the most beautiful of all natural objects.

I don't know why a gall should have a distinctive or specific form. There is no evidence that the form is of any adaptive importance, and the answer may be that the formation of any specific form is purely mechanical. But the remarkable thing about galls is that those made by the same species of insects are all of the same form, are all formed on the same species of plant, and are always on the same part of the plant, so that those versed in gall lore may know the identity of the gall-maker by merely looking at the gall.

The study of gall insects is in some respects difficult, for we cannot always be sure that the insect which emerges from the gall is the one that made it, since many insects make no galls but lay their eggs in those made by others. Such insects are called "guests."

Furthermore, the fact that both the gall-makers and "guests" are attacked by parasitic hymenoptera adds to our confusion, for it is not always easy to determine the interrelations of these insects. Many galls, indeed, are complicated communities. In one case, as many as thirty different kinds of insects, belonging to almost all the orders, were reared from a single species of gall.

I have often been asked if galls are injurious to the host plant. In a few cases, they may do considerable damage, but generally they are not harmful and some are even useful. Certain oak galls have long been used in the manufacture of ink; others are used in medicine for their astringent properties; and a few serve as food. In Missouri and Arkansas, the deciduous oak gall is fed, when abundant, to cattle, hogs, and sheep, as well as to chickens and turkeys, with excellent results.

Few of us give much thought to the leaves of trees except in the early spring when we await their emergence, or in the fall when they paint the landscape with vivid reds and golden browns. Only those of us who have studied them know how marvelously they are put together and what mysterious food-making processes take place within them. Also, despite their paper thinness, they provide a dwelling place for various insects.

It almost passes belief that there are creatures so small that they can live and grow between the upper and lower surfaces of a leaf and yet be visible to the naked eye. Hold a leaf, more or less discolored with white or grayish blotches or with long twisting lines, up to the light and you will find the blotch or twisted line inhabited by a tiny worm-like creature.

These twisting lines and blotches are passages and tunnels which the larvae of insects — beetles, flies, sawflies, and moths — excavate in the tissues of the leaves, and, as they are known as mines, the insects making them are called leaf miners. The patterns which these insects trace are of as many designs as the species that make them. As in the case of the galls, each species makes its own characteristic pattern, so that those familiar with the insects can usually identify the species by the form of the mine; as one writer puts it, "they write their signatures on the leaves."

I wonder if James Russell Lowell had these little animals in mind when he wrote:

> And there's never a leaf nor blade too mean
> To be some happy creature's palace.

Whether they are happy is a moot question, but assuming they are, if shelter and plenty of food alone are conducive to happiness, they do not live an altogether carefree existence. Sometimes they find the veins of the leaves a barrier to further progress and must cut through them or confine their operations to a limited area. They must be careful, too, not to cut latex cells, lest the secretions pour out and drown them. But their gravest problem is waste disposal. Some miners merely distribute the wastes over the floor of the mine; others go to the trouble of excavating side chambers in which to dispose of their refuse; and many others have developed the habit of cutting holes in the surface of the leaf through which they push out their fecula.

The leaf miners attack nearly all families of plants, and needless to say, some of them can prove quite destructive. Even garden vegetables are not immune, for several species attack spinach and beets, often with disastrous results. Quite frequently, a leaf may serve as a habitation for an entire family, and if you hold such a leaf up to the light, you may see several larvae, each making a little bag and all eventually joining together to make a great blister. It would be well before preparing "greens" for the table to examine them.

Because a few members of a group of animals are harmful or dangerous is no reason to accuse all, yet that seems to be a practice. The snakes and hawks are a case in point; the spiders are another. These animals seem generally to be regarded with suspicion and often with fear, even though the vast majority are entirely harmless. It is true they are poisonous — that is how they kill their prey — but, with the exception of the tarantulas of the Southwest and the black widows, none of our spiders can eject enough venom into a wound to cause any trouble. They are considerably less dangerous to handle than many of our common insects, and we have more reason to fear the sting of a bee or the bite of a mosquito, which, incidentally, are more disposed to attack us.

Not only do I know people who become terrified at the sight of spiders and shun them as something evil and loathsome, but I also know people who consider them ugly and repulsive. That is a matter of opinion, but personally I find many of them rather beautiful and some exceedingly quaint. However you feel about them, remember they are your friends and, like the earthworms, work for you night and day, destroying flies, mosquitoes, grasshoppers, and other "bugs" that harm us.

Spiders, moreover, are infinitely interesting once you get to know them. They are skilled civil engineers: watch one at work and you will marvel at the precision with which it constructs its web, and at the uncanny skill with which it measures angles and calculates stresses and strains.

It may surprise you to learn that spiders may spin several different kinds of silk and that they have a use for each kind. They have a silk with which they lower themselves from an elevated position and which they spin as they move from place to place; it also forms the permanent frame of their webs. They have a viscid sort of silk with which they entrap their victims, and a silk with which they swathe them. Then they have a fourth kind — a thick, often brightly colored silk — that they use to encase their eggs, forming what might be called a baby blanket. Of course, all spiders do not spin all these different kinds of silk.

Originally, spiders used silk only to wrap their masses of eggs. Then they began to line their retreats, and after a while they began to build platforms of silk outside these retreats. It was then but a step to construct snares which at first were quite primitive but which gradually developed into the intricate, beautiful webs that now excite our wonder and admiration.

Snares differ greatly. They may be merely a maze of threads extending in all directions, such as are built by the domestic or house spider and commonly known as a cobweb; they may consist of a more or less closely woven sheet on a single plane with threads extending in all directions with no apparent regularity of arrangement, like those built by the hammock spider; they may be of finer workmanship like the funnel-shaped web of the grass spider; or they may be of the orb type — the most intricate and exquisite structures made by any of the lower animals.

August seems to be the heyday of spider life, for these animals appear to be more commonly seen during this month than at any other time of the year. Certainly they appear to be everywhere, and their webs — particularly the orb webs — may be found almost without searching. I have only to go into the neighboring field or down the road to find the beautiful web of the garden spider, and directly outside my window, I can see the web of the shamrock spider stretched between the branches of a honeysuckle shrub.

The orb weavers usually spin their webs vertically as they are thus more apt to be in the path of flying insects. The radii are usually fastened to a silken framework, which is supported by guy-lines to surrounding objects such as plant stems, and are connected by a continuous spiral thread or line spaced regularly except at the center or hub which is of more solid silk and usually surrounded by an open space.

The radii, the guy-lines, the framework, and the center of the web are all made of dry, inelastic silk, but the spiral line is very viscid and elastic and adheres to any object that touches it. This is the trapping part of the web. Any unfortunate insect that touches one of the spirals and tries to escape becomes inexorably entangled in the neighboring lines and held fast until the spider can reach it. If you have access to a microscope, examine one of these threads and you will find it consists of two strands bearing a series of globules and looking very much like a string of pearls. The strands are the elastic part of the thread and the globules the sticky portion.

Some orb weavers, when they have completed their webs, rest on the hub and there await their prey. Others have a retreat or den above or to one side of the orb in which they lie in wait. These spiders spin what is called a trapline from the hub to the den; it serves as a means of passage to and from the web and vibrates as a signal when an insect has been trapped.

The moment an insect has been caught, the spider rushes toward it, wraps it in a band of silk called the swathing band, and rolls it over and over. If hungry, the spider proceeds to feast at once; otherwise, it leaves the trapped insect for a future meal. You can observe the swathing act by throwing a grasshopper into a web. As the spider rushes toward its victim, you will observe it travels on the dry, inelastic radii and not on the viscid spiral, in which it would become entrapped like its prey. The webs, as strong as they may be, are frequently damaged, and during the hunting season a spider is likely to make a new web every twenty-four hours.

Not all spiders spin snares. The crab spiders and the wolf spiders lie in wait for their prey or chase them over the ground. The jumping spiders are also hunters. They are small or medium-sized, rather stout, with conspicuous eyes, a body usually thickly covered with hairs or scales, and with thick front legs, which, in the males, are covered with peculiar bunches of hairs that serve as ornaments. Many of these spiders, moreover, are brightly colored, even iridescent.

These spiders may often be seen jumping about on plants, logs, and fences. They are aptly named. They can move sideways or backward and can jump surprising distances. If you observe their habits, you will discover that they believe in "safety first," for before they jump they spin a line of silk which they fasten to the "jumping-off" place and with which they can regain their original resting place if necessary.

These jumping spiders are quite ardent in their love-making. The males put on a display that compares favorably with the court-ship antics of many larger animals. At mating time, the males dance before the females and strike the most singular postures, holding their legs extended or sideways or over their heads to show their ornaments, or moving them about to attract attention.

As in July, the birds and mammals are, for the most part, rather quiet, although occasionally I hear the song of a red-eyed vireo, the song sparrow, or the wood pewee. In the fresh morning air or in the twilight of the evening, the barn swallows swoop above the garden; chimney swifts, with quivering wings and shrill twitterings, describe a lacework of disappearing lines against the sky as they pursue fast-flying insects. And in the neighboring field, young and old chipping sparrows feed on the seeds of weeds. The swallows often call to mind a summer's day many years ago. I was about nine at the time, and my father and I were sitting on the porch waiting for supper to be served. It had been a hot, sultry day, unrelieved by even the slightest breeze, and it was, I thought, with more hope than expectation that my father voiced the belief we would soon have rain.

His remark might well have passed had it not been for my natural curiosity. I pondered the matter of rain for some moments, scanned the sky for likely signs, but except for some gathering clouds deep in the western sky through which the setting sun was weaving its way, I saw nothing that could possibly have established my father as a weather prophet. He must have sensed my thoughts, for he suddenly suggested I observe the flight of the swallows. I watched them intently for several minutes but saw nothing unusual in their behavior. He pointed out how low they were flying and went on to explain that as the moisture in the atmosphere increases, insects are found nearer to the ground, thus making it necessary for the birds chasing them to fly much lower than they would normally.

Our discussion was shortly interrupted by the call to supper, and for the time being I forgot all about my father's prediction. I was reminded of it a few hours later when I was awakened by a violent clap of thunder. As I lay in my bed watching the flashes of lightning through the window and listening to the raindrops on the roof, I kept thinking of the swallows. The next day I got a book on birds, and, by reading the descriptions and looking at the illustrations, I learned that the birds we had observed were barn swallows. I also learned that they build their nests in barns, cup-shaped affairs of mud and grass built on the beams and rafters.

In August, red bats mate, and in a newly-mown meadow, jumping mice may often be seen searching for new homes. And as night falls, raccoons steal from the woods by moonlight to feed on juicy kernels in corn patches, and flying squirrels gambol in the nearby woods.

A woman once wrote me to ask how to get rid of a family of flying squirrels that had taken possession of her attic. "They are lovely little animals," she said, "but I am afraid my house comes first, and they are being destructive. They are not a bit afraid of me, but they keep me from sleeping, to say nothing of the damage they are doing. They play in the attic all night and sleep in the partitions all day." I could sympathize with her and knew how she felt about getting rid of the squirrels, for they are delight-ful little animals and a joy in the house, *if* properly confined. Unrestrained, however, as in her case, they can prove quite a nuisance. It doesn't take much imagination to picture them in her attic, up to all sorts of tricks, chasing each other, squealing and scratching, playing about like puppies and kittens.

My correspondent reveals much of their habits when she says they play all night and sleep all day. You can arouse them by rap-ping on the trees in which they have their nests to get them out in the daylight, but the only thing you will learn about them is the manner in which they "fly." I cannot guarantee you will learn even that, for they are as likely to go right back to sleep, clinging to the bark like lichens and looking for all the world like some fungus growth. Even on a cloudy day, I have never succeeded in getting them to do much except leave the nest and take one or two flights. More often, they ignore me and resume their slumbers.

You must forego part of your night's sleep if you wish to observe them during their hours of frolic, but these beautiful, dreamy-eyed little forest folk are worth it. As dusk falls and the moon begins to shed its soft glow over the landscape, they venture forth; but only when the night hawk is on the wing and the bat has taken the place of the chimney swift do they scamper and gambol among the trees and glide through the air like ghostly spirits.

Find a comfortable seat in the woods on a bright moonlit night and be quiet and patient. Perhaps you will not see them at once; you may have to wait for what seems an interminable time. Suddenly, you hear a slight rustle among the leaves overhead and the next moment you see a shadowy form glide swiftly through the air and alight on the bole of a tree. Then you see another come sailing after it; then another and another until you think the night air is full of them. After a while, you lose all thought of time until aching muscles finally tell you to go home, and as you leave these elfin creatures to their nocturnal enjoyments and wend your way homeward, you will rejoice in a memorable experience.

During the dry, hot days of August, the red newts remain hidden beneath logs and stones or in the moist humus of the woodland floor, but on a foggy or rainy day, they emerge and wander about in search of insects or other small animals which they can eat. I usually find them after a rainy night crawling along the road or woodland path, occasionally by the hundreds. They are very pretty little animals, albeit very timid, and will often peer out from among the leaves with an expression of alert shyness. Sometimes they remain motionless for so long they appear carved out of stone, but then without warning, they will dart away with lightning speed.

These red newts are the young form of the spotted newt. They live on land only until they become mature when they return to the water whence they came. It may take them one, two, and even three years to mature, but when they feel the urge to take up a water-dwelling existence, they assemble from all directions and begin moving to the nearest pond or stream. They crawl over the ground, through tall grasses, over and around obstacles of all kinds with a persistency that seems beyond the powers of such small animals, and even though they may be far from any body of water, they seem to know instinctively where to go. Before or as they enter the water, they change their coats of red to one of a more somber hue, but they retain the pepper-like spots and the red ones along the back. Minor structural changes also take place, but these do not greatly change their form.

During my August rambles, I sometimes come upon a female garter snake and her newly-born young. This snake, like many others, is supposed to take her young into her mouth and throat for protection against threatened danger, but I have never seen her do it nor do I know of anyone who has. If the phenomenon were actually as common as the stories about it, there would be no difficulty in subjecting it to actual proof. It is merely another snake superstition that has gained credence because of unreliable eyewitnesses.

The brown snake also gives birth to young during August; the eggs of the black snake hatch during the month; while the green snakes are just beginning to lay their eggs under flat stones, logs, and in sawdust piles. I know of no reptile, or, for that matter, no other animal, more gentle than the green or grass snake. Never have I been able to induce one to bite, and even when newly captured, it will submit to the most vigorous handling without showing the least sign of anger. A beautiful green, it blends so well with its surroundings that it is usually found only by chance. One time when examining some tangles, I found it twined about a stem, but I question if I would have seen it had it not moved when I inadvertently rubbed against it. It is fond of crawling beneath flat stones that have been warmed by the sun, but if discovered in such a place will escape into the surrounding vegetation with bewildering speed. Once in the vegetation, it will perceptibly slacken its pace as if aware of the protection afforded by its color.

Despite its reputation, August is not altogether a month of heat and sultriness. Frequently after a night of showers, the morning will dawn bright and clear, and cool breezes will blow gently over the landscape as the sun chases lingering clouds merrily on their way and dissolves glistening dewdrops. It is not the kind of a morning to spend indoors, but one on which to follow the narrow woodland path, where the flowers of the false foxglove gleam like yellow stars, and tick trefoils rise in the purplish haze, or to stroll down a winding country lane, where the bright blossoms of the purple-flowering raspberry rise above the tangles and the dodder winds its bright threads about the herbage and shrubbery like tangled yellow yarn. This is also the season when the hog peanut opens its small showy blossoms in drooping clusters among the blossoming skullcaps and the graceful lilac-blue spires of the bellflower.

It is the sort of morning to loiter by the pond, where countless insects swarm about the odd-shaped flowers of the turtlehead and the dense white globes of the buttonbush that perfume the air with a jasmine-like fragrance; where the rose-pink flowers of the swamp mallow, growing among the tall sedges and cattails of the marsh, flutter like banners in the breeze; and where recently transformed leopard frogs chase flying insects and take to the water as some unseen danger threatens.

It is the sort of morning when you want to pause by the meadow, where the boneset spreads its soft lead-white bloom and the joe-pye weed its magenta flower clusters, to watch the redwings dart over the pinkish hoods of the swamp milkweed, the New England aster, and the slender spikes of the vervains, or to see the nesting goldfinches as they break up the silvery cushions of the thistles for the down with which to line their nests. And before the day is done you want to climb the distant hillside, where the hardy bells of the harebell sway with exquisite grace on tremulous hairlike stems; or to visit a field, where the vetch forms lakes of blue, the milkwort and the fuzzy heads of the rabbit's foot clover bloom among the grasses, and the spreading dogbane opens its tiny rose-veined bells and plays host to hundreds of beautiful and iridescent dogbane beetles, where bees and butterflies feed on the sweet nectar of the burdock and ironweed. And as you wend your way homeward you "discover" the beautiful spikes of the butter-and-eggs and the yellow buttons of the tansy, and you begin to realize that everywhere sunflowers are lifting their yellow heads and goldenrods are waving in the breeze. Autumn is near at hand.

There are other signs that autumn is fast approaching. Cranberries and blackberries are beginning to deepen in color; the curved stems of the Solomon's seal are heavy with blackish berries; currantlike clusters of the chokeberries are hanging from the thicket; and the scarlet berries of the nightshade shine like red lanterns in shady tangles by the roadside. The first transient birds are beginning to appear: olive-sided and yellow-billed flycatchers, bay-breasted, Cape May, and magnolia warblers. Northern water thrushes pause on their southward flight by slow-moving streams whose winding paths through swampy woods and low-lying meadows are traced by brilliant spikes of cardinal flowers and the golden-centered flowers of the arrowhead. Tree swallows are gathering in flocks and flying to the seashore, where the sea lavender appears like a blue-gray mist blown in from the sea; where the sea pinks gleam like rosy stars and plovers whirl and shout their plaintive cries; where the beach pea blossoms, drab-colored sparrows search for seeds, and nimble sandpipers scurry over the sands, chasing retreating ripples and skipping back out of reach of each advancing wave. And above the open sea where a flock of cormorants pass, high in the sky, herring gulls and terns, having left their breeding grounds, wheel, dart, and tip from side to side with outstretched wings, their bodies glistening in the bright sunshine and casting moving shadows upon the water.

NATURAL EVENTS IN AUGUST

- The curved leafy stem of the Solomon's seal is heavy with blackish berries.

- Nesting goldfinches break up the silvery cushions of the thistle for the down with which to line their nests.

- On warm nights many kinds of crickets and long-horned grasshoppers join in a nocturnal chorus.

- Red bats mate.

- Along the streams and in thickets, sunflowers lift their yellow heads to the sky.

- Red-eyed vireos, song sparrows, and wood pewees are still singing.

- The caterpillars of the hickory tiger moth crawl about on hickory, butternut, and other forest trees.

- Eggs of the black snake hatch.

- Burdock and ironweed are in blossom, and insects feast on the sweet nectar.

- Herring gulls leave their breeding grounds.

- The flowers of the false foxglove gleam like yellow stars in open woods.

- Buffalo treehoppers lay their eggs in stems of young trees, particularly pear and apple.

- Recently transformed leopard frogs abound along the margins of ponds.

- Joe-pye weed decorates the August landscape with its magenta flower clusters.

- Northern water thrushes may be seen in swampy woods and along the borders of streams on their southward migration.

- The vetch forms lakes of blue in fields and meadows.

- The caterpillars of the white-marked tussock moth frequent linden, maple, and elm trees.

- The young of the garter snakes are born, also those of the common brown (DeKay's) snake.

- The New England aster floods low meadows and moist hollows along the roadsides with color.

- Redwings play in wet meadows.

- Larvae of the painted beauty feed on everlastings.

- Raccoons, stealing from the woods by moonlight, appear in corn patches to feed on juicy kernels.

- Cranberries and blackberries deepen in color.

- Plovers whirl and shout their plaintive cries about the grassy downs along the seashore.

- Rosy maple moths are frequently found asleep, or intoxicated with nectar, in the flowers of the evening primrose.

- Jumping mice search for new homes after the meadows have been mown.

- The boneset spreads its soft lead-white bloom in low meadows.

- The bright blossoms of the purple-flowering raspberry burst forth above the roadside tangles and shady woodland dells.

- Flycatchers are on their way to the south.

- The dodder winds its bright threads about the herbage and shrubbery of moist thickets like tangled yellow yarn.

- Yellow bears are common in gardens.

- Green snakes lay eggs under flat stones, logs, or in sawdust piles.

- The rose-pink flowers of the swamp mallow, growing among the tall sedges and cattails of the marsh, flutter like banners in the breeze.

- Common terns begin to gather in flocks and leave their breeding grounds.

- Adults and immature forms of the two-marked treehopper, resembling a flock of miniature partridges, are found on bittersweet.

- Spiders are abundant; their webs may be found everywhere.

- The hardy bells of the harebell sway with exquisite grace on tremulous hairlike stems.

- In the fresh morning air or in the twilight of the evening the barn swallows swoop above the garden, and the chimney swifts, with quivering wings and shrill twitterings, describe a lacework of disappearing lines against the sky as they pursue fast-flying insects.

- Adults of the eight-spotted forester appear amid grapevines and Virginia creeper.

- Flying squirrels gambol in the moonlit woods.

- The dense white globes of the buttonbush perfume the air with a jasmine-like fragrance.

- Nimble sandpipers play on the sands of the sea beach.

- Leaf miners are busy tunneling in leaves.

- On foggy and rainy days red newts wander about the woodland floor in search of insects.

- Along shady streams stand brilliant spikes of the cardinal flowers.

- Magnolia, Cape May, and bay-breasted warblers fly southward.

❦ Insects visit the flowers of the turtlehead, blossoming beside brooks and ponds.

❦ Sea lavender, blossoming in salt meadows and marshes, suggests, from a distance, blue-gray mist blown in from the sea.

❦ Cormorants appear on their southward migration.

❦ The tiny rose-veined bells of the spreading dogbane attract bees, flies, moths, and butterflies; hundreds of the beautiful iridescent dogbane beetles play about on the foliage.

❦ Currant-like clusters of the chokeberries hang from the thicket.

❦ Tree swallows arrive at the seashore to roost in the marshes.

❦ Spiny rose galls appear on rose bushes; other galls may be found on trees and shrubs.

❦ The fuzzy flower heads of the rabbit-foot clover appear in fields and pastures.

❦ The gold-centered flowers of the arrowhead trace the path of slow streams.

❦ The scarlet berries of the nightshade shine like lanterns in tangled thickets.

❦ Sea pinks, gleaming like rosy stars, rise above the grasses on the seashore.

❦ Roadsides are bright with the graceful lilac-blue spires of the bellflower.

❦ The pinkish hoods of the swamp milkweed may be seen in wet places.

❦ Tick trefoil color thickets, woods, and river banks a pinkish purple.

❦ In moist thickets and along shady roadsides the hog peanut opens its small showy blossoms in drooping clusters.

❦ The beach pea flowers among the sand dunes of the coast.

❧ The yellow buttons of tansy brighten roadsides.

❧ Beautiful spikes of the butter-and-eggs relieve the cheerlessness of waste places.

❧ Meadows are bright with the cloverlike heads of the milkwort.

❧ The slender spikes of the vervains mount skyward.

❧ Goldenrods wave in the August breeze.

❧ Spiny caterpillars of the mourning cloak feed on the foliage of various trees.

❧ The spotted pelidnota beetle is a frequent visitor to the grape arbor.

❧ Stag beetles and prionid beetles fly about porch and street lights.

❧ Jumping spiders are common on plants, logs, and fences.

❧ In gardens and weedy cultivated fields young and old chipping sparrows feed on weed seeds.

❧ Along the seashore drab-colored sparrows search for seeds.

September

It seems as if it were only yesterday I wandered down the road listening for the sweet melody of a newly-arrived songster or followed the winding trail through the neighboring woods looking for an early spring flower. As I now wander down the same road or follow the same winding woodland trail, there is a hint of autumn in the air and once again,

The sultry summer past, September comes;
Soft twilight of the slow declining year.

Upon the distant hillside red maples show touches of crimson; in the orchard apples are reddening and peaches, wearing the blush of mellow ripeness, hang from slender branches; and along stone walls grapes may be found in purple clusters. In the thicket, the purple berries and gaily painted leaves of the Indian cucumber vie with the curving stems of the false spikenard, heavy with the weight of red-speckled berries. Along the roadside the juicy buttons of the pokeweed are "all on fire with ripeness." The berries of the Canada mayflower, the curious doll's eyes of the white baneberry, and the bright red lanterns of the painted trillium decorate the woodland scene and in soft, wet ground the hooded flower of the jack-in-the-pulpit has become a brilliant, clustering berry-like fruit. Meanwhile, along margins of swamps the red-cheeked apple-like fruit of the cockspur thorn opens against the dark oval leaves, in marshy meadows the scarlet beads of the black alder glitter in the sunshine, and in upland fields the brilliant fruit of the haw flashes against the sky. Everywhere wild cherries and elderberries, the red, blue, and lead-colored berries of the dogwoods, and the red and purple sprays of the viburnums provide a banquet table for migrating birds that disperse the seeds far and wide.

This afternoon I came upon a flock of starlings greedily feeding on the berries of the red osier dogwood, and though I saw many of the seeds voided, many others were doubtless carried away to be dropped in some other spot. I have wondered how great a role color plays in attracting the birds, or if color has anything at all to do with seed dispersal. Certainly a great many brightly colored fruits and berries seem to have no appeal whatever to the birds, whereas many dull colored ones are eagerly sought after. At any rate, the brightly colored berries and fruits of September have a charm and beauty for which we should be grateful.

I have also wondered why birds can feed with impunity on

berries which poison us and other animals. I have thought about it particularly when I have seen them feeding on the grayish-white berries of the poison ivy and the poison sumac, or the purplish-black berries of the deadly nightshade. We are all familiar with the toxic properties of the ivy and sumac berries; there are other berries equally as dangerous. Most of us leave unfamiliar berries alone. Children, however, are thoughtless and often do not realize, until too late, that many fruits and berries should not be eaten. I have known children to become violently ill from eating harmful fruits or by putting into their mouths leaves and stems of plants that have toxic or acrid properties. The translucent ruby red berries of the nightshade and the green, prickly, egg-shaped fruit capsules of the jimson weed or thorn apple seem especially attractive to them. The nightshade berries if eaten in quantities can cause violent gastric disturbances, and the seeds of the jimson weed contain a powerful narcotic which can prove fatal.

Birds were not too much in evidence during July and August. But with the coming of September they reappear in the open to gather in flocks and to gorge themselves on ripening seeds and fruits in preparation for their southward flights. It is no uncommon sight to see them descend "en masse" on a clump of shrubs heavily laden with fruit, or on a patch of weedy field, methodically cleaning the shrubs and field plants of their food and then rising as one to fly to another feeding place.

In the early morning ducks move toward the coast to spend the winter in the salt marshes. And later in the day neatly uniformed redwings wheel and advance in military platoons over the marsh. Woodland birds flit from thicket to thicket, quickly scudding to shelter as the ominous form of a hawk appears overhead, for now that the mating season is over the hawks may frequently be seen sailing and gyrating high in the air.

Many birds have already left for the South; others are beginning to leave; and some of those whose breeding grounds are farther north are now passing through. Go out on some moonlit night and you may see hundreds of birds flying across the bright face of the moon, at heights of a quarter of a mile or so, or go out on a dark and misty night and you will hear them calling to one another in an effort to keep together as they grope their way over the treetops. My heart goes out to these invisible travelers as they hurry through the night, braving unknown terrors until morning dawns, when they can feed and rest until night, to resume their hurried flight to the still verdant vegetation of the tropics some thousands of miles away.

Not all our birds migrate by night. The memory still lingers of a September day many years ago when I saw the first wild geese in flight. It was a beautiful day, cool and crisp, the blue cloudless sky hanging like a canopy over the painted landscape, the air fragrant with the smell of burning leaves. I watched with awe as the birds soared across the sky to disappear in the distance and wondered what it would be like to take wing and fly to some distant place.

Today we need only to step into a modern airliner to have such dreams come true, but reality is often disillusioning. I doubt if I could get as much of a thrill in flying now as I might have experienced if I could have stepped on a magic carpet and followed the birds to their distant goal.

In our conquest of the air we have come a long way since the early days of aviation, but we are still far from being masters of it. The birds can still teach us much about flying; it is doubtful if we will ever acquire their perfection and grace of flight.

We have instruments to guide us over large bodies of water and through dense fogs, but they are not wholly reliable and often deceive us. The birds, however, can strike out over a body of water, such as the Gulf of Mexico, or fly through the heaviest fog, and unerringly arrive at their destination. Every year scarlet tanagers cross the Gulf a distance of five hundred to seven hundred miles, and bobolinks, black-billed and yellow-billed cuckoos, bank swallows, vireos, kingbirds, and others fly the five-hundred-mile stretch of ocean between Jamaica and South America guided only by their sense of direction.

How well this sense of direction is developed in birds is shown in species in which the immature birds and adults migrate at different times. The belief still persists, I know, that young birds are first led over a route by older, experienced birds and thereafter regularly follow such a course year after year from memory and sight. This is doubtless true in some species, but it does not apply to those in which the young migrate at a different time. The young of such species apparently have an inherited migratory instinct and a sense of direction, for they instinctively follow more or less the same course as that taken by the adults, though they have never been over it before.

The distances some migratory birds travel each year seem almost incomprehensible when we consider their size and the difficulties and hazards they encounter in their flights. Scarlet tanagers that nest in Canada and New England migrate to Peru; bobolinks, barn swallows, and some thrushes that summer with us, winter in Brazil. To the blackpoll warblers that nest in Alaska such flights must seem a mere jaunt, for these birds travel to northern South America. The nighthawk, however, puts all land birds to shame when it comes to long-distance flights; this bird migrates from the Yukon to Argentina, over 10,000 miles!

The migratory flight of the nighthawk, however, is exceeded by some of the shore birds. There are many species of shore birds that breed north of the Arctic Circle and every one of them visits South America in winter, six of them penetrating to Patagonia. When we see the small and seemingly frail hummingbird darting about our garden flowers we may not realize that it flies non-stop across the Gulf of Mexico. But if you think this is a record flight, consider the golden plover which makes a non-stop flight from Nova Scotia to South America, a jump requiring probably forty-eight hours of continuous flying. The bird accomplishes this feat with a consumption of less than two ounces of fuel in the form of body fat.

Insects migrate, too. Most of them travel only short distances, such as from tree or shrub into the ground, or from a field to a nearby house or barn. There are several species, however, that journey considerable distances.

The most notable example is undoubtedly the monarch butterfly. As cold weather approaches the monarchs gather in flocks and, like the birds, fly south. How these butterflies find their way or how they endure such long journeys we do not know. These butterflies have not been in the south before. Even if they had, how could they tell their children of distant lands and the routes to follow when we are not sure they can communicate with one another? Furthermore, they do not see their children. We believe that the battered monarchs we see in the spring are those that migrated southward the preceding fall, but we are not sure of it, nor do we know that they have ever been in the north before.

Why do they migrate at all? A lack of food is not the reason, for butterflies eat very little and their food supplies are by no means exhausted when they start on their migratory journeys. Neither is the migration to escape crowding, for they are not crowded when they leave; on the contrary, they become more crowded than ever, since they gather in great flocks, numbering in the hundreds. Nor is it to escape their natural enemies, such as the birds, for the birds let them alone. Other enemies might lead them to migrate elsewhere, but then why should they return?

Like the birds, the mammals, too, are more in evidence than they have been for the past two months. Of course, with the ripening of fruits and berries, with the setting of seeds by flowering herbs and wild grains, and with insects plentiful, this is the time for the mammals to store supplies in their granaries and to fatten themselves against their winter's sleep. I often see a chipmunk scurrying away to his underground burrow with full cheek pouches, looking as if he had a bad case of the mumps. I don't know what purpose this store of food serves. The chipmunk is not particularly fat when he goes into hibernation and some naturalists think he eats some of this food before he goes to sleep for the winter, leaving the remainder for a spring breakfast. Others are of the opinion that he makes use of it during the long winter months underground. Whichever the reason, he certainly stores an abundant food supply. As much as half a bushel or more of seeds, nuts, and other edibles has been found in a single chamber.

The deer mouse is also busy storing up all sorts of edibles. He seems to prefer beechnuts — as many as a peck has been discovered in his home — but he is also fond of basswood seeds and the bright red berries of the black alder; on occasion I have seen him climb up the twigs on a moonlit night and gather the berries.

Instead of storing food for the winter, the woodchuck prefers to build up a thick layer of fat on which he can draw while he sleeps the winter through in his underground burrow. And so, since early summer, he has been stuffing himself with food and growing so fat and sluggish that now he seems hardly able to move. No longer do I find him waddling along in the field or by the woodland border; instead, I more often see him sitting by the entrance to his burrow, a picture of listlessness and immobility. But he is not altogether indifferent to what goes on about him, for the moment he hears me approach he pops into his burrow. Not many more days of wakefulness remain to him, and before the month is out he will have gone down into his winter retreat, not to reappear until next spring.

Like the woodchuck, the bear is stuffing himself with the nuts and berries he finds in the hill thickets because he also spends the winter asleep in his den. The deer, which during the summer come out of the thick woods at night to feed on water lilies and other succulent water plants, are beginning to forsake the watercourses, as the water and marsh plants wither and retire to the deep woods where there is now plenty of food, especially the beech mast, of which they are very fond and upon which they get amazingly fat. And before long the bucks, having rubbed the velvet from their antlers, will begin wooing, battling rivals for their mates. Both sexes, incidentally, have begun to shed their summer coats and to take on the warmer "blue" pelage of the winter; and the spots of fawns are disappearing.

Other mammals are also shedding their summer "furs" and

putting on their winter overcoats. During this transition period their fur is ragged and uncertain in color and, in the case of the fur-bearers, of little value to the trapper. Birds, too, are molting, exchanging their bright tints for the duller hues of traveling and winter dress; and the nuptial glow which many fishes acquired in the spring or early summer has also faded.

Meanwhile, muskrats have begun to plan their winter homes, and in some instances have even begun to build them. Although they may sometimes construct their houses among willow sprouts or in masses of sweet flags, they usually select a site where the water is about two feet deep, either in the middle of a stream or a few feet offshore in a pond. Sedges, pondweeds, cattails, and other coarse vegetation are gathered and mixed with mud. This material becomes more or less immovable as it continues to pile up, and when the animals have a dome-shaped pile sufficiently large they make a tunnel or plunge-hole from the bottom upward and hollow out a chamber just below the surface of the dome. As the roof sinks, more mud and stalks are placed on top of the chamber, and the entire house is finally wadded and plastered with mud and water-soaked vegetation until the structure is firm and able to withstand the buffeting of winter storms.

The chamber, which is carpeted with a soft bed of leaves and moss, may be a foot or more in diameter and sufficiently high to enable the occupants to move about freely. Since it serves as feeding and sleeping quarters, it may occasionally contain several alcoves slightly partitioned from one another. Sometimes there are two chambers, each with its own plunge hole, but such chambers are probably occupied by different families. As a rule, the largest houses seldom provide quarters for more than five or six rats. There is a case on record, however, where an enormous lodge harbored fourteen animals.

One of the methods by which plants obtain transportation for their seeds to distant places is by covering them with flesh and pulp, thus making them attractive to the birds as food. In some instances, the seeds are enclosed in a sticky pulp which adheres to the birds' beaks and even to their feet and, as the birds move from place to place, the seeds drop off as the pulp dries or when the birds rub their beaks against the twigs and branches. But when the seeds are indigestible, as in the case of the hard-shelled "pits" of cherries, haws, and other fruits, they are voided with the excrement.

If the seeds are not tricked out in a fashion which renders them attractive to the birds, the plants obtain free transportation in some other manner. You may discover a pleasant pastime in wandering along the country lane or through the fields and woods, observing the many ways plants have developed for seed dispersal. Note how the September breezes break up the silvery cushions of the thistles and how the shimmering gossamer-winged seeds are borne off into the air. Open a milkweed pod and you will find symmetrical packs of golden-brown seeds, each with a tuft of silken sails; or better still, watch a pod open and see how the silken sails spring out and, catching the faintest breath of air, sail off to unknown destinations.

Go down to the nearby brook and touch the pods of the jewelweed, and you will see the seeds fly out with startling suddenness. The first time I touched these seed pods I was so fascinated with the ingenious mechanism that causes them to open at one's touch and to shoot the seeds into the neighboring thicket that I was loathe to leave until I had sent many of these tiny travelers on their way.

Other plants have developed barbs and hooks that make the seed pods cling to your clothing or the fur of animals. In this manner, they get free transportation to places where they can find room in which to germinate and grow. You are doubtless familiar with the troublesome barbs of the beggar ticks and the prickly heads of the burdock that literally steal a ride on every switching tail, woolly dog, trouser leg, or skirt and coat. But I daresay you have never examined them under a magnifying glass; do so and you will see why they cling to your clothing so persistently. And when you find the tick trefoil look at the flat pods and you will discover why they cling with even greater stubbornness; why they are so irritatingly difficult to remove. As a matter of fact, I have just spent fifteen minutes trying to get rid of them from my trousers and I am not sure I have wholly succeeded. Tomorrow I will surely find some more; I usually do.

Whenever I roam through the countryside at this time of the year, I am impressed with the diversity of fruiting structures. Berries and similar fruits are all essentially alike, but seed pods are as different as the plants that make them. In size and shape, they range from the small oval pods of the peppergrass, which I still occasionally place in my mouth for their peppery taste, and the slightly larger triangular pods of the shepherd's purse, to the long-curved, cylindrical, cigarlike capsules of the catalpa, or the shiny, leather-looking, maroon-brown pods of the honey locust, which may be sixteen or eighteen inches long.

The seed capsules of the seed box, in which the seeds become loose and rattle when the plant is shaken, are known to most of us; but less familiar, perhaps, are the slender, curved, violet-tipped pods of the fireweed, the spiny, inflated, berrylike capsules of the wild cucumber (which often burst open so forcibly that they eject the large seeds several feet), or the green, burlike spheres of the burweed, which are composed of nutlets, wedge-shaped below and flattened above, with an abrupt point in the center so that the general appearance of the surface is somewhat like the pineapple.

The seed pods, as well as berries and similar fruits, are as characteristic of our plants as their floral structures. If you have learned to recognize various plants by their flowers, you could as easily learn to recognize them by their seed pods. Certainly, you would have no difficulty in recognizing the inflated, prolate-spheroidal fruit capsule of the Indian tobacco, the three-sided capsule of the bellwort, the lawl-tipped, egg-shaped pod of the wild indigo, or the curious fruiting umbel of the wild carrot that looks so much like a bird's nest. Since many of the fruiting structures remain after the flowers have faded and the leaves have fallen, they serve as a reminder of your summer flower companions as you roam afield during the bleak days of November or later when the snow covers the ground.

Although September may justly be called the month of fruits, the color of the September scene is not entirely due to the glittering varieties that hang from countless boughs along the wayside and in the orchard. True, many flowers are rapidly fading, yet many others remain to decorate the landscape. Where the wet meadow fringes the woodland border, the slender spikes of the ladies' tresses — the last of the orchids to flower — bear small white flowers among the tall sunflowers, whose nodding heads tower in the sky. Roadsides glow with the rose purple flower heads of the blazing star and the still-flowering celandine, whose saffron juice stains whatever it touches; where the meandering brook flows merrily on its way, the great lobelia continues to blossom in an attempt to outlast its twin sister, the cardinal flower. In stony pastures, the everlasting perfumes the air with a faint, elusive odor, and the blue curls, with their clammy, balsam-scented leaves, continue to open their little blue corollas, which have long curling stamens. Bur marigolds still enliven cheerless ditches, and along the woodland trail, the little bell-like flowers of the rattlesnake root nod in graceful open clusters from the tops of shining colored stalks. Asters are now at the height of their flowering and flood with color the wayside and woodland thicket, while the joe-pye weed tints the swamps with drifts of pink, and waving wands of goldenrods dress the fields in a cloth of gold.

It is said that no flower attracts as many insects as the goldenrod. I don't know how true this is, but countless insects certainly visit it for the pollen which it generously shares with all. Among the most frequent visitors are the locust borer, a beautiful black beetle with numerous wavy yellow bands, and the blister beetle, a black beetle which frequently is found in such numbers that the golden plumes appear as if sprinkled with soot.

Despite the decline of summer, insects are still rampant. Crickets and grasshoppers abound in the fields and meadows, and these, together with the katydids and tree locusts, continue their incessant chirping both day and night. If you are an observant naturalist, perhaps you may have noticed that the chirping of the crickets varies with the weather. During warm weather, it is high-pitched and rapid; during cold periods, it slows down and becomes a rattle. Indeed, the frequency of stridulation and temperature are so closely related that several formulas have been worked out for determining the temperature from the number of chirps per minute:

(T = temperature Fahrenheit and N = number of chirps per minute)

$T = 50 + (N - 92) / 4.7$ for the tree cricket

$T = 50 + (N - 40) / 4$ for the house cricket

$T = 60 + (N - 19) / 3$ for the katydid

Crickets, incidentally, make delightful pets and are most companionable, especially on winter nights when they evoke memories of the summer with their chirping. Keep them in a cricket cage, which can be made by setting a lamp chimney in an earth-filled flower pot, and feed them lettuce, moist bread, and various fruits. Should they start eating one another, give them some bone meal, which should reduce any cannibalistic tendencies.

Second broods of butterflies and moths, which have not been seen since early summer, appear now, and certain late larvae are busy feeding on the foliage of various plants. The caterpillars of the silver-spotted skipper may often be found on the locust, each caterpillar making a nest within which it remains concealed by fastening together, with silk, the leaflets of a compound leaf. This is one of the very few skippers that winter in the pupal state, most of them wintering as larvae, either partly grown or in their cocoons. The caterpillars of the fall webworm may also be found on such trees as the apple and ash, as well as many others, and their webs are a conspicuous feature of the September landscape. They are unlike those made by the tent caterpillars in the spring, being much lighter in texture and being extended over all the leaves on which the caterpillars feed. There is some question as to whether there are one or two species of this insect. In the North, the adults are all snow white in color and there is only a single generation each year; but in the South, some of the adults have forewings thickly studded with dark brown points, while others are pure white, and there are two generations annually. Someday, I suppose, the question will be answered.

Another late-feeding caterpillar is the red-humped apple worm. There have been times when I have found these caterpillars in large numbers feeding on the wild blackberry, although they are more common on apple. The caterpillars have a coral head and a hump of the same color with black tubercles on the first abdominal segment. They are more or less gregarious, especially when resting, when they crowd so close together as to cover the branch completely.

The caterpillars of various dagger moths may also be seen during this month, feeding on trees and shrubs. Frequently, I find the yellow hairy caterpillars of the American dagger moth, which feed on maple and elm, crawling along a city sidewalk searching for a place to pupate. And we are all familiar with the evenly clipped red and black furry caterpillars which are so often seen at this time, hurrying over the ground in their haste to find a snug place in which to curl up for the winter.

The term woolly bear is commonly given to this caterpillar, but actually there are other woolly bears — in fact, some two thousand of them. They transform into small moths, collectively called tiger moths, many of which are exceedingly pretty. It was these insects Keats had in mind when he wrote:

> "All diamonded with panes of quaint device,
> Innumerable of stains, and splendid dyes,
> As are the Tiger Moths' deep damask wings."

As the days gradually become cool, the toads stop feeding and hop restlessly around or sit in protected corners. The toads are among the first of the amphibians to go into hibernation and on cool days, not one will be seen, though on warm nights they may venture forth if they have not taken to their winter quarters. They winter in soft soil a few inches below the surface in our gardens or in the banks of the ponds in which they breed. If you have not seen a toad dig his way into the ground, you might be surprised to learn that he works his way into the soil backwards, throwing the earth outward with sidewise movements of his hind legs and wedging his way downward by pushing with his front feet. I have kept toads in a terrarium and have found it amusing to watch them dig into the soil. They leave no opening at the top of the burrow, for the earth falls in after them as they work their way downward. They do not actually hibernate in the burrow but in a chamber, and as the ground freezes, they dig deeper and deeper, leaving a series of chambers in which they have rested. Sometimes, they freeze to death before they have had a chance to dig deep enough, but the percentage of mortality is low, if experiments which have shown a death rate of about three percent can be taken as a criterion.

Usually, about this time, the gilled larvae of the spotted newt transform into lunged air breathers, turn an orange red, and climb up on land as the red newts which I have already mentioned. They range over the woodland floor together with older newts that emerged from the water the previous year, and when the weather turns cold, go into winter quarters beneath fallen leaves and branches.

During September, the copperhead brings forth its young alive, although sometimes it may do so toward the latter part of August. The young, which number from five to ten, are about ten inches long and have bright sulphur-yellow tails. The rattlesnake also gives birth to a dozen or more young, which are born with one button on the tail. In both cases, the young are born from egglike envelopes, retained within the mother's body until the embryos have fully developed, and they are able to tear their way out and to look out for themselves.

I have often been curious to know why we are inclined to view with contempt or indifference things that are common or that we see in such abundance that we scarcely note their existence. The dandelion, for instance, when viewed dispassionately and examined wholly for itself, is an exceedingly beautiful flower, and yet it is generally considered an obnoxious weed. By the same token, our grasses are ignored, except when we have to trim our lawns or weed our gardens, and little attention is ever paid to them, except by those whose business it is to supply us with food. I daresay that most of you who read these words are unable to recognize many of them by name. Yet from the time when the mayflowers and violets and other flowers of early spring open their blossoms to the sky until the delicate autumn flowers of the witch-hazel bloom above the fast-falling leaves, the grasses bloom along every wayside and woodland trail, in gardens and orchards, along the banks of winding streams and in waste places, fields, and meadows. We are too intent upon growing our garden flowers or collecting the flowers of fields and woods to know that the blossoms and wind-blown anthers of the grasses rival them in richness and variety of coloring. Examine the flowering heads of the nearest grasses, and you will find an infinite variety of forms and coloring; you will be amazed at the delicacy of tiny blossoms tinged with rose and purple; and you will be charmed by the grace of swaying stem and drooping leaf. Wander along the wayside and roam through field and meadow with an eye only for these most common and least known of plants. You will find grasses higher than your head and others barely rising above the earth; grasses whose flowering spikes are so small they are barely noticeable; grasses that are stout and robust and others so slender that their dying stems are like golden threads.

Where the farmer has tilled the ground, the old witch grass lifts its blossoming heads like shower fountains of green, and about the dooryard, the crab grass raises its deeply colored spike to spread like the fingers of your hand. Foxtails, both yellow and green, decorate the wayside with cylindrical spikes of seedlike flowers; the tall redtop opens its beautiful flowering head of shining purple spikelets where fields are dry; and the purple Eragrostis rises like a reddish purple mist in the bright September sun. About the borders of ponds, the reed grass with panicles of frosted silver lends an air of enchantment, and in wet meadows, the wool grass, which is a sedge and not a grass despite its name, waves in the passing breeze.

September is the month for mushrooms, too. Along the woodland trail, the Russula hygrophorus may be found lifting its pink-tinged cap under a mat of leaves; the sharp-scaled Pholiota, growing in dense tufts on prostrate trunks or old stumps, relieves the gloom of shady thickets. Occasionally, I find the broad white caps of the elm Pleurotus, and I still recall the first time I found the masked Tricholoma and became enchanted with its delicate violet-tinged beauty. Less conspicuous is the conelike boletus, which is difficult to find among the bewildering lights and shadows that play upon the dead leaves covering the woodland floor.

There are many others, such as the smooth Lepiota, which resembles the meadow mushroom, the blushing Lepiota, the poisonous fly Amanita, and the honey mushroom which is very common and abundant. And puffballs, small and large, are everywhere, sending up their puffs of smoke like miniature volcanoes.

NATURAL EVENTS IN SEPTEMBER

- Foxtails decorate the wayside with cylindrical spikes of seed-like flowers.

- The old witch grass lifts its blossoming heads like shower fountains of green.

- Wild grapes, in purple clusters, garland stone walls.

- Peaches, with downy cheeks, wearing the blush of mellow ripeness, droop from slender boughs.

- Woodchucks gorge themselves in preparation for their winter's sleep.

- Deer forsake the water courses and retire to the deep woods, where food is plentiful.

- Pelts of fur bearers are ragged and uncertain in color.

- Birds exchange their bright tints for the duller hues of traveling and winter dress.

- Bears stuff themselves with nuts and berries.

- Woodland birds flit cautiously from copse to copse, hurrying to shelter as the ominous form of a hawk appears overhead.

- Neatly uniformed redwings wheel and advance in military platoons over the marsh.

- The young of rattlesnakes and copperheads are born.

- Larvae of spotted newts transform into the red newts which leave the water for the land.

- Muskrats are planning their winter homes.

- Where the meandering brook flows merrily on its way, the great lobelia continues to blossom.

- Feathery clusters of the wild carrot develop into fruiting umbels that look like birds' nests.

- Apples are reddening on orchard trees.

- Transient birds feast on wild cherries, elderberries, and dogwood berries.

- At night hundreds of migrating birds may be seen flying across the face of the moon.

- The barbs of the beggar ticks, the prickly heads of the burdock, and the pods of the tick trefoil become attached to the fur of animals and are carried to distances near and far.

- Bur marigolds still enliven cheerless ditches.

- Along the woodland trail the little bell-like flowers of the rattlesnake root nod in graceful open clusters from the tops of shining colored stalks.

- Asters flood with color the wayside and woodland thicket.

- The Joe-Pye weed tints the swamps with drifts of pink.

- Waving wands of goldenrods dress the fields in a cloth of gold. Second broods of various butterflies and moths appear.

- The caterpillars of the fall webworm may be found on such trees as the apple and ash.

- The caterpillars of various dagger moths feed on trees and shrubs.

- Woolly bears hurry over the ground in search of a snug place in which to curl up for the winter.

- The dark green stems of the crab grass spread over the ground and lift their narrow, deeply colored spikes which spread widely like the fingers of a hand.

- The tall redtop opens its beautiful flower heads of shining purple spikelets where fields are dry.

- The purple Eragrostis rises like a purple mist in the bright September sun.

- Ducks begin to move toward the coast to spend the winter in salt marshes.

- Blister beetles and locust borers feed on the blossoms of goldenrod.

- Caterpillars of the red-humped apple worm can be found feeding on wild blackberries.

- Robins and starlings feast on the berries of the red osier dogwood.

- The September breezes break up the silvery cushions of the thistles.

- The nodding heads of tall sunflowers tower into the sky.

- The conelike boletus is inconspicuous among the bewildering lights and shadows that play upon the dead leaves covering the woodland floor.

- The masked Tricholoma lends an air of enchantment to the woods with its delicate violet tinged beauty.

- The sharp scaled Pholiota, growing in tufts on prostrate trunks or old stumps, relieves the gloom of shady thickets.

- Along the woodland trail the Russula hygrophorus may be found lifting its pink tinged cap under a mat of leaves.

- The broad white caps of the elm Pleurotus are common on stumps of elm and maple.

- The red and purple sprays of the viburnums decorate the landscape and provide a banquet for migrating birds.

- About the borders of ponds the reed grass with panicles of frosted silver lends an air of enchantment.

- In wet meadows the wool grass waves in the passing breeze.

- Crickets, grasshoppers, and katydids are still calling noisily on warm nights.

- The small white flowers of the ladies' tresses — the last of the orchids to flower — bloom on slender, twisted spikes in wet meadows.

- The jewel weed shoots out its seeds from exploding pods with startling suddenness.

- Roadsides are aglow with the rose-purple flower heads of the blazing star and the celandine whose saffron juice stains whatever it touches.

- Male white-tailed deer begin to rub the velvet from their antlers and the spots of fawns disappear.

- Red maples begin to turn crimson.

- Pods of milkweed crack open, revealing symmetrical packs of golden brown seeds which are wafted away on silken sails.

- Mice, squirrels, and chipmunks gather nuts and seeds for their granaries.

- Monarch butterflies begin their southward migration.

- Toads begin to disappear.

- The dark berries of the pokeweed are "all on fire with ripeness" and hang heavy with juice.

- Omnipresent puffballs, large and small, are sending up their puffs of smoke like miniature volcanoes.

- The stems of the wild spikenard curve from the weight of numerous pale, red-speckled berries.

- In marshy meadows the scarlet beads of the black alder glitter in the sunshine.

- The speckled berries of the Canada mayflower line the woodland trail.

- The curious doll's eyes of the white baneberry gleam in shady woods.

- The bright red lanterns of the painted trillium light the woodland brook.

- The hooded flower of the jack-in-the-pulpit has become a brilliant clustering berrylike fruit.

- Birds begin to gather in flocks and gorge themselves on ripening seeds and fruits in preparation for their southward flights.

- The purple berries and gayly painted leaves of the Indian cucumber relieve the shady thicket.

- In stony pastures the everlasting perfumes the air with a faint elusive odor, and the blue curls, with its clammy, balsam-scented leaves, continues to open its little blue corollas with their long, curling tongues.

- Hawks soar through the sky on long sustained flights.

- Along the margins of swamps the red-cheeked apple-like fruit of the cockspur thorn open against the dark oval leaves.

- In upland fields and thickets the brilliant fruit of the haw flashes against the September sky.

- The caterpillars of the silver-spotted skipper may often be found on the locust.

October

Even as the cool nights of declining summer herald the approach of autumn, the red maples unfurl their scarlet flags to advertise the great annual show which Nature stages before ringing down the final curtain on the dying year. Almost before we realize it, the golden days of October are with us once again and beckon us to roam about the countryside amidst all the splendor of the autumn landscape.

Much of the brilliancy of the autumnal coloring is due to the red maples. As in the spring, when the opening crimson and scarlet flowers spread a suffused glow over the countryside, the scarlet or crimson leaves stand out against the azure October sky. The sumacs, sometimes hardly more than shrubs, are no less wonderful and contribute their share to the autumnal pageant. They glow in scarlet and gold, often deepening to crimson and orange. The staghorn sumac makes thickets of its own and frequently brightens waste places and neglected fields which otherwise would remain drab and cheerless, while its smaller brother, the smooth sumac, flings its magnificent beauty along the fences, over deserted fields, and up rocky, gravelly mountainsides through all the October days.

> Like glowing larva streams the sumac crawls
> Upon the mountain's granite walls.

Even the dreaded poison ivy adds its brilliant crimson to shady copses and hidden nooks, while the Virginia creeper, with sprays of rich cardinal, decorates the somber boles of dark evergreens, and the brilliant clusters of orange-red bittersweet berries brighten old walls and fence rows. Along some well-bordered stream and on the distant hillside, the red oak becomes clothed in a rich, dark, purplish red, while here and there the scarlet oak, robed in full panoply of its scarlet dress, stands aglow with fire in the bright sunshine.

On the uplands the beech, with leaves of palest Naples yellow, serves notice that all is not crimson and scarlet on the autumnal landscape. The birches, too, take up the challenge with yellow tints, and where no other trees grow — in rocky barrens, old fields, and waste places — the gray birch adds a touch of beauty with brilliant, golden-yellow leaves that glisten beneath dancing sunbeams. But much of the radiant splendor of the October foliage would be lost without the gorgeous coloring of the sugar maple, whose foliage is as uncertain as that of the weather. It may have leaves of yellow or crimson, scarlet or orange, of green with a spot of crimson, or crimson with a spot of pink; it may even have leaves with a patchwork of yellow and purple and scarlet. We may overlook such charming details and we may not see all the complexities of color — there is so much that may escape us — but the overall effect of Nature's handiwork is certainly not lost upon us.

Everywhere nuts are ripening — acorns, beechnuts, hickory nuts, and butternuts — and as I wander through the woods they fall from the branches and beat a tattoo upon the ground. When a boy I often went nutting, but now I prefer to leave nut gathering to the chipmunks and squirrels. The chipmunk hasn't many more days to spend outdoors; the time is rapidly drawing near when he must retire for the winter. If the weather turns really cold he will have disappeared before the month is out, but if autumn is unseasonably warm he may wait until December. At any rate, for such an active, sun-loving animal, the first few weeks of confinement underground must be a harrowing experience. We can imagine how it must feel for him to leave the bright October sunlight and descend into a narrow, torturous tunnel and there grope about in the dark, perhaps dimly aware that he must remain for weeks to come, meanwhile eating and sleeping in cramped quarters, becoming drowsier and drowsier until at last he loses consciousness altogether.

Whether the chipmunks have a better time of it than the squirrels who remain active all winter is a matter of conjecture. These animals must also provide against the coming months of scarcity, and they, too, are busy laying in supplies. One day this week, when I paused to listen to a bobwhite calling from a stubble field, where sparrows were flitting about like blown leaves, I heard a rustling in the underbrush and a moment later I came upon a gray squirrel sitting on his haunches, alert with the sense of danger and with an acorn in his little paws.

After a while, satisfied he had nothing to fear, he dropped on all fours and began scratching among the leaves, his plumelike tail quivering excitedly. He worked steadily for a few minutes. When he had dug a hole deep enough, he dropped the acorn into it, replacing the soil and leaves, and scampered off — obviously intent on repeating his performance. At one time it was believed the habit of burying nuts was merely an idle pastime, for it seemed impossible that nuts buried in the ground in various places could ever be recovered. Yet burying nuts is no mere pastime, for the squirrels can locate them weeks later even when the ground is covered with snow. I have frequently seen them during the winter, sniffing about on top of the crusted snow, then stop suddenly, and start digging and come up with a nut a few moments later.

The red squirrel is as industrious as his cousin, and when the cool days of October arrive he begins to prepare his winter home and to stock his larder so he will not go hungry, for, though he is up and about throughout the winter, there might be days when food is scarce and driving storms keep him home. Several years ago I chanced to be in a particularly wooded part of the state, where these animals were abundant, and whenever I went into the woods they barked and spit at me from the branches and observed my every move with considerable curiosity, as if they resented my being there.

As the October days become shorter and cooler the insects begin to disappear. The cicadas cease their incessant chorus; ground beetles retire beneath logs and stones; and termites begin their downward migration into the soil. The wasp and bumble-bee colonies, too, are dying out, and the queens take up their search for likely winter retreats. But although these insects and many others either die or seek winter quarters, there are others that remain active. Gnats and flies still dance in the golden sun-shine, the field crickets continue their nightly serenades unless the nights are too cold, and the snowy tree crickets may still be heard if not hushed by early frosts. Occasionally a red admiral may be seen visiting still blossoming flowers, but most of the butterflies that last into the fall are the dull-hued species which are inconspicuous among the falling foliage.

Down at the pond, dragonflies still dart through the air over the water where whirligigs play and striders skate on the glassy surface, while diving beetles speed through the submerged vegetation and water scorpions crawl along the water's edge; but one by one the dragonflies will die and the others will crawl into the mud to keep the caddis worms company until the returning warmth of the early spring sun calls them forth.

Meanwhile, the worker honeybees are driving the drones from the hives and are otherwise preparing for the winter. The drones have but one function — to fertilize the queen's eggs — and apart from this they are of little or no service. Their tongues are not long enough to get nectar from the flowers, and they have neither baskets in which to carry pollen, a sting with which to fight enemies, nor pockets for secreting wax. During the summer when nectar flows in abundance into the hive, the workers without complaint support these sluggards, whose very name has become a synonym for laziness. There is sufficient honey not only for the immediate needs of the community but also a surplus for the winter. But when fading flowers and shortening days herald the arrival of autumn and the end of the honey flow, the workers change in their attitude toward the drones. Now that they must visit the smallest flower and venture farther afield in order to fill their honey bags, they are not so keen on parting with the precious drops of honey which they must feed the drones. With winter in the offing and the flow of honey reduced almost to the vanishing point, economy must henceforth be the watchword, and with an instinctive thrift, they begin figuratively to reckon up profit and loss and to place the greedy appetites of the drones on the debit side of the ledger. These unproductive, oversized members of the community — now that their excuse for living is over — have become a burden that might jeopardize the safety of the community. So without hesitation, the workers turn upon them and drive them from the hive, thus fulfilling the primal law of nature that the useless must perish.

To the drones, this sudden change in the attitude of the workers must be incomprehensible and bewildering — an unexpected and devilish piece of treachery. One wonders what they must think if they can reason at all when they suddenly find their friends of yesterday now their most implacable enemies bent on their utter destruction.

At one time, it was believed the drones were stung to death. Such an end would be quick and merciful, but the drones seemingly must atone for a life of ease and luxury. Instead of attacking them directly, the workers gradually starve them to death by barring them from the hive. Cut off from their food supply, the disconsolate drones seek refuge in flight, but unable to gather nectar themselves, they return to the only source of food they have known, only to be driven away by the worker "guards" who rush at them menacingly or otherwise bar their way to the honey vaults. At last, famished and weak, the hapless drones crawl away among the grass blades and perish. Sometimes the drones are too feeble to crawl away but lie helpless before the entrance to the hive. They are shown no mercy but are picked up by the workers, carried away, and dropped to the ground. Frequently, while numbly awaiting their end, predatory insects put them out of their misery or the autumn chill provides a quick, merciful death, for the drones seem less able to withstand the cold than the other members of the community.

The driving off of the drones normally takes place at the close of the honey flow and after the swarming season, but there have been cases reported where the workers have driven off the drones during the lull between the flow from apple orchards and from the clover fields. At the other extreme, there have been times when the workers have permitted the drones to remain alive until late fall, and in the case of a queenless colony, they have even kept them through the winter. Such instances, however, are exceptions and occur only under abnormal conditions. The instinctive behavior of the bees is to get rid of the drones in preparation for their approaching struggle with the hazards of winter.

On a bright, sunny day I may hear a peeper or two, but before many more days have passed these diminutive little frogs will nestle down under the moss and leaves for their winter's sleep.

Leopard frogs are not so common in their usual haunts as they were a few weeks ago, and as the days go by, more and more leave the meadows and deep woods for marshes, ponds, springs, and shallow streams. Nearly mature adults of the spotted newt, still bearing traces of their youthful orange-red coloration, are gathering from many directions and move toward the nearest pond or brook. The spotted salamanders are still active, but as the days become colder, they crawl into holes beneath the leaf cover of the forest, where they remain for the winter. The cold-blooded reptiles are also beginning to feel the pinch of frosty nights: the garter snakes are congregating at their wintering places, and wood turtles are digging into the bottom mud of ponds and streams or retiring into holes along the banks.

Most species of land snails are very hardy and survive cold far below the freezing point. They are, however, dormant during the winter, and as the air cools in October, they cease eating and begin to crawl beneath stones, into tree trunks, or bury themselves in moss, leaves, or earth. As a rule, they hibernate alone, but sometimes they gather in groups. They draw their bodies into their shells and secrete a thin curtain of mucus over the opening, which prevents them from drying out, and thus boxed in, they remain quiet from four to six months.

You can observe for yourself how the snails secrete this parchment-like wall of mucus by subjecting them to a gradually cooling or drying environment. Many people keep snails as pets and find them interesting little animals. They may be kept in a terrarium having soil not too acid or of the bog type. Since they appreciate a moist or humid atmosphere, the plant life should be frequently sprinkled and the top of the terrarium covered with glass. In such a moist environment, they remain quite active and soon learn to find berries, fruits, lettuce, and other succulent morsels which you may give them.

In spite of their means of locomotion and the burden they carry around with them, snails get about remarkably well. Actually, a snail's foot is one of the most wonderful means of locomotion ever devised by nature. If you doubt it, watch a snail climb up the side of a glass tumbler. Observe how the foot stretches out and holds on. Observe, too, how a slime gland at the anterior end of the foot deposits a film of mucus on which the animal moves; it lays down, as it were, a sidewalk ahead of itself, and this sidewalk is always the same whether the path is rough or smooth, uphill or downhill.

You will note, too, that the snail's pace is always about the same. It may be two inches per minute, ten feet per hour, or two hundred and forty feet per day if the animal constantly keeps on the move. As I watch one of these animals crawl over a surface weighed by the unbalanced shell, I marvel at how the forward progress of the creature can seem so unconnected with any apparent muscular effort — it appears, as someone once remarked, that the slow, even progress is as mysterious and inevitable as the march of fate.

I have yet to see any living creature as loose-jointed as one of these animals. When the snail retires within its little house, it folds its foot lengthwise and gradually draws it up within the shell, the head end first and then the tail end. Conversely, when the animal emerges, the tail end comes out first and then the head and "horns." The "horns," of course, are not real horns but stalks with round knob-like tips. On the longer stalks, they serve as eyes and on the shorter probably as organs of smell.

It is amusing to watch a snail use its eyes and to see how it extends one eye over the edge of a leaf to observe what is beyond. It is said the animal can locate food hidden as far away as twenty inches. The mouth is directly below the stalks and is provided with one or more chitinous jaws and a long, ribbon-like tongue covered with horny teeth. The snail's table manners leave much to be desired. Give it an apple, and you will find it will soon make a fair-sized hole in it, but you will also discover it to be a hopeless slobberer.

As frosty nights become more frequent and the ground grows colder and harder, the mole digs deeper into the soil, and when winter has finally come, he may be as far as ten inches below the surface. I once felt sorry for this little animal, doomed forever to live in darkness and always having to dig for enough food to keep alive. I felt that Nature must have been in one of her capricious moods when she fashioned this creature, but since then I have veered to the opinion that she may not have been unkind after all when she destined him to a subterranean existence. The mole always has an abundance of food at hand, even though he may have to dig for it; he is always sheltered from the elements; and he is relatively free from attacks by enemies except at such times as he works too near the surface when the moving soil may be detected by a hawk or when a weasel may enter his burrow.

Like the shrew, the mole has an insatiable appetite and will eat most of his own weight in a day. Again like the shrew, the mole is an exceptionally active animal. But what I never could understand is why he doesn't live at a more leisurely pace. He certainly doesn't have to be on the constant lookout for enemies, nor must he prowl about for food, for the things he eats — grubs, earthworms, and other ground-dwelling insects — are usually near at hand. There may be times when food is scarce — all animals experience periods of scarcity — but why doesn't he put on extra fat which he can draw upon? On the contrary, he is forever on the move, snatching his sleep whenever he feels the need, although the common belief is that he works only during certain times of the day. Even during the winter, when other animals are asleep or otherwise inactive, he is either traveling along his runs in search of food or extending his tunnels where the ground is not frozen, particularly after a winter thaw when the soil is easy to excavate.

Just to give you an idea of how much a mole eats, one of these animals was given, as an experiment during a twenty-four hour period, fifty large grubs, one "chestnut worm," one wireworm, one cicada nymph, forty-five larvae of "rose bugs," and thirteen earthworms. In another experiment, he was given a pint of earthworms at eight o'clock in the evening, and on the following morning, he was found to be very feeble and cold and soon died.

On examination, the stomach was found to be empty, although he had eaten every worm.

Not only is the mole a most active animal, but he is also an exceptionally fast workman; the speed with which he can tunnel through the earth surpasses belief. There is one instance on record of a mole tunneling a distance of seventy-five yards in a single night. His tunneling activities often seriously interfere with our use of the soil, and they often result in an uprooting of plants and a cutting off of the moisture supply. In spite of his feeding chiefly on worms and insects, he will at times eat seeds and roots. Much of the injury usually charged to him, however, should rather be laid at the door of other small mammals, such as shrews and meadow and pine mice, which use his underground galleries for traffic and marauding and which actually are responsible for much of the injury to tubers, bulbs, roots, and planted seeds. There is also some evidence that the mole is a carrier of plant disease; however, his destruction of noxious insects places him in a more favorable light. Hamilton, for instance, tells of moles having almost entirely eliminated the larvae of the Japanese beetle from a friend's grounds.

The harvestmen, also known as "daddy longlegs," are more often observed in the fall when they may be seen running over boulders in the pastures, their favorite hunting grounds, although they also frequent fields and woodland borders. The young, which hatch from the eggs in the spring, are very timid creatures and usually hide under stones and other objects until they become full-grown, which is in late summer when they become more venturesome and come out in the open.

It is astonishing how these animals can support their bodies on such long, thin, fragile legs, and how they can move over the ground and through the grass without getting them caught in the grass blades. Yet eight legs, I suppose, should be enough to carry a body not much larger than a grain of wheat; and doubtless there are times when their legs do become entangled. Getting a leg caught, however, is a trifling thing, for the animal will merely "throw it off" and grow a new one if it cannot extricate itself. The legs are unquestionably much stronger than we suspect; strangely enough, however, they separate easily from the body. This fact, combined with their unusual length, has led some observers to believe they serve as a sort of protective fence when the animal is attacked; that the enemy grasps a leg as the nearest thing to seize and is left with it as the harvestman "throws it off" and escapes. I have never seen harvestmen use their legs for this purpose and doubt very much if they would use such means for protecting themselves, as they have a scent gland that gives off an odor strong enough to scare off any enemies inclined to attack them.

Many spiders are still active: you have only to examine the goldenrod to find crab spiders lurking in the blossoms, or to look about in the fields to see wolf spiders running over the ground. This is the time of the year when small spiders, and especially the young of the wolf spiders, delight to fly, apparently "just for fun." On a warm and comparatively mild day they mount to the top of a bush, fence, or twig, or the summit of a clod of earth and spin out a silken thread or sometimes a brush-like cluster of threads. The threads are caught by the air currents and carried out until enough has been spun to support them. Then they let go and sail through the air on their silken parachutes until they strike a foothold. Here they may rest and "take off" again, or they may cut loose and let their parachutes go wherever the wind may carry them. Perhaps you have seen these gossamer threads shimmering in the sunlight or clinging to your clothes and wondered what they were.

Some spiders have the habit of drawing out a thread behind them as they walk. These threads often become attached in a kind of lacework to such places as the pickets of a fence or the sides of a barn. Other spiders, such as the jumping spiders, spin a silken thread to let themselves down from the branches of trees and other supports, and these tenuous cables are blown about by the wind, adding to the silvery gossamer that embroiders the countryside in this most delightful of months.

About the second week of October the brook trout begin to move upstream to their spawning grounds. For some time the male has been preparing for this annual event, and by the time he is ready to perform his courtship act his sides have become a glowing red, his lower jaw has become upwardly hooked, his teeth have become larger, his body has become flattened, and his skin has thickened. The female, on the other hand, has remained relatively unchanged, except that her body has grown larger to accommodate the developing eggs.

On reaching the spawning grounds, the female fashions a shallow basin by fanning her tail against the gravel. She works more or less steadily for about two days or until she has a basin usually deeper and longer than her own body. Meanwhile, the males approach and one of them stations himself near the down-current of the basin and drives off any other male bold enough to dispute his claim. Sometimes the female takes part in driving away the rivals, but for the most part she leaves this task to the male and confines her activities to nest building. When the nest nears completion the two of them engage in a period of court-ship, and then the female settles herself close to the gravel. As if by a prearranged signal, the male now darts toward her and arches his body against hers so that she is pressed closer to the gravel. In this position the female lays her eggs, and the male deposits his sperms over them. Immediately after the eggs have been laid the female begins to cover them with gravel by swinging her body from side to side. The entire process of egg-laying takes only a few seconds; when it is over the male swims away, but the female may continue at her task of covering the eggs for hours.

Since insects are not as abundant as they have been, October birds are chiefly those that subsist on seeds and berries. Although a few, such as the phoebe, still remain, most of the insect eaters — the whippoorwill, nighthawk, chimney swift, kingbird, flycatcher, and swallow — have departed, leaving the robins, bluebirds, purple finches, sparrows, thrushes, and others to feast on the harvest of seeds which the weeds and grasses provide and the bountiful supply of fruits and berries with which the shrubs and vines are heavily laden. And millions of nuts — acorns, beechnuts, and the like — serve the nuthatches, woodpeckers, and blue jays.

The jays are particularly noisy in October, for their nesting duties are long since completed, and they are free to revel in the plenty that Nature has provided. Whenever I walk in the woods, they announce my presence with a raucous chorus and fly among the tree tops, a boisterous, rollicking crew, screaming as if in great terror or pain but apparently for no other reason than to exercise their vocal cords. Yet their din is not without value: as the hunting season opens, it serves as a warning to the four-footed creatures to scurry for cover.

The catbirds are still about my house, and occasionally on a warm day I hear their whispering song. In the neighboring field chipping sparrows have gathered in a flock, but before very long both they and the catbirds will have gone. In October the south-ward flight of migratory hawks is at its height, and frequently flocks of grackles may be seen in a cornfield or apple orchard where they often do considerable damage to the apples by pecking at them. Meanwhile, our winter visitors are beginning to arrive. Several days ago I saw a white-throated sparrow in a clearing and a ruby-crowned kinglet in a roadside thicket, but as I have not seen either of them since, they presumably are miles away by now. Yesterday I saw a northern shrike on the top of a telephone pole; only a minute ago, as I stood by my window, a junco flew over the strawberry patch.

October is a delightful month to wander about the countryside. The days have not the chill of spring nor the heat of summer and, though the sun may be bright, the air is cool and invigorating and fragrant with the undefinable smell of autumn. Everywhere the rich coloring of the foliage meets the eye; the birds in merry flocks dart through the sky; you find the pumpkin on the vine; and you thrill to the joy of living. You linger longer outdoors than you are wont to do, for perhaps tomorrow purple shadows will lie softly upon snowy fields, howling winds will sigh through leafless boughs, and another year will have passed, leaving only memories to cherish amidst less inspiring surroundings.

Barring the asters and goldenrods, few flowers are in bloom at this late date, but these we affectionately regard as staunch friends who have remained when others have faded away. The daisy fleabane, whose kinship to the asters and daisy is apparent at a glance, continues to blossom in fields and similar places; along the roadside where shaggy manes have magically appeared, the bright yellow flowers of the Jerusalem artichoke gleam like miniature suns above the thickets and fence rows, while the dying fronds of the hay-scented fern, looking like wraiths, perfume the air with the odor of decay. The blazing star still decorates waste places with its soft rose-purple flower heads, and in ditches and along the fringes of ponds and streams the bur marigold continues to bloom. We may still find the ladies' tresses in wet meadows, where patches of the lavender-pink gerardia peep above the grass, and almost everywhere we come across the chickweed and shepherd's purse, which seem never to stop flowering. And where the long, silvery, decorative plumes of the wild clematis festoon woodland and wayside thickets, the ragweed and tropical galinsoga are still in flower. But despite all these late-blooming flowers, October is rightly the month of the gentian.

> Thou waitest late, and com'st alone
> When woods are bare and birds have flown,
> And frosts and shortening days portend
> The aged year is near his end."

These words of Bryant's are not strictly accurate, and yet they are not altogether without aptness, as those can testify who have had the unexpected joy of finding the fringed gentian blossoming when the flowers of summer have withered and died and when nature's prospect is bleak and frosty.

I have never forgotten the day when I chanced, for the first time, upon this gay and lovely flower in a shady copse that fringed a woodland pond,

> "Whose sweet and quiet eyes —
> Looks through its fringes to the sky
> Blue, blue as if the sky let fall
> A flower from its cerulean wall."

It is, indeed, a happy adventure to come upon the dainty gentian, for it is becoming altogether too rare. And then, too, since it is an annual and its little hairy seeds seat themselves on the winds and often ride great distances, we do not know when or where we will next find it; a year hence we may revisit the spot where we find it today and search for it in vain.

As October draws to a close the ferns, already chilled by early frosts, turn brown and die; the needles of the larch become yellow and drop. And as the winds grow stronger the leaves fall more rapidly, transforming the character of the landscape, denuding the woods where the bucks of deer range in search of does to woo and rivals to battle, with tempers so uncertain that they will charge a man, to stab with antlers and strike with hoofs.

NATURAL EVENTS IN OCTOBER

- Shaggy-mane mushrooms magically appear on lawns, along roadsides, and in pastures and waste places.

- Yellow crab spiders lurk in goldenrod blossoms.

- Chipping sparrows begin their southern journey.

- Gnats and flies still dance in the golden sunshine.

- Ferns, chilled by early frosts, turn brown and die.

- Termites begin their downward migration into the ground.

- The whispering song of the catbird may be heard on warm days.

- A red admiral butterfly may be seen visiting flowers still blossoming.

- The brilliant flower heads of the Jerusalem artichoke, towering high in the air, decorate roadsides and fence rows.

- Bumblebees and wasp queens search for winter retreats, as the drones and workers succumb to falling temperatures.

- Wood turtles dig into the bottom mud of ponds and streams or retire into holes along the banks.

- The Virginia creeper, with sprays of rich cardinal, festoons the somber boles of dark evergreens.

- A northern shrike, newly-arrived from the northland, may be seen perched on top of a small tree or post.

- Ground beetles retire beneath logs.

- The scarlet oak, robed in full panoply of its autumn dress, stands aglow with fire in the bright sunshine.

- The southward flight of migratory hawks is at its height.

- Brilliant clusters of orange-red bittersweet berries brighten old walls, copses, and fence rows.

- Spotted salamanders are still on the move, but as the days become colder they crawl into holes beneath the leaf cover of the forest and remain there for the winter.

- Nuts ripen.

- The needles of the larch turn yellow and fall. No other cone-bearer is leafless in winter.

- Grackles pass through New England cornfields and orchards in large migrating flocks.

- Snowy tree crickets may still be heard, if not hushed by early frosts.

- Sumacs paint the landscape with their beautiful foliage.

- Garter snakes congregate at their wintering places.

- Young adults of the spotted newt, still bearing traces of their youthful orange-red coloration, migrate into weed-grown brooks.

- Squirrels are busy gathering acorns and beechnuts.

- The blue gentian, blooming in moist meadows and woodland borders, strikes a contrasting note amidst the reds and yellows and browns of autumn.

- The woods resound with the cries of blue jays.

- Juncos reappear. They will soon be seeking bird feeding stations.

- Brook trout move upstream and begin to spawn.

- The long, silvery, decorative plumes of the wild clematis festoon woodland and roadside thickets.

- Poison ivy turns a fiery red.

- This is the period of great leaf fall.

- Deer mate.

- Spring peepers may be heard on bright, sunny days.

- Ladies' tresses still blossom in wet meadows, where patches of the lavender-pink gerardia peep above the grasses.

- The red maples unfurl their scarlet flags.

- The blazing star decorates waste places with its soft rose-purple flower heads, and in ditches and along the fringes of ponds and streams the bur marigold continues to bloom.

- Leopard frogs leave their haunts in the meadows and deep woods and go into marshes, ponds, springs, and shallow streams.

- The red oak becomes clothed in a rich, dark, purplish-red.

- The beech, with leaves of palest Naples yellow, serves notice that all is not crimson and scarlet on the autumn landscape.

- In rocky barrens and waste places the gray birch adds a touch of beauty with brilliant golden-yellow leaves that glisten beneath dancing sunbeams.

- Chipmunks go into their winter homes.

- Cicadas cease their incessant chorus.

- Field crickets continue their nightly serenades.

- Dragonflies may still be seen flying over ponds and streams.

- Worker honeybees drive the drones from the hive.

- Land snails cease eating and begin to crawl beneath stones, into tree trunks, or to bury themselves in moss, leaves, or earth.

- Moles dig deeper into the ground.

- Harvestmen are common in pastures.

- Young spiders "balloon" through the air.

꙳ Asters and goldenrods are still in flower.

꙳ In thickets and along fence rows the dying fronds of the hay-scented fern seem like wraiths and perfume the air with the odor of decay.

꙳ The ragweed and the tropical galinsoga are still in flower.

꙳ The daisy fleabane, whose kinship to the asters and daisy is apparent at a glance, continues to blossom in fields and similar places.

꙳ Chickweed and shepherd's purse are still in flower.

꙳ Transient white-throated sparrows may be seen in clearings and ruby-crowned kinglets in roadside thickets.

November

I have been sitting by my study window, watching swirling gusts of wind blow fallen leaves crazily over the ground. It seems only yesterday that they were resplendent in yellows and golds, russets and browns; but now, tattered and torn, they lie scattered about, the playthings of every passing breeze and a poignant reminder that the season of biting winds, icy pendants, and whirling snowflakes is near at hand. Only the rosy glow in the sky, as the sun disappears behind the distant hillside, remains as the essence of October's brilliance. Yet the woods, though not wholly leafless, are not without a certain beauty as purple and brown shadows silently steal over them and the twilight blends into the blackness of the night.

Traditionally November is a month of...

> wailing winds and naked woods
> and meadows brown and sere,

and all is bleak and cheerless. But there are days when the sun shines sweetly and the air is warm and soft like that of May; when a red dragonfly may be seen winging its way in the golden sunshine and an evening primrose belatedly opens its blossoms in the hope that some still-active sphinx moth might visit it; when a meadowlark may be heard singing one last song before he sets out on his southward flight.

Today was such a day. As I wandered down the road, the light golden-yellow flowers of the fall dandelion, perched on long, slender flower stalks, waved in the breeze, and the small, pale lavender flowers of the wood aster, crowded in dense clusters, created the illusion of a mist hanging above the ground. Along the woodland trail, the yellow caps of the fat Pholiota, growing in tufts on a fallen log, gleamed like unset jewels, and the yellow-green flowers of the witch hazel, studded on leafless twigs, glittered in the bright sunshine like clusters of golden stars. One could well wonder if the calendar had been turned back or ask with the poet:

> Has time grown sleepy at his post
> And let the exiled Summer back?
> Or is it her regretful ghost
> Or witchcraft of the almanac?

You should be aware of the witch hazel because the large, bony, shining black seeds, which have been maturing since the preceding fall, are now discharged through the elastic rupture of the capsules and bombard the neighborhood with all the violence of an artillery barrage. The force with which these seeds are projected is shown by the distance they travel, which sometimes is as much as forty-five feet, or by the intensity of the sting, should one of them hit you on the face. If you are minded to take home an armful of the twigs to decorate your living room, be sure to protect yourself, for the missiles play no favorites.

November has always seemed to me a somewhat capricious month, a struggling mixture of summer and winter, with its moods changing with the varying winds. Certainly, as I strolled through the woods and came upon a number of brownish-gray moths flying about like so many tiny ghosts, I found it difficult to reconcile the summer-like day with the thought that on the morrow legions of cold might sweep in from Canada and sprinkle the landscape with snowflakes. Yet the thought was not unreasonable, for as a boy I expected skating and coasting on Thanksgiving Day, and I doubt if the passing years have brought any marked change in our seasons. Only three years ago we had a heavy fall of snow in November, and the winter developed into the worst one we have ever had, when snowstorms followed one another with clockwork regularity and the snowdrifts, like white tents, became heaped upon the fields and meadows and clogged the roads and woodland paths with impassable barriers. Many weather prognostications relate to the month, and I was reminded of the following quatrain, about the whiteness of a goose's breastbone, when a wedge of geese, pointed southward, honked overhead:

> If the November goose bone be thick
> So will Winter weather be;
> If the November goose bone be thin
> So will the Winter weather be.

The moths I saw were the males of the fall cankerworm. They emerge from their cocoons in November and fly about in search of the females. The females, lacking wings, do not fly but are not quite as sedentary as other wingless moths. As soon as they emerge from their cocoons, they scramble up the trunks of trees, where they await the males. The eggs, which they fasten to the bark of the trees with a strong gluey secretion, are covered with gray hairs which they rub from their abdomens. They look like tiny gray flower pots arranged in somewhat regular clusters and number several hundreds.

Although insects are not as abundant as they have been, they are not entirely absent. Houseflies still linger outdoors before seeking their winter quarters, and I saw quite a few honeybees flying about the last of the wildflowers in search of nectar. These worker bees, now that they have gotten rid of the drones, are making their final preparations for winter. They make fewer and fewer trips afield, venturing forth only during the midday sunny hours, and the loads which they carry home become steadily lighter.

It has been estimated that some 480 pounds of honey are required to maintain an average-sized colony throughout the year. Of this amount, 400 pounds are used to support the bees themselves, 70 pounds to feed the brood, and 10 pounds for the making of wax. To accumulate this amount of honey, the bees must make 17,760,000 trips afield. These journeyings represent an intense industry during the summer, for it is then that the bees must accumulate enough food so that when their immediate needs are taken care of, they will have some left over to store as a reserve supply for the winter. And this reserve, stored in thousands of waxen cells, must be enough not only to carry them through the winter, but also to provide for brood rearing in the spring. Under such circumstances, it is understandable that they cannot afford to be prodigal of their reserves and find it necessary to get rid of the drones.

This hoarding instinct — of such vital importance to the survival of the community — would in itself serve no useful purpose during the winter if the bees were not able to generate and conserve heat since they are unable to survive temperatures below 57°F. They meet this difficulty by drawing together into a single compact cluster and, by vibrating their wings, generate enough heat within it to produce the necessary warmth.

The cluster consists of a hollow sphere of bees several layers thick. It is a most excellent non-conductor of heat, being so effective that a point inside may sometimes be 100°F. warmer than a point a few inches away, outside the cluster. Within the hollow sphere are bees, which move about freely, and which generate heat by vibrating their wings. The remaining bees are inactive and form a shell. They constantly shift their position, however, and exchange places with the bees within the cluster. The number of inactive bees varies with the outer temperature, being larger at warmer temperatures when less heat production is needed, and smaller at lower temperatures.

To maintain the muscular activity necessary for heat production, the bees are forced to draw upon their food reserves. The undigested material, which forms excreta, is retained in the hind intestine until the bees have an opportunity for flight, for normally no feces are deposited within the hive. During the cold winters of the North, there are times when the bees cannot fly for several weeks, and the generation of heat during such a period of cold weather requires an increased consumption of food and results in an increased amount of feces. The presence of feces, moreover, causes the bees to become restless, to generate still more heat, and to accumulate still more feces. To escape such a vicious circle, they often fly out when it is so cold that they die before being able to return.

We might well marvel at the ingenuity displayed by the honeybees in meeting the hazards of winter, but at the same time, it is doubtful if they are happy at being imprisoned and forced to a life of relative idleness after months of honeybee activity in a world of sunshine and flowers.

The crickets are also about and on warm days scrape their fiddles, but as the cold weather sets in, they huddle under boards and loose stones, where many of them may be found dead in early winter. A few other insects are also active, but by far the great majority have by now snuggled into winter quarters. Insects that have spent the summer on trees and shrubs have sought refuge beneath the bark and in the stems and buds, or have descended to the ground cover of leaves and grass; wasps have left their paper nests for secluded roof corners; and the ground-dwelling species, such as wireworms, the larvae of May beetles, and mound-building ants, have burrowed below the frost line or have retired to lower parts of their nests.

Other animals, too, have taken to their winter quarters. Except for such species as the water spiders, which may be found in large numbers on bridges, the spiders have largely disappeared; snails, slugs, and myriapods have sought refuge beneath the leaf mold; and earthworms have huddled together in rounded chambers deep in the ground. The toads, frogs, and turtles have buried themselves in the soil or the mud of ponds and streams; except for rattlesnakes, which may appear for one last sunning before vanishing for the winter, the snakes have slipped into deep cracks and crevices of piled-up rocks and ledges, where they have knotted themselves into torpid tangles; the woodchucks and chipmunks have descended into their underground burrows; the bats have retired to their caves; and other hibernating mammals have either sought their winter dens or will soon do so, depending on the weather.

Why some animals brave the winter and remain active while others seek a cozy nook and sleep is a question to which we have no answer. Investigators have found that such environmental conditions as cold, hunger, darkness, and quiet may induce hibernation, but all these factors together will not induce a non-hibernating animal to become dormant. Hibernating animals, moreover, often go into hibernation while food is plentiful and the weather is still warm, simply because they are scheduled to do so.

Most people apparently think that going into hibernation is a sudden step taken on an impulse, that the hibernating animal retires to his winter quarters and goes to sleep. But this is not true. Whether they are wasps, toads, or woodchucks, animals usually go into hibernation slowly, often a step at a time, sleeping for a while and then waking, then sleeping some more and again waking, until finally they slip into a long, continual lethargy.

In some instances, the animals prepare for hibernation weeks in advance. Chipmunks begin to lay up large stores in September and woodchucks, needing a large amount of fat to carry them through the winter months, start eating vast amounts of grass and clover as early as mid-July. This fat is stored in layers around the animal's chest and shoulders, in the axillae of the legs, and about the internal organs and muscles, but in other animals, it is concentrated in variously shaped structures such as the multi-fingered bodies of frogs and toads, familiar to all biology students.

Some animals descend into a deep torpor; others become only slightly sluggish and are more or less aware of what transpires about them. Even the deep sleepers are susceptible to noise, touch, and other disturbances, the woodchuck being extremely sensitive to all kinds of stimuli. Hibernating animals, especially those which are deeply dormant, are entirely motionless and manifest no signs of life except for their breathing. Their sleeping positions differ, but usually most of them are curled up with their heads between their hind legs so that their eyes are hidden. There are exceptions, of course; dormant wasps hold themselves strictly straightened out, their bodies, legs, and wings all parallel; the thirteen-lined squirrels sit on their hind legs with their backs arched and their heads bent at an angle so that their noses rest against their bodies; and bats often hang by one arm for a long time and then change to the other.

We usually think of mammals when we speak of hibernation; yet actually, few mammals hibernate. By far the largest number of winter sleepers are the protozoans, rotifers, earthworms, clams, snails, crustaceans, spiders, insects, toads, frogs, turtles, snakes, and salamanders. Most of them hibernate alone, but some gather in large or small companies. Bats, for instance, hibernate in hollow trees by the dozens or in caves by the thousands; termites cluster together deep in tree trunks or in underground chambers; and garter snakes congregate in very large numbers deep in crevices of rocks.

Meanwhile, the animals that have not gone into hibernation but intend to remain active are preparing for the winter in various ways. The deer wander about in family parties and fatten on the food to be found in the woods; the squirrels are industriously completing their winter stores; the muskrats are putting the finishing touches to their homes; the furbearers have donned their winter overcoats; and the varying hare and weasel have acquired their winter colors.

Colors are so commonplace that we subconsciously accept them, not thinking about them unless some vivid or unusual combination catches our eye or, perhaps more accurately, our imagination. This is another way of saying how few of us realize how much colors mean to us and more specifically how much they mean to animals; indeed, they often determine an animal's chance of survival.

When we look at a tiger or zebra in a zoo, we think they are quite conspicuous, but in their natural habitat, their colors blend with their surroundings so well that they are practically invisible. Without his peculiar color pattern, I dare say the zebra would fall prey more often to a hungry lion or some other carnivore, for what other defense has he against such enemies?

But what of the tiger? This animal certainly doesn't need to be protected! His peculiar color pattern has another purpose: it permits him to lie unseen in wait for his prey. In the final analysis, it is just as essential that the tiger be protected against starvation as the zebra against slaughter.

There are exceptions, of course, but the coloration of most animals makes them inconspicuous in their natural environment. Polar bears, arctic foxes, and snowy owls that live where the ground is covered with snow are white, and animals that live among the green leaves, such as the praying mantes, katydids, and certain tree frogs, are usually green, while those that live on flowers are likely to resemble those they are accustomed to visit. I have already mentioned the crab spiders; there are also the Catocala moths, popularly known as the underwings, which look so much like the bark of trees that they are difficult to detect when they rest on them.

Lizards and other animals that live on the desert are usually sandy or gray in color, while those that live in swampy places and meadows are, for the most part, gray or yellowish with parallel stripes, which make them blend with the stems and leaves of small trees, rushes, and grasses. The vesper sparrow, a drab, somber-colored little bird, harmonizes so well with the ground that it is almost impossible to find it among the meadow grass. The same thing can be said of the bittern, whose colors are so inconspicuous as to make the bird practically invisible among the rank growth of a marsh and swamp. The bittern, moreover, is adept at concealment and has the habit of standing among the grass or reeds with its bill cocked up at such an angle that even when in full sight it remains unnoticed because of its resemblance to a stake or rail.

With most animals, the color scheme remains constant, but with some, such as the varying hare and weasel, it changes with the seasons. In summer, the varying hare is reddish brown and in winter completely white, except at the tips of the ears. This seasonal change of color is of great value, for the hare has many enemies—the bald eagle, the snowy and great horned owls, the hawks, lynx, wolf, fox, weasel, mink, and sable. Were he to retain his summer pelage he would be a highly conspicuous object on the snow-covered landscape, but by changing to white he becomes almost invisible, as he is in summer when his dun-colored dress blends with the browns of leafy soil and rock.

The weasel also undergoes a seasonal change. In summer, he is uniformly chocolate brown above (except for the tip of his tail, which is black) and white below, and in winter completely white except for the final third of his tail, which remains black. But only in the northern parts of their range do the weasels change color. In southern parts, they retain their summer coloration, while in the intermediate regions, such as New York and southern Michigan, some turn white and others do not. The change of color, according to recent investigations, is due neither to temperature nor snow but is the result of a long selection occurring in an arctic environment.

The artist views the human form as a medium of expression, and so too might we look upon the trees as they stand naked and all-revealing. Silhouetted against the sky, they are the most conspicuous living elements on the landscape, things of beauty and poetic charm. And when they become buffeted by the winter storms and so burdened with loads of snow that they creak and groan as if in protest, they evoke our sympathy. With this feeling comes the realization that trees are not the characterless things that many persons believe but familiar companions in a different guise — companions whom we can learn to recognize all over again. And if we did, we would soon learn to recognize them not only close at hand by various distinguishing features, as we know our friends by such facial characteristics as the color of the eyes or of the hair, but also from afar, as we know our friends at a distance by some indefinable peculiarity of form or habit of gait. Certainly it is no great task to learn to know the birch with its feathery, brushlike head; the poplar with its powdery skin; the dogwood with its curled-in branches and twigs studded with the curious turban-shaped flower buds; and the hop hornbeam which, retiring and usually concealed by other trees, now stands revealed by its hoplike fruit clusters.

In the marshes that border the river, the redwings have gathered in large flocks, and any day they will set off on their southern flight. On the second day of November, while walking down the road, I saw a hermit thrush feeding on the berries of the Virginia creeper in a wayside thicket. Despite the lateness of the year, many of our summer visitors are still with us. The same day I saw the hermit thrush, as I was returning home to dinner, I came across a flock of cedar waxwings dining on the scarlet berries of the mountain ash. These birds are usually gone by now, but if there is a bountiful supply of wild fruits of the kind that persist during the winter, many of them remain in flocks of various sizes. One year I counted a flock of thirteen in late December, when the ground was covered with snow and a biting wind blew across the fields. I have always been partial to these sleek and dandified

Beau Brummels of birdland, and as I stopped to watch them feed I could well understand why there is never a feather out of place nor a speck of dirt on their velvety coats — they dined with all the poise and dignity that bespeak good breeding. Elegance is the word to describe the cedar waxwings, for they combine beauty of plumage with a grace of movement that a professional mannequin might well envy. Certainly, they have a right to be called the "tip-tops of feathered aristocracy," but I think they would resent being called snobs. Though they appear "stand-offish," they are actually sociable and affectionate birds and ever ready to help others in distress, whether their own kind or not. They have their foibles, too, being somewhat inclined to indolence and gluttony and other trifling dissipations. I thought they would never stop eating, and I fully expected to see the berries sticking in their throats for want of room below. I left them sitting on the branches well content with the world but probably eager to get at the berries again.

Occasionally on my November rambles, I see pipits in a marsh or pasture, but the frosty nights soon send them on their way. More frequently, I come upon a myrtle warbler feeding on the berries of the bayberry. Warblers feed on insects, but the myrtle warbler can subsist on berries and seeds. The bird is especially fond of bayberries and will eat nothing else so long as the supply holds out; but when they become exhausted, it will eat the berries of the red cedar, the Virginia creeper, the viburnums, honeysuckles, and others. Along the seacoast where this warbler winters, it prefers the bayberries, even though mild weather brings forth countless flies from the seaweed.

The seacoast, even in bleak November, is not entirely cheerless and melancholy. Along marshes and tidal rivers, the white silky cockades of the groundsel bush relieve the drab monotony of withered grasses and the unattractive prospect of exposed mud flats. And along the beach, where migrating sanderlings and redbacked sandpipers patter over the sands, the seaside goldenrod adds its golden touch to the barren shoreline.

The beach yields much of interest if you are willing to brave the chill sea breezes. High on the beach where the tide and storm waves have left them you can find innumerable shells mixed with rows of dead eelgrass and seaweed or scattered about in the sand—cockles, boatshells, moon shells, whelks, and many others. You can also find sponges, sea urchins, sand dollars, the remains of crabs and fishes, the molted shells of the horseshoe crab, and a variety of other creatures, including the omnipresent beach fleas. But instead of these mute reminders of what were once living animals you prefer those still throbbing with the pulse of life, then follow the beach toward the sea and along the low tide mark you will find the curious porcelain-like sand bug, about the size and color of a pigeon's egg, the quahog and razor clam, mud crabs and mantis shrimps, and the sandworm Nereis. Among the rocks, draped with rockweeds hanging in great olive-brown clusters, and covered with countless barnacles, you will find starfishes and crabs hiding in the crevices, green crabs underneath loose stones, hermit crabs carrying their homes with them wherever they go, and periwinkles crawling in the tidepools in aimless fashion or over the wet sand, tracing irregular paths as they wander about.

NATURAL EVENTS IN NOVEMBER

- Honeybees are still active, seeking nectar from the last of the autumn wildflowers.

- A red dragonfly may be seen occasionally, swinging into the sunshine.

- Water spiders are to be found in large numbers on bridges.

- Migrating thrushes feed on the berries of the Virginia creeper.

- Rattlesnakes may enjoy one last sunning before disappearing for the winter in deep cracks and crevices of piled-up rocks and ledges.

- A few houseflies still linger outdoors before seeking their winter quarters.

- The witch hazel is in bloom. (The witch hazel is the last of the shrubs to flower.)

- The moths of the fall cankerworm emerge from the ground and the males mate with the wingless females on the trunks of trees.

- Wedges of wild geese, pointed southward, honk overhead.

- A few migrating sanderlings and red-backed sandpipers still patter over the ocean beaches.

- Myrtle warblers feed on bayberries.

- The varying hare and weasel assume their winter coloring.

- Flocks of cedar waxwings may be seen feeding on the coral-red berries of the mountain ash.

- The still blooming seaside goldenrod adds a touch of color to a bleak and barren shoreline.

- Mound-builder ants retire to lower parts of the nest.

ᴓ Squirrels are industriously completing their winter stores.

ᴓ Redwings flock in numbers and begin their southward flight.

ᴓ Wireworms and the larvae of May beetles burrow below the frost line.

ᴓ The light golden-yellow flowers of the fall dandelion, perched on long slender flower stalks, wave merrily in the November breeze.

ᴓ Muskrats are putting finishing touches to their houses.

ᴓ Occasionally an evening primrose belatedly opens its blossoms in the hope that some still active sphinx moth might visit it.

ᴓ As cold weather draws near, crickets huddle under boards and loose stones.

ᴓ Fur bearers have acquired their winter coats.

ᴓ The song of the meadowlark may still be heard.

ᴓ Along the marshes and tidal rivers the groundsel bush relieves the drab monotony of withered grasses and the unattractive prospect of exposed mud flats with its white silky cockades.

ᴓ Deer wander in family parties and fatten on the food to be found in the woods.

ᴓ Migrating pipits feed in marsh and pasture, but frosty nights soon send them southward.

ᴓ The small, pale lavender flowers of the wood aster, crowded in dense clusters, create the illusion of a mist hanging above the ground in woods and shady roadsides.

ᴓ The yellow caps of the fat Pholiota (mushroom), growing in tufts on a fallen log, gleam like unset jewels.

ᴓ Snow falls and the nature year begins to ebb.

ᴓ The hop hornbeam, retiring in its habit and usually concealed by other trees, stands revealed by its hoplike fruit clusters.

- Wasps leave their paper nests for secluded roof corners.

- Earthworms huddle together in rounded chambers deep in the ground.

- Snails, slugs, and myriapods seek refuge beneath the leaf mold.

December

We are well into December. The trees stand draped with ermine cloaks and the withered asters, goldenrods, and sunflowers that blossomed only yesterday but now wreathed in snow present a singularly graceful and fantastic appearance. Down by the woodland border, where a brook murmured its way not so long ago, the catkins of the alders, cased in ice, sparkle and quiver in the sunshine like jeweled pendants. The monotony of white is broken only by the green of pines and hemlocks.

Officially, winter does not arrive until the twenty-first of December, but I have known years when the first of the month has brought us weather which we normally associate with January and February. I can also recall years when we did not have our first snowfall until after the first of the year, and when the weather during the month was almost springlike. Whatever the December weather may turn out to be, the plants and animals have long since made their preparations for the winter and are quite indifferent as to when it comes.

The adjustments which some plants and animals make to meet the exigencies of winter are varied and often quite ingenious. As autumn grows old and falling temperatures and leaden skies warn of approaching winter, the grouse grows fringes of sharp points on his toes to serve as snowshoes so he can run more easily over the snow in search of partridge berries, of which he is especially fond, and other fruits, such as the red berries of the bearberry, which prove a welcome addition to his menu, even though they are dry and flavorless.

At the time the varying hare changes his color and puts on his white winter robe, he also grows long stiff hairs along the margins of his feet. These hairs serve the same purpose as the pectinations of the grouse, permitting the hare to race with complete abandon over deep snow where other animals flounder. Many years ago, I saw a fox chase a hare over the snow, but the fox was easily eluded; an owl or a hawk would have been more successful if it had followed the white, bounding figure, practically invisible against the snowy background.

Neither the weasel nor the hare turns completely white when he changes color. To do so would nullify the adaptation, even though it might seem that the black tip of the weasel's tail and the dusky tips of the hare's ears would make them conspicuous on the snow. If you ever have the opportunity to perform the experiment, place one of these animals on the snow in such a way that it doesn't cast a shadow. You will find that, although you may be able to see the tip of the tail or the tips of the ears at a short distance, it is difficult to distinguish the outline of the animal. But cover either, and after a few moments, you can begin to detect the form of the animal; in other words, as long as the tip of the tail or the tips of the ears are visible, only these parts will hold your attention.

As a special protection against the cold, animals that remain abroad have winter underwear in the form of very dense short hairs that sprout among the roots of the longer and true fur. The birds that remain or visit us during the winter are also protected against the cold in a similar manner, for their plumage (duller in hue and hence less conspicuous) is denser and more closely interlocked than that which follows the spring molt. Ducks and related birds have a downy undergrowth which not only serves the main purpose of preventing water from reaching the breast but also helps to keep out the cold. And it is this down, which loosens in the spring, that the females pluck out and use as a bedding for their eggs. The down of the eider duck is highly valued for its lightness and warmth and yet, ironically, by the time we use it, it is actually third-hand material.

The invertebrates, too, take special care to protect themselves against the winter. The egg sacs or cocoons of the spiders, in which the eggs or young spiderlings pass the winter, we find attached to all sorts of places, such as the undersurfaces of stones, the loose bark of trees, the sides of buildings, and the stems or twigs of plants. They are not flimsy coverings made in a haphazard manner, but actually fairly elaborate structures made in a definite manner characteristic of the species. The drassids, for instance, make a white or brown papery disc; the domestic spiders, a cocoon more or less spherical in outline and about the size of an orange seed; the banded garden spiders, a cup-shaped cocoon with a flat top; and the yellow garden spiders, a cocoon about the size of a walnut but as light as cotton and hung airily from weed tops such as the steeplebush and thistle. If you find a cocoon of the yellow garden spider, open it and you will discover the eggs enclosed in a silken cup surrounded with a thick layer of flossy silk, which in turn is enclosed in a firm, brown, closely woven outer covering that gives it its characteristic shape. In some species, the cocoon is further covered with a protective layer of some foreign substance such as mud, or, as is the case of the grass spider, with bits of rubbish.

Some insects, including the thrips, escape the cold and winter storms by crawling down between the woolly leaves of the mullein, whose tall dried spikes rise into the air like church steeples; others, like the woolly aphids, throw thick warm coverings around themselves; and still others make dense cocoons in which they spend the winter as pupae. On the side of the nearby shed, there are a number of ashen-gray chrysalids of the cabbage butterfly, fastened with tufts of silk, and as I write, the nests of the viceroy butterfly come to mind. They are tube-like structures made by the caterpillars of rolled leaves, lined with silk, and fastened to the twigs with the same material in such a manner that they cannot fall during the winter. It is interesting to note that, although this species has two or three broods, only the autumn brood of caterpillars makes these nests, so that the nest-building instinct appears only in alternate generations, or even less frequently when the species is more than two-brooded.

Occasionally, galls serve as winter homes for their makers. The willow pine galls, which are conspicuous on the tips of willow twigs, provide a snug retreat not only for the little gnats that make them but for a number of guests. Open one of the spherical galls that are so common on goldenrod stems, and you will likely find a tiny fat grub resting quite comfortably in its little house.

No less than animals, the plants also prepare for the winter in various ways. The woolly leaves of the mullein, for example, are a protection against the intense cold which the exquisite rosettes formed by year-old plants must endure through the winter before they can send up a flower stalk the second spring. Trees and shrubs, on the other hand, protect the tender inner parts of their buds against the cold and moisture by providing them with thick scales or coating them with a waxy resinous substance, and against sudden changes of temperatures by lining them with down or wool that serves the same purpose as the underfur of animals.

The reason why berries of certain trees and shrubs remain on the branches well into winter may be an adaptation to prevent the embryos from being killed by the frosts and rains of autumn were they to fall at that time. Beechnuts, acorns, and other nuts and berries that fall in the autumn apparently find the moisture of the ground and the leaf coverings to their liking, though too much warmth or moisture causes them to germinate prematurely. I have often found acorns anchored with purple sprouts during the winter, but it seems that the winter following such untimely growth usually proves fatal to them.

All our hibernating mammals are now in their winter quarters. Even the bears, who are the last to seek their dens in hollow tree trunks, beside upturned roots, and in natural caves in ledges, have vanished from their former haunts. The females go to cover before the males, but in years when the weather is mild and food continues to be available, even they will not go into hibernation until midwinter, or just before their cubs are born. As a matter of fact, the males often remain active all winter and when they do sleep are likely to lie in a hollow in the ground, half-covered with brush, or in a thicket on the lee side of a log. Frequently, a bear will crawl into any convenient shelter and snow and ice will accumulate about the animal, imprisoning it, with only a breathing hole open to the outside and without food or drink, until liberated by the warm rays of the spring sun.

Although deer do not hibernate, they are probably more affected by winter conditions than any other non-hibernating mammal. When the winter is open and the snow cover is thin, they can wander about and seek fresh feeding grounds, but when the snowfall is heavy, they are restricted to the paths or "yards" which they are able to open up, where they must depend for food on the tender buds and twigs of maple, birch, cedar, and other conifers. Winter is the season of hardship for the deer, particularly if it is a severe one, and many perish from exhaustion and starvation and the attacks of such predators as wildcats and wolves.

As the ice gradually creeps over the inland ponds and streams, golden-eyed ducks are forced to fly to the seacoast and muskrats to forage for the submerged roots and stalks of lilies, cattails, and other water plants. The muskrat's smaller relatives, the field mice and deer mice, have more freedom, since they are able to run along their pathways and over the snow to feed on blanched shoots of grasses and the bark from trees. Mice are especially destructive in the winter by girdling such trees as the apple, but the screech owls do their best to help us by preying upon them.

On a warm December day, I may hear a cricket or grasshopper making lonesome calls from the lee of a fence or ledge. Insects, of course, are noticeably absent, but there have been times when I have found caddis worms crawling over the bottoms of streams or clinging to the stalks of submerged water plants, and many beetles are still active under bark and stones. The vast majority of insects, however, are in a dormant state. Yesterday, I found glittering backswimmers hanging by the hundreds from tangles of half-decayed chara plants, and on the bark of a nearby elm tree were the egg masses of the white-marked tussock moth, attached to the loose cocoons of the wingless females. And when I came upon the graceful green crowns of the leatherwood fern rising above the snow-covered rocks in a woodland ledge and found the velvet-stemmed collybia growing in tufts on a dead stump, it occurred to me that December outdoors does not present the bleak and barren prospect that many envisage. Even the green twigs of the sassafras strike a spring-like note in the midst of winter snows, and as I passed the meadow, where I stopped a few brief months ago to watch the kingbirds chase flying insects, a flock of starlings rose from the ground and settled in a towering roadside tulip tree, its branches still covered with the light brown fruiting cones. In an alder thicket, I came upon a feeding flock of pine siskins and redpolls; when I emerged from the woods to follow the path that leads across the snow-swept field, I found some purple finches dining on the blue berries of the cedar. And just as I was about to step indoors, I noticed that the privet is still fresh, bright, and green. It called to mind one day last winter when I motored along the seacoast, where buffleheads played in the surf and horned larks in merry companies ran along the beach, and discovered how the bright, glossy evergreen leaves and the shining black berries of the inkberry provided a touch of unexpected beauty on the sandy shoreline.

With all its shortcomings and discomforts, winter has its compensations. I know of nothing more exhilarating than to put on my heavy boots and winter jacket and take to the outdoors, where I can feel the icy crust beneath my feet and the biting wind on my face, where I can see flocks of goldfinches feeding in a wind-swept field or the inimitable chickadees searching the red fruit of the sumac for hiding insects, and where I can hear the crows breaking the frozen silence as they streak across the sky. Nor do I know of a greater peace than to sit beside the fireplace in the evening and watch the burning birch logs cast dancing shadows on the walls and split and crackle and send flashing sparks into the air, while the night wind sings its way beneath the eaves and an owl breaks the silence with its eerie call far in the distance.

NATURAL EVENTS IN DECEMBER

- Pine-cone galls, conspicuous on the tips of the willow twigs, serve as winter homes for their makers and other guest hibernators.

- Between the woolly leaves of the mullein, whose tall, dried spikes rise into the air like church steeples, may be found numbers of hibernating thrips.

- Meadow mice and deer mice, undaunted by the cold, feed on the blanched shoots of grasses and gnaw the bark from trees.

- Crows break the frozen silence as they fly to and fro between their feeding and roosting places.

- Dead grasses and withered asters, goldenrods, and sunflowers, wreathed in snow or encased in ice, present a graceful and fantastic appearance.

- Muskrats forage for the submerged roots and stalks of lilies, cattails, and other water plants.

- Crickets and grasshoppers may sometimes be heard making lonesome calls from the lee of some fence or ledge.

- All hibernating mammals are now in winter quarters.

- Flocks of goldfinches may be seen in sheltered pastures, feeding on the seeds of goldenrods and other composites.

- Many beetles are still active under bark and stones.

- Purple finches feed on the blue berries of the red cedar.

- The catkins of the alders, enclosed in ice, sparkle and quiver in the sunshine like jeweled pendants.

- The ruffed grouse searches eagerly for partridge berries.

❧ The larvae of the caddis flies may be seen crawling over the bottoms of streams or clinging to the stalks of submerged water plants.

❧ Chickadees visit the red fruit of the sumac.

❧ The nature year appears at its lowest ebb.

❧ Though dry and flavorless, red bearberries, clustered on trailing and spreading branches, prove a welcome addition to the scanty winter menu of grouse and other wintering birds.

❧ Privet is still fresh, bright, and green — the last plant to succumb to winter storms.

❧ Buffleheads play in white-crested surf along the coast.

❧ The bright, glossy evergreen leaves and the shining black berries of the inkberry provide a touch of unexpected beauty on the sandy stretches of the seacoast.

❧ Glittering backswimmers hang by the hundreds from tangles of half-decayed chara plants.

❧ The light-brown fruiting cones, from which the winged seed-like bodies have partially fallen, persist on the branches and serve to identify the tulip tree.

❧ Screech owls search for mice. Mice are especially destructive in winter by girdling such trees as the apple, and the owls help us by preying on the rodents.

❧ Fastened to fences and buildings by tufts of silk may be found the green or ashen-gray chrysalids of the cabbage butterfly.

❧ In rocky woodlands, the graceful crowns of the leatherwood fern, conspicuous in their fragile greenness, rise above the black leaf mold.

❧ Birch and alder thickets are alive with feeding flocks of pine siskins and redpolls.

❧ Starlings form winter flocks.

- The green twigs of the sassafras strike a spring-like note in the midst of winter snows. The dainty green buds are pleasing to the taste.

- Conspicuous on the bark of elms and maples are the egg masses of the white-marked tussock moth, attached to the loose cocoons of the wingless females.

- Pines and hemlocks relieve the monotony of white with a touch of green.

- The velvet-stemmed Collybia, easily recognized by its tawny cap and velvety stem, appears in tufts on dead stumps and decaying wood.

- The slender stems of the moth mullein, set with round, brown seed vessels, rise above the snow and serve as banquet tables to hungry birds.

- As ice gradually creeps over the inland ponds and streams, golden-eyed ducks are forced to fly to the seacoast.

- Horned larks, in merry companies, run along the beach.

- The trees stand draped with ermine cloaks.

- The ruffed grouse dons its snowshoes.

- The egg sacs or cocoons of spiders may be found attached to all sorts of places.

- Fat grubs spend the winter within the spherical galls on goldenrod stems.

- The half-grown caterpillars of the viceroy butterfly spend the winter in silken cases on willow and poplar twigs.

THE END